MISS SEETON
RULES

THE HERON CARVIC MISS SEETON MYSTERIES

By Heron Carvic

By Hampton Charles

By Hamilton Crane

Heron Carvic's Miss Seeton

MISS SEETON RULES

HAMILTON CRANE

BERKLEY PRIME CRIME, NEW YORK

MISS SEETON RULES

A Berkley Prime Crime Book
Published by The Berkley Publishing Group
200 Madison Avenue, New York, New York 10016

First edition: October 1994

Library of Congress Cataloging-in-Publication Data
Crane, Hamilton.
    Miss Seeton rules/Hamilton Crane.—1st ed.
        p.   cm.—(Heron Carvic's Miss Seeton)
    ISBN 0-425-14354-6
    1. Seeton, Miss (Fictitious character)—Fiction. 2. Women
detectives—England—Fiction. I. Title. II. Series.
PR6063.A7648M57 1994
813' .54—dc20   94-8657
                                                        CIP

Printed in The United States of America

10 9 8 7 6 5 4 3 2 1

Remember, remember the fifth of November—
The Gunpowder Treason and Plot.
I see no reason why Gunpowder Treason
Should ever be forgot.
—*Traditional children's verse, based on historical
events of November 1605*

Trea•son: 1 the action of betraying; betrayal of the trust undertaken by or reposed in any one; breach of faith, treachery.
2 law a: High treason or treason proper: Violation by a subject of his allegiance to his sovereign or to the state. Defined 1350–51 by Act 25 Edward III, Statute 5 c.2, as compassing or imagining the king's death, or that of his wife or eldest son, violating the wife of the king or of the heir apparent, or the king's eldest daughter being unmarried . . .
In 1795 the offence was extended to actual or contemplated use of force to make the king change his counsels, or to intimidate either or both of the Houses of Parliament . . . **c:** Constructive treason: Action which though not actually or overtly coming under any of the acts specified in the Statute of Treason, was declared by law to be treason and punishable as such.
—*Shorter Oxford English Dictionary*

CHAPTER 1

"Call me . . . Catesby."

One by one, taking care that nobody should notice their absence and remark on it, they had slipped away from their everyday concerns to the appointed place. The heavy door had creaked open, had whispered shut behind each new arrival; the blinds had been drawn across windows where no light could risk being seen.

The last of the four had taken his seat in safety. The meeting was about to begin.

Catesby, natural leader of the little group, surveyed with a long, careful look the other three around the table. "Catesby—is that clear? Whenever we have . . . important matters to discuss, Catesby is my name—and nothing else."

"Catesby," came the obedient echo, accompanied by nods.

"Real names," Catesby went on, "are dangerous—the very least slip could betray us. You will all remember that."

More obedient nods. Catesby smiled—a lopsided smile which did not soften the desperate purpose gleaming in those haunted, steel-grey eyes.

"You will all," commanded Catesby, "take new names." The lopsided smile widened; the grey eyes for a moment held a glint of mischief as thin fingers drummed on the table. "You will remember them—you will write nothing down. What is written on paper can be too easily read by those with no business to read it."

A thin finger pointed. "Rookwood."

The newly-christened Rookwood blinked, then nodded, with an air of resignation. "Rookwood," he repeated.

"Keyes."

"Keyes," agreed he who had been given that name.

"Winter."

"Er—Thomas, or Robert?"

Mischief faded at once from Catesby's eyes, though its ghost danced still in those of the reluctant Winter.

"This is no time for joking." Catesby frowned. "There is no need for Christian names. Winter by itself will do."

"I'd rather be Digby," suggested Winter. "Or Percy, at a pinch." Then he sniggered. "Well, perhaps not—but not Winter, either. Winter's so—so ambiguous. Boring."

Catesby slapped a sudden, furious hand on the table. It sounded like a gunshot. Everyone jumped.

"Boring? You fool! We aren't doing this for fun! If you can't be serious . . ."

Rookwood and Keyes stared, too startled to protest. Was Winter to be lost to them before the plan had even begun to mature? They were so few in number—they needed him!

"No," said Catesby, slowly, as if answering the unspoken thought. "No, you have to be serious—you have no choice. Because"—the eyes were steel darts, the voice an icicle—"you already know too much, Winter."

There was menace in every syllable, and it held Winter silent. Catesby's smile was bitter in triumph. "No, we certainly can't risk letting you . . . retire. You are in this with the rest of us, Winter. It's too late for you—for anyone—to back out now."

Once more, steel and ice chilled the hearts of the three around the table in the darkened, anonymous room. "Is that clearly understood?" enquired Catesby.

And there came uneasy murmurs of acquiescence from the others: from Rookwood, from Keyes, and—without protest—from Winter: whose eyes had lost their sparkle as he realised that for him—for all of them—there could be no escape until their purpose had been finally accomplished.

The village of Plummergen is in Kent. Rye, at five miles distant the closest town, lies across the county border, in Sussex; and yet, despite its closeness, Rye is not the most convenient centre for Plummergen shoppers needing rather more than the well-stocked local establishments can supply. That honour goes to Brettenden, six miles to the north but, like its smaller neighbour, in Kent—though it is not so much parochialism as convenience which prompts Plummergen to shop from time to time in Brettenden. There is no direct bus service to Rye; the bus to Brettenden, although drastically curtailed from its glorious twice-daily run of older, affluent days, is nevertheless still regular, convenient—and cheap. Indeed, the official county service (once a week on market day) is so shamed by the greater efficiency of the additional twice-a-week bus provided by Plummergen's Crabbe family, owners of the local garage, that the trip—on whichever day of the week it is taken— is thought to give some of the best value for money for miles.

Plummergen's shops, it has been said, are well-stocked. There are three main retail outlets in the village: they all carry a remarkably similar range of items, although with sufficient variety to keep everyone happy. Along with the regulation groceries (green and otherwise), sweets, tobacco, wines and spirits, and deep-frozen pre-packaged foods, Mr. Takeley the grocer sells more Reduced goods than his competitors combined, owing to the temperamental nature of his deep freeze.

Mr. Welsted the draper is not given, as is Mr. Takeley, to Liquidation Sales—Mr. Takeley has a sense of humour—but, in addition to the standard stock, provides Plummergen with general haberdashery, knitting wool and patterns, dressmaking fabrics, and—since Plummergen's second place in the Best Kept Village Competition—a wider range of picture postcards than before.

Postmaster Mr. Stillman has a larger floor area than Mr. Takeley and Mr. Welsted on which to display his wares. His shop, moreover, is on much the best-placed site for gossip-loving Plummergen. It stands, its windows shaded by a striped awning, next door to Crabbe's Garage, and opposite the bus stop. Shoppers in the post office miss no coming nor going of any who travel, in whatever direction. With a little judicious craning of necks they may observe those who post letters in the nearby wall-mounted box, and will freely speculate on the purpose and destination of their friends' correspondence. By blatant snooping, they may study the drivers and passengers of passing cars, for every vehicle which either leaves or enters the village must pass the post office in so doing: Mr. Stillman's invaluable premises are situated in Plummergen's main—its only—street: The Street, as it is known.

And from the windows of Mr. Stillman's invaluable premises, one crisp autumn afternoon, busy eyes were keeping their habitual watch even as busy tongues wagged over the most interesting of the various items of news which were currently in circulation.

"Pretty little thing, she is," said Mrs. Spice, in tones of fond approval. "A real picture. Not like some, with great clodhopping feet in them platform shoes, and hair all over her face." She paused, and pondered briefly. "Dainty, that's the very word."

And no voice was raised against her choice.

"Not a bit of side to her, neither, by all accounts," said

Mrs. Henderson. "Her poor mother'd be proud of her if she was still alive, no doubt o' that."

A general chorus sighed that it did not doubt it. Even Mrs. Skinner, who had once quarrelled with Mrs. Henderson over the church flower rota and had barely exchanged two civil words with her since, could not bring herself to disagree.

Indeed, she went further. "Her mother *and* her poor dad, if you ask me. Reckon he's sorry now things happened like they did, him being thrown out o' the country that way, and her left to be brung up respectable—and so popular, too."

"Better for her he *was* thrown out," said someone more realist than romantic. "Stands to reason he'd have done her reputation no good at all, carrying on the way he was afore they got rid of him, and her near grownup now, bless her. She's a sight better off without him . . ."

And again no voice was raised against the remark.

"Georgy Girl," mused Emmy Putts sadly from behind the grocery counter, as someone murmured knowingly of morganatic marriage. "Princess Petite—that's what they call her. Allus in the papers, she is, as good as a film star." She sighed. "Some folk have all the luck "

"Some folk," said Mrs. Stillman sternly, "are born to it, Emmeline, and some aren't. You keep your mind on your work, my girl, and let's have none of your nonsense about being in the papers. Plummergen's good enough for the likes of you, not being royalty, nor even gentry-born. At least," she pointed out, "you'll be free to marry who you want, when the time comes, and no argument. But there'll be checking, and Acts of Parliament, and—and everything o' that sort for young Georgina, so it said in the paper the other day. You count your blessings, Emmy Putts, and be thankful your blood isn't blue like hers—poor lamb," she added.

The Princess Georgina was one of the youngest, and one of the most popular, members of the current royal scene.

No more than five feet tall, and in perfect proportion from her bubbly blonde curls to her tiny feet, she had been dubbed ''The Petite Princess'' from her first appearance in public. Her immaculate grooming, coupled with her sparkling personality and apparent enthusiasm for whatever task she might be given to perform, made her a role model the battle-weary parents of teenage England would have been only too glad for their offspring to emulate. Never once had Georgina put a finely-shod foot wrong. When, at the launching of a nuclear submarine, the naval brass band had followed the National Anthem with a spirited version of the Seekers' hit from seven years earlier, Georgy Girl's place in the hearts of the nation was assured, as front-page photographs next day showed Her Royal Highness clapping her hands and laughing with genuine delight for the unexpected compliment.

Georgina's name had never been involved with scandal—unlike that of her father, whose lurid behaviour had led, some fifteen years before, to what the racier elements of the media had dubbed *Exile—by Royal Decree!* It was hinted that she was being groomed as a future Princess of Wales: it was rumoured that half the eligible bachelors in the country would go into terminal decline on the announcement of her betrothal, no matter who the lucky man might be—and, whoever he was, even Prince Charles, he couldn't possibly be good enough for Her Royal Highness. Georgina's postbag—so voluminous that Mount Pleasant Sorting Office had allocated an entire room to her incoming mail—was swamped with well-meant advice and delicate embroidery from doting pensioners, with declarations of platonic affection from an age-range of males between fifteen and seventy-five, with cards and presents from schoolchildren, and with heartfelt offers of marriage and lifelong devotion from daydreamers on whom she had once, in passing, allowed her golden glance to fall.

Georgina, bewildered but flattered by the attention, had been wisely reared: her curly blonde head remained resolutely unturned. Her secretary issued statements that Her Royal Highness had no mind, as yet, to settle down, deeming her public duties fulfilment enough. Such wisdom in one so young was hailed as a rare and wholly admirable quality; Mount Pleasant had to allocate another room. Georgy Girl was England's darling. Not a voice could be heard to speak against her; she was mobbed and adored wherever she went . . .

And now she was coming to Kent.

"I still don't know's they oughter risk it, though." Mrs. Spice returned to her original argument. "Her being so young, and with nobody knowing what that radiation mightn't do, if you know what I mean." She cast a quick, suggestive glance at Emmy Putts, unmarried and wide-eyed behind the bacon slicer. "In the long term," she enlarged cryptically, nodding in a way which spoke volumes to every mother in the room, but which left Emmy still staring.

"There's . . . shields and things, they say," said Mrs. Henderson, hopefully. "Lead. They'll take no chances with her, you can be sure o' that."

"There's tales," said Mrs. Skinner swiftly, "of some poor soul Murreystone way, her husband used to work there—and out it popped with two heads, poor little thing, and never lived above a day or so, though he'd had all the lead shields and special clothes you like."

"They'll say anything," countered Mrs. Henderson, "over to Murreystone. Two heads, indeed! First I've heard of it. Might as well say as it had—had webbed feet, and a tail—if it had anything at all, that is, which with Murreystone you can be sure it never did, on account of never bin born in the first place."

The post office now perceived a great conversational dilemma. Should Mrs. Skinner's tempting Radiation Mutant Monster theme be pursued? It could not be doubted that the possibilities were virtually endless—but their development required, inconveniently, a credence in Murreystone news it was not in Plummergen's nature to give. Would it be better to follow the traditional lead of Mrs. Henderson, in scorning any claim to veracity or reliability on the part of the rival village? After all, no Plummergenite had been known to trust a Murreystoner in thought, word, or deed for several hundred years. A feud believed to have begun during the fifteenth-century Wars of the Roses was in full swing by the Civil War, two centuries later, and had never been allowed to lapse since that time.

Torn between two so violently opposing points of view, the shoppers turned, as they often did, to Mrs. Flax for the final decision. Mrs. Flax, Plummergen's Wise Woman, was a person of much authority in the village. Were she to cap Mrs. Skinner's story with one of her own—a new-born baby with a full set of teeth, an infant smothered from head to foot in hair—they would joyfully narrate horrors of their own immediate invention. Should she, however, second Mrs. Henderson in dismissing the two-headed child as a figment of Murreystone's (or even of Mrs. Skinner's) imagination, the topic would be abandoned forthwith.

Mrs. Flax, with every eye upon her, drew a deep, portentous breath. She wagged her head in meaningful fashion. "If they'd come to me," said the Wise Woman, never slow to reinforce her reputation, "Murreystone or no, there would've bin herbs to spare them their sorrow—ah, and more besides, being the devil's work . . . which is no more than a body can expect from that heathen band across the marsh, o' course." She made her decision. "Allus bearing in mind," she added, "as there's no cause to believe a word they devils say in the first place. And even if there was"— for, in the manner of oracles, Mrs. Flax was skilled at hedging her bets—"there was babies born hare-shotten and with clubbed feet—ah, and worse—long afore anyone invented atom bombs and nuclear power."

Any lapse in her logic was overlooked in the relief of having a clear conversational lead at last. The Murreystone Mutant was no more than a myth: they could return to less disquieting topics of conversation—yet, on consideration, not so very much less. There could be no doubt that Murreystone would be as interested in the proposed visit of the Princess Georgina as Plummergen, of whatever age, could be; and Murreystone's reaction to local events involving Plummergen—no matter how indirectly—was seldom of a tranquil nature.

"Poor little mites," said Mrs. Skinner, snatching a face-saving cue from the Wise Woman before anyone else— Mrs. Henderson in particular—could speak. "Oh, there was hard times if you was a kiddie, right enough—and not so very long ago, neither."

Her audience brooded on children pushed up chimneys and sent down mines, or driven, barefoot, out into the fields to pick stones, scare rooks, and herd sheep. Some of the older women muttered grimly of the Union, informing their younger friends that nothing today could match the horrors of the— happily defunct—Workhouse . . .

"But things is better nowadays, you can't deny," Mrs. Henderson reminded them, in accents which dared Mrs. Skinner to make such a denial. "I mean, how many Plummergen folk've had the chance to meet any of the Royal Family the way they've got now?"

"Only the kiddies, though," pointed out Mrs. Scillicough. As the mother of Plummergen's infamous triplets, Mrs. Scillicough felt herself better qualified than most to pronounce on matters juvenile. "On account of 'em learning all about it at school, the paper says, which is what none of us did, nuclear power not being in the Eleven Plus nor nothing."

"The school over to Murreystone's not so big as ours," someone said, thoughtfully.

The fact was hardly surprising: Murreystone's inhabitants number around three hundred and fifty, while Plummergen has a population of just over five hundred.

"And nobbut the one teacher," someone else added, more thoughtful still.

"But one or two o' their dads works down in Dungeness," said Mrs. Skinner, reluctant—despite the opinions of Mrs. Flax—to abandon entirely her Radiation Mutant theme. "And there's not a soul from these parts but works on a farm, or in Brettenden or suchlike—nothing to do with nuclear power at all. Seems to me they'll take unfair advantage, if we're not careful."

"Unfair it may well be," came the automatic retort from Mrs. Henderson, "but I'd like to know what's anyone's notion of what anyone can do about it—because there's summat got to be done, there's no denying." She sighed. "Not as if any of us knows the editor of the *Beacon* for putting in a word, is it? Fine chance! Open to all, so the paper said this competition is, and a daft idea it is, too— all the kiddies, anyway," as she saw Mrs. Scillicough draw breath to protest. She closed her eyes in an attempt to recall the exact wording of the notice which had appeared at the end of a thrilling feature in that week's *Brettenden Telegraph and Beacon (est. 1847, incorporating [1893] The Iverhurst Chronicle and Argus).*

"For the best essay from a child at present in full-time primary education in the county of Kent, on the subject of Nuclear Power, first prize, a ten-pound book token. Plus"—and Mrs. Henderson opened her eyes—"the honour of presenting a—a bucket to Her Royal Highness Princess Georgina on the occasion of the Grand Opening of Dungeness D Nuclear Power Station."

This feat of memory was received with nods and murmurs of appreciation from everyone save, inevitably, Mrs. Skinner.

"And there's the one advantage we've got over Murreystone," she said. "Alice Maynard, that's to say, on account of presenting bookays"—the pronunciation was scornful— "needs 'em to curtsey nice, and Miss Maynard's a-going to teach the kiddies dances and stuff for the Christmas pantomime, remember. So if it's one of ours as wins the competition, whoever it is'll not disgrace the village by falling flat on her face or tripping over her feet when she gets to meet the princess.''

"There's worse things than tripping over people's feet, where Murreystone's concerned," said Mrs. Flax sagely. "It's for no good reason, you mark my words, they'll want one of theirs to—to give her the flowers." Mrs. Flax was wise enough to know when, and how, to mask ignorance with adroit turns of phrase. "They'll be up to summat, make no mistake about that, if they've half the chance . . . ''

Everyone nodded. During the Civil War, Murreystone had been strong for Protector Cromwell: Plummergen had even more strongly backed the Royalist side. Neither village had ever changed its stance on matters political; and if the Princess Georgina wasn't Royalty, Plummergen would like to know who was. There could be no doubt that the selection of a Murreystone candidate for the presentation honour could lead to nothing but embarrassment, at the very least, for everyone concerned. If the editor of the *Beacon* had his wits about him, for all the vaunted freedom of the press he wouldn't even consider any entries which came from the village five miles to the east of Plummergen . . .

And when someone voiced the opinion that Murreystone—for whatever purpose—was bound to play dirty, not a single voice was raised against this view.

CHAPTER 2

No voice, indeed, was raised for some moments, as everyone grimly contemplated many previous instances of Murreystone's undeniable rascality. Then mother-of-four Mrs. Newport, sister to the triplet-bedevilled Mrs. Scillicough, ventured the opinion that—for all the *Beacon* said the essay was for the youngsters to write—she wouldn't mind betting there'd be a few Murreystone mums and dads'd want to give their kiddies a helping hand, and in a way you couldn't blame them, could you? Because it was only natural. But if Murreystone was going to do it, well, she didn't know but what Plummergen wouldn't have to, too, to stand any chance of winning, when all was said and done. Not (added Mrs. Newport hastily) as she'd any cause to say such things on her own account, of course, being as hers were all under five and even the eldest not due to start school for another year, but you had to look at it from both sides, didn't you?

It was as everyone was attempting this Janus-like mental manoeuvre that the doorbell jangled.

Heads turned at once to see who had come to join their number: they had all been so busy brooding on Perfidious Murreystone, and pondering the uneasy sophistry of Mrs.

Newport, that their attention had drifted from the world
outside the post office. What part of that world was now
coming in to join them?

"Morning, Mrs. Blaine." The relieved and welcoming
chorus came from those who realised that nobody now need
commit herself to the merits or otherwise of stooping to
Murreystone's anticipated level. "Morning, Miss Nuttel!"
And The Nuts, somewhat startled by the intensity of the
greeting, responded with appropriate salutations of their
own.

"The Nuts" is the collective title by which these two
ladies are almost invariably known to impertinent Plummergen. Some say the name derives from their being as
nutty as fruitcakes; others hold the (more probable) theory
that it is the rampant vegetarianism of the pair which has
resulted in their nuxial nomenclature. Whatever the reason,
Miss Erica Nuttel and Mrs. Norah Blaine have around the
village been referred to as "The Nuts" for nearly as long
as the village has been their home: a home which they set
up together a dozen or so years ago in Lilikot, a plate-glass-
windowed dwelling of modern style situated almost exactly
opposite the bus stop, Crabbe's Garage, and the post office.

If shoppers in the post office blatantly observe each coming and going of those who travel or post letters, there is
a recognised—and regretted—restriction in such observation. The Nuts, on the other hand, may observe as much,
and for as long, as is their pleasure: and their pleasure is
very great. Living where they do, Miss Nuttel (who is also
known as Nutcrackers) and Mrs. Blaine (the Hot Cross
Bun) are not restricted, as are Mr. Stillman's customers, by
his hours of business. Mr. Stillman stays open only from
eight in the morning to six in the evening: the inhabitants
of Lilikot, during the summer at least, can maintain—
should they so wish—a constant vigil on outside events
from dawn (around four) until dusk (almost ten). And the
ladies would be among the first to support the installation
of street lighting, so that their vigilance might be increased.

The Nuts, it must be emphasised, are vigilant from no unworthy cause. Their motives are pure, their intentions philanthropic in the extreme. Their only wish is to serve their fellow citizens to the best of their ability: and they pride themselves that serve them they definitely do. Their devotion to this self-appointed task, they feel, cannot be questioned; and the value of that service (to Plummergen, at least) has never been in doubt—although the editor of the *Brettenden Telegraph and Beacon* has been known to hold forth at some length on the topic of sales and circulation figures in the Plummergen area. For with Miss Nuttel and Mrs. Blaine ever ready to pass on gossip, to indulge in scandal, and to monger all manner of rumour on the slightest excuse, why would anyone in the same community even think of paying good money for a newspaper?

Miss Nuttel is tall, thin, and equine of feature. Mrs. Blaine is short, stout, and black-eyed with either malice or mischief, depending on her mood. When thwarted, she is given to flashes of temper, followed by long, brooding sulks or by providential migraines, which last are known to the village as "one of my heads." Their main purpose, Plummergen agrees, is to make Miss Nuttel feel guilty . . .

And it now seemed clear, from the way in which both Nuts had responded to the greetings of their fellow shoppers, that this current excursion was taking place in a post-sulk (or post-migraine) period; and everyone wondered why the Hot Cross Bun should be so cross today with Eric.

Miss Nuttel, having nodded to the assembled company, marched across to the revolving book-stand, where she stood in a grim silence thumbing through the pages of one of the popular *Mastery* series. These slim volumes held out the tantalising promise of near-professional skills or knowledge upon the expenditure of a modest sum of money and a minimum of effort; *Master Banking in Thirty Minutes* had been selling in considerable numbers since the recent appointment of a new manager to one of the most prestigious financial houses in Brettenden.

Norah Blaine's blackcurrant eyes darted around in search of a sympathetic face. They fell upon Mrs. Skinner, still feeling a little peeved at her worsting by Mrs. Flax in the matter of the Murreystone Mutant, yet too nervous of the Wise Woman's likely reaction to say so out loud. "If you aren't in a hurry, Mrs. Skinner," said Mrs. Blaine in a winning tone, "would you mind too much if I just popped in front of you to make my few purchases? They're really rather *urgent,* you see," with a pointed glare for Miss Nuttel, whose interest in *Master Fancy Needlework* was as deep as it was unexpected.

"You go right ahead, dear."

Mrs. Skinner's was not the only nose to twitch at the scent of scandal when it became clear that Miss Nuttel had no intention of following her friend to the Ironmongery and Kitchenware section of the shop. Mrs. Stillman, frowning in what she knew was a vain attempt to quench the curiosity of her customers, moved across to the other counter.

"Anything in particular you're looking for, Mrs. Blaine?"

Mrs. Blaine made to consult a crumpled envelope. "Well, to begin with, two new sieves, please, the large ones with fine metal mesh. And two buckets, but they must be galvanised. If you've only got plastic, I suppose"—with a sigh suggestive of martyrdom—"it will have to wait until market day ... although I'm sure I don't see why I should."

"Well, you don't have to." Mrs. Stillman gestured behind her. "Large sieves, you said? We've three different sizes to choose from, and as for galvanised buckets, was it the double sort for floors you wanted, or ordinary?"

Mrs. Blaine opted, loudly, for the ordinary style; Miss Nuttel slammed *Master Fancy Needlework* back on the shelf. Clearly, the thought of even thirty minutes' dedication to drawing threads and weaving fine silks had depressed her.

"I don't suppose," said Mrs. Blaine, absently banging

the buckets one against the other as Mrs. Stillman placed them on the counter before her, "that you stock glass-cloths, do you? I thought not," with another martyred sigh. And her mood remained resolutely glum even when Mrs. Stillman reminded her of the propensity of drapers to stock tea-towels among the rest of their Manchester goods. It seemed that the very idea of having to cross The Street to Mr. Welsted's little shop was too much for Mrs. Blaine to bear, even though it stood no more than a few score yards from Lilikot's front door.

"I'll pay for these." Mrs. Blaine, wilfully oblivious of the approach of Miss Nuttel, took out her purse as Mrs. Stillman spoke the total. "Goodness, so much? Really, I do think—but there," with a third exhalation indicative of martyrdom, "the housekeeping will simply have to stretch this week, that's all. And if people don't like it, they have only themselves to blame."

Beside her, Miss Nuttel cleared her throat in a whinny, and stared haughtily down her nose. "Rubber tubing?" she enquired, as Mrs. Stillman sorted out change. "Couple of yards," she added.

"Some more home-made wine, Mrs. Blaine?" It was too good a chance for Mrs. Skinner to miss. Mrs. Henderson's attempts at Strong and Wholesome Barley Beer had given her neighbours their biggest shock since the council announced the latest rent increase, and the glaziers of Brettenden their most lucrative employment for months. Gleeful rumour had set the decorators' estimates—their vans and ladders had never, in fact, appeared—at astronomical levels. "I know you takes a pride in your dandelion, o' course, but if you don't mind me saying so it's a bit on the late side, isn't it?"

Mrs. Blaine clashed her buckets together as she lifted them from the counter, but made no reply beyond another long-suffering sigh, and a shake of her head as the sieves rattled in their galvanised receptacles. Miss Nuttel, her nose in the air, ignored Mrs. Blaine to watch Mrs. Stillman wrestling, Laocoön-like, with her tape-measure and scissors against black rubber coils; and she was as deaf to Mrs. Skinner's words as ever Mrs. Henderson could be.

"Yes. Six feet," said Miss Nuttel, as Mrs. Stillman put the inevitable query. "Plaster of Paris, too, if you've got it." She paused, and shot a triumphant look in the direction of Mrs. Blaine. "Twenty pounds."

Mrs. Blaine uttered a squeal of fury, turned on her heel, and, with a bucket in either hand, headed—reproachfully clanking—for the door. She needed only apple cheeks and a wooden shoulder-yoke to be everyone's ideal of the country milkmaid—that is, had the apple cheeks been plumped in a winsome smile. But Norah Blaine was far from smiling now.

"I'm sorry, Miss Nuttel. Plaster of Paris is more what you'd get in craft shops, though I believe we've a bag or two of cement round the back that's old stock I could let you have half price, if you'd like it."

Mrs. Blaine's plump frame vibrated on the threshold as, waiting for a volunteer with unencumbered hands to open the door, she waited also for Miss Nuttel's reply. It might have been supposed that the prospect of so tempting a bargain must please Norah Blaine: but the dark, dangerous gleam in her eyes, and the narrow set of her mouth, suggested that such supposition would be wrong.

"No, thanks." At Miss Nuttel's words, Mrs. Blaine seemed to brighten. "Just this. Fine."

And, as Miss Nuttel forced the slim black rubber serpent into the capacious pocket of her coat, Mrs. Blaine, herself serpentlike as she hissed through clenched teeth, dropped her buckets with a discordant clang, snatched open the door, and, to the tinkling accompaniment of the bell, picked them up again and clanked her way crossly out.

Miss Nuttel paid for the rubber tubing and strode after her in triumph, leaving everyone staring. As Mrs. Stillman tidied away her heavy-duty scissors and the reel of tube, Mrs. Henderson spoke.

"Well!"

Nobody could have summed up the general sentiment more exactly.

"Which isn't to say," Mrs. Henderson went on, she having tacitly been granted the floor, "as there han't bin summat strange about that pair over the past few days, because there has."

"I'd call it more than strange," said Mrs. Skinner at once. "What with digging that hole the way she was, deep as a grave if Mrs. Putts is to be believed, and I'm sure I don't see why not, if you ask me it's a wonder they're still both alive to tell the tale. Ain't that right, Emmy?"

Emmy Putts, thus addressed, jumped. She had been lost in a daydream inspired by thoughts of Princess Georgina, and wishing that the crown she herself, for the second time, had crammed over her long blonde wig as this year's Miss Plummergen, had been as real as the gorgeous tiaras and diadems worn by the fortunate Georgy Girl.

She blinked. "Pardon, Mrs. Skinner. What say?"

"Miss Nuttel's hole," prompted Mrs. Skinner. "Remember, your ma said she saw her digging it when she popped along to the admiral to borrow a jar of honey, and happened to look over the fence?"

Everyone crowded close, though this was a tale they had heard told many times in recent days. Indeed, it had been the main topic of village speculation for almost a week, only being relegated to second place once the forthcoming visit of Princess Georgina had been announced.

Rear Admiral Bernard "Buzzard" Leighton, a relative newcomer to Plummergen, had from his arrival occasioned much discussion in the village, not only by sporting a ginger beard, but by keeping bees: neither of which activities anybody was ever known to have pursued within living memory. The bees—or the beard—alone would have been a cause of suspicion: both together gave Plummergen a field day, and, though rumour had it that Major-General Sir George Colveden planned to go into melliferous partnership with his new friend next spring, these rumours were not enough to place the seal of respectability on the Buzzard's hobby (the beard was reluctantly accepted as beyond Plummergen's control) until his honey won a prize in the Preserves section of the recent Produce Show.

People at once began to recall old country remedies and recipes which, without honey, were sure to fail. Sugar was denounced as pure, white, and deadly. The admiral, overwhelmed by this sudden interest, regretted that four hives—especially hives which had not long since been transported from another part of the country—were unable to supply the needs of his new neighbours: the odd jar or two, perhaps, as a present, but he'd no intention of setting up in business at his age. Of course, with winter coming on, if anyone wanted to sample his recipe for a hot toddy, they'd be more than welcome to drop in for a few drinks one evening . . .

Mrs. Putts, in her own words a respectable widow-woman of several years' standing, had no intention of joining the Buzzard in one of his by now (undeservedly) notorious push-the-boat-out parties, when the green-and-white Gin Pennant flew from the flagpole in his front garden, issuing its unspoken invitation to all former officers within the vicinity to consider themselves Bernard Leighton's guests. Guest? For her, plain Clarissa Putts, to mix with the likes of Sir George and Colonel Windup? Not to mention Major Howett, who being female and a nurse did ought to have known better than encourage menfolk to pickle their livers . . . Though far too sensible to voice the sentiment aloud while asking a favour, Mrs. Putts was resolved that she would do no such thing. On the other hand, if the admiral could spare just *one* jar: not that she held with beautification on her own account, of course, but young Emmy had read in one of her magazines that honey and glycerine, in equal parts, would soften and beautify the complexion, and, being too shy to ask on her own account . . .

Which intelligence had come as a surprise to Emmy Putts, a regular and appreciative recipient of much bluff naval gallantry whenever the admiral entered the post office, or encountered her outside it. Emmy had been sworn to secrecy by her mother about this aspect of the story.

The admiral had been delighted to offer Mrs. Putts—he hastily begged her pardon, to offer on her daughter's behalf—not one, but two jars of honey, along with the chance to watch his bees at their work. A quiet time, October, but interesting, he was sure she'd agree, if she cared to accompany him; which Mrs. Putts, prepared to sell her honour dear, was happy to do. Around the side of the admiral's house went Mrs. Putts in the admiral's wake, hearing him talk with eloquence of brood chambers, and queens, and sugar syrup; and hearing also, as the pair neared the far end of the garden where the four hives were set on their brick-and-wood stands, the unmistakable and energetic sound of digging from over the fence.

The admiral heard it, too, and paused. Was not one of the traditional naval toasts "Sweethearts and wives"? The ladies, God bless 'em, shouldn't really be burdened with the heavy work—though he'd always understood his neighbours to have tended their topsoil so well that it as good as looked after itself.

But the rhythmic chink of spade on stone, the thud of falling soil, still floated over the fence separating Ararat Cottage, home of the Buzzard, from the little house next door. It sounded like very hard work indeed; and—with Mrs. Putts by his side—the admiral popped his head over the top of the fence to enquire:

"Need any help there, Miss Nuttel?"

Erica Nuttel, knee-deep in orange subsoil, and breathing hard, shook her head without speaking. The admiral regarded her with kindly interest.

Mrs. Putts stared with blatant curiosity, and proved the weaker of the two. "My goodness, Miss Nuttel, whatever d'you want with such a great big hole? You'll not be planting a tree so deep, all clay and stones as it is.''

''No,'' agreed Miss Nuttel, and dug on.

Mrs. Putts suffered in silence for a while, then coughed. ''We're on the main drainage, so it can't surely be a new septic tank,'' she said, in a pleading tone.

''No,'' said Miss Nuttel, digging yet deeper.

''Another well, maybe?'' The Nuts, when they had first arrived in Plummergen, had employed the services of a water-diviner to find them a spring, and had sunk their own well, insisting that tap water was full of who-knew-what unhealthy chemicals.

''No,'' said Miss Nuttel, by now almost invisible behind an upthrown pile of sticky clay.

''Then what,'' demanded Mrs. Putts, who could bear this no longer, ''*do* you want that hole for, Miss Nuttel?''

And Miss Nuttel's reply had sent—Clarissa Putts reported later to an enthralled Emmy—ice-cold shivers down her spine, as if she knew what dreadful fate had been foretold and yet could do nothing about it. Miss Nuttel had paused at last in her digging, and wiped an earthy hand across her brow, and uttered those three terrible words that had turned the heart of Clarrie Putts to water . . .

''For the body,'' said Erica Nuttel.

CHAPTER 3

Although circulation of the *Brettenden Beacon* was not high in the Plummergen area, there were still those who read the newspaper every week in great detail, down to the Notices of Bankruptcy, Auctions, and Planning Applications. One of these was Martin Jessyp, efficient headmaster of the little village school; and, on the afternoon of the day on which the visit of Princess Georgina had been announced, he had gone into lengthy consultation with his deputy, Miss Alice Maynard, on the subject of Nuclear Power.

It was not, of course, that they wished to encourage the spirit of feuding which any mention of Murreystone was sure to inflame. If, on the other hand, there was a competition open to all local children, neither he nor Alice saw any good reason why a Plummergen child should not win it, fair and square, given sufficient encouragement and help. Early on Saturday morning, therefore, he gave Miss Maynard a lift into Brettenden. The two entered the public lending library with enthusiasm and stout canvas bags, and borrowed as many books on Energy as they could find.

They spent an industrious and productive weekend in

their respective cottages, making notes, planning lessons. And on Monday morning, after Assembly, the fifty-odd pupils of Plummergen School gathered, Bigguns and Tiddlers amongst themselves but Junior Mixed Infants to the authorities, in their appointed classrooms for initiation into the mysteries which their forthcoming trip to Dungeness D would reveal in even greater depth.

"*What is Energy?*" chalked Miss Maynard, at the top of the blackboard; and, underneath, wrote as she spoke that it was the ability of matter to move, to change. It was the power of something—anything—to work, to perform. Without the energy they had that breakfast-time consumed in the form of food, none of them would have been able to walk to school afterwards, especially on such a blustery day.

"Pity we had breakfast, then," muttered someone with a sideways elbow-dig into the ribs of his neighbour. "Fancy a day off school, I do."

His neighbour sniggered, and Miss Maynard, whose hearing was acute, smiled in sympathy while she shook her head. She herself, she pointed out, liked Monday mornings no better than anyone else: unfortunately, just as there was little that could be done about the weather, there was little that could be done about Monday mornings.

"Except," she added, "to make them more interesting, perhaps. I thought we would start today's lesson with some experiments to blow away any weekend cobwebs that the wind hasn't already blown away. Now, who's going to volunteer to bring some water from the cloakroom?"

Every hand shot up as Miss Maynard took a white enamel jug from behind the desk, and held it aloft. She studied the twenty eager faces turned towards her. "Thank you, Paul. As full as you can comfortably carry it, please—you aren't to go straining yourself."

Young Paul jumped to his feet, hurried to take the jug from Alice's hands, and trotted away to the cloakroom while Miss Maynard produced three matchboxes, some rubber bands, a stout pair of scissors, and an empty plastic bottle of the squeezy sort which holds dish-washing detergent.

Three children were chosen to wield the scissors turn and turn about. Christopher cut the top off the detergent bottle, Rachel removed the base, and Laura sliced it down the middle. Sally opened it out and tried to flatten it, so that it lay, a curving rectangle, rocking to and fro on Miss Maynard's desk as Paul reappeared, bright-eyed and slightly out of breath, with water splashing over the blue rim of the jug, assuring Alice that it hadn't been a bit too heavy, Miss, honest.

"Thank you. And now," said Miss Maynard, with a quiver in her voice, "I believe that Miss Seeton left a large bowl here after the Conker Contest, didn't she? Gemma, could you fetch it for me, please?"

Tactfully, Alice ignored the ripple of laughter which ran around the twenty Tiddlers, and Lizzie's ritual moaning for the playground loss of her twenty-oncer in the bout with Rachel's seventeener, the memory of which contest made her friends snigger all the more . . .

Unless, reflected Alice Maynard, they were giggling— and who could, in honesty, blame them?—at the memory of cheating Murreystone's defeat in the official inter-village Conker Contest. Even Miss Seeton's patent soaking mixture, disclosed to the village through the courtesy of her friend Miss Wicks, had not been proof against perfidious Murreystone's use of, not honestly-hardened horse chestnuts, but the more devious painted pebble which only the quick eye of Nigel Colveden had observed. The resulting fracas, of which young Plummergen had been an enthusiastic audience, would live long in village legend . . .

"Thank you, Gemma. Paul, would you fill the bowl with water? Thank you. Now, children, you are too young to use matches, and so . . . "

The Tiddlers of Plummergen range in age from Under Five to Over Seven. Miss Maynard was taking no chances, although she imagined that Mr. Jessyp, teaching the Big-guns (Between Eight and Eleven), would allow his class to carry out this part of the energy experiment, supervised, themselves.

Alice emptied out all the matches, then struck six into flame, and allowed six different children to extinguish them with hearty puffs. More children, following her instructions, inserted the dead matches into the ends of the boxes, one on either side; others ruled and measured on the white curved plastic for still more to cut three small rectangles, while rubber bands were fastened between the protruding matches, followed by the insertion of one white rectangle and its repeated twisting until each rubber band was taut.

The tiny motors thus primed, Miss Maynard took upon herself the honour of launching the first paddle-boat on young Paul's mixing-bowl pond, with Christopher and Ra-chel next, the envy of their friends: but all, they knew, would have their fair turn—as they did.

"And that," said Miss Maynard, as Paul's matchbox craft beat Lizzie's in the final race, "is only one sort of energy—one sort of power. There are, as you will see, a great many others even before we come to nuclear power."

From egg-boxes cut into segments, fastened between two circles of cardboard spinning around a central nail, they made a tiny water-wheel, suspended on string beneath Paul's pouring jug, varying its speed with the speed of his pouring. Wrapping a length of coated flex around a pocket compass, fixing the ends to steel nails stuck in a potato, they made a flicker of electricity. Christopher, trying not to laugh, with much heavy breathing blew up a balloon, then rubbed it repeatedly against his shirt-front before sticking it in triumph to the wall, indisputable proof of the power of static electricity . . .

"And this will be for when we go outside at break time." Miss Maynard, with a smile, produced from her can-vas bag two lengths of balsa wood, a long metal knitting-needle, another washing-up bottle, a collection of small stones for weight, and four disposable paper cups. "Very suitable," said Miss Maynard, "on such a blustery day. We couldn't have asked for anything better. We are going to make a turbine to show how wind power works . . ."

The wind, reflected Miss Seeton, was certainly powerful. It was as well that there was no sign of rain, for the risk of having one's umbrella blown inside out must be very great—so great, indeed, that there had been no question of taking one's best umbrella, in case it should be damaged. Miss Seeton's best umbrella was one of her proudest possessions. Of fine black silk, it had a sensible crook handle rather than a knob, or a strap: and that handle, with part of the shaft, was indeed—the proud owner would tell the astonished enquirer—made of gold.

"Not *solid* gold, of course," she would add, fearing to be thought ostentatious, and blushing for the very idea that anyone might suppose her to have caused any added expense to the courteous gentleman who had given her so generous and rare a gift all those years ago. Detective Superintendent—as he had then been—Delphick, one assumed, although of course one would never have been so impertinent as to ask the question direct, had at that time surely not been paid the sort of salary which would allow him to distribute gold-handled umbrellas to anyone he chose, even if perhaps, since his most gratifying promotion, he now might be. Not—Miss Seeton would further explain, paying tribute—that the handle was gold *plated*, either. One would not wish to give the impression that dear Mr. Delphick might have been, well, deceitful, or stingy. The handle was of real gold—though admittedly hollow—but it had been hallmarked for proof by the Royal Mint, or by whoever it was who had stamped those tiny official numbers and symbols in an unobtrusive place.

"A—a token, that is to say a reminder, of a—a little adventure we shared," the explanation would continue, if the enquiry was pursued; and Miss Seeton would blush once more. "The superintendent was kind enough to say that I had been of—of some assistance to him, and . . . "

And Miss Seeton's voice would tail modestly away as she smiled, sighed, and gently changed the subject.

Miss Seeton has no call to be so modest. Chief Superintendent Delphick would be the first to admit that, without her help, Scotland Yard could never have solved the vicious Covent Garden knifing of a prostitute by her drug-dealing colleague, the infamous Cesar Lebel. The breaking of even part of a drugs ring by the forces of law and order has to be a cause for some celebration; the capture of a murderer, effected mainly through the innocent offices of a retired schoolteacher, has to be a triumph.

In Miss Seeton's case, the triumph is regarded by everyone else as miraculous, while by Miss Seeton herself— and not entirely through the little spinster's innate humility—it is, to say the least, misunderstood. Gentlewomen, Miss Seeton knows full well, do not have adventures: therefore she, Emily Dorothea Seeton, does not have them. No matter that, by poking one or other of her many brollies into whatever criminal hornets' nest she might encounter as she goes on her unconscious way, she not only stirs the hornets into confusion, leading to their ultimate capture, but somehow also contrives to blunt their stings before such capture is effected, thereby making the job of the police a good deal easier than they would otherwise expect it to be; no matter that the police have in the past found such poking and stirring to be of so incomparable a kind that Miss Seeton has been co-opted as a consultant into the force . . . Miss Seeton hardly ever realises that she has poked, stirred, and blunted, and certainly never appreciates that her actions have been so productive for good, pleasing though the intelligence would be should anyone ever induce her to accept it. Though she was trained, and for many years practised, as a teacher of art, Miss Seeton cannot—does not allow herself to—see what others see . . .

And yet it is for the peculiar—the unique—character of her Seeing that Miss Seeton is so valued by the police. The very title of her official position—like the lady herself, unique—reveals her true worth and purpose. She is retained, and paid, by the Yard as an Art Consultant, liable to be called on by her constabulary colleagues whenever they encounter a case of an unusual, irregular, or outré nature. As some fight fire with fire, so the police confront the unusual with the unique . . .

Miss Seeton, on the odd occasions when she takes time to consider the matter, thinks of her appointment as that of an IdentiKit artist. She believes that the meticulous, detailed, and—in the eyes of everyone else—dull drawings she makes of witnesses, scenes of the crime, or certain items of evidence, are required only because the IdentiKit system has, for some reason, on that occasion broken down. Perhaps the Kit has been mislaid, or the operating officer— Miss Seeton is hazy as to details—is for some reason absent from work. In such circumstances, why should someone with a little skill in sketching not be called upon to sketch?

And sketch she does, in painstaking line and shade and hatching, doing no more than a camera could do, and doing it far more slowly: which slow sketches are as much use to the police as a broken umbrella would be to Miss Seeton. But when Miss Seeton's eye Sees as no other eye can see— when eye signals brain to set hand swooping across the pristine page in swift and instinctive movement—when the resulting doodle, cartoon, call it what you will, makes Miss Seeton blush for having Seen beyond what is there, for having taken the type of imaginative liberties only permitted to genius, which she sadly knows herself not to possess . . . it is then that those who can interpret her work—which she has always to be coaxed into showing, blushing for what she regards as her frivolity as well as for her lack of talent—it is then that those who interpret her work use their interpretation, reluctant though it at first may be to reveal itself, to clear a welcome path through the perplexing tangle of nefarious branches to the final resolution of the crime.

It was in gratitude for having presented him with Cesar Lebel, and his associates, gift-wrapped on toast that Superintendent Delphick had in turn presented Miss Seeton with her gold-handled, black silk umbrella. It was after the umbrella had been damaged during a contretemps with a member of an unorthodox and sinister cult—who, pursuing its owner up a ladder with homicidal intent, had in innocent retaliation been bombarded to a well-deserved demise by brolly and handbag and borrowed coat together—it was after this that the suggestion was made by Ashford's Superintendent Brinton, friend to Delphick of the Yard, that Miss Seeton should keep her gold umbrella for comparatively safe occasions, such as afternoon tea with friends; which suggestion Miss Seeton, fearing to risk further damage to her treasured trophy, followed as closely as she could.

On such a blustery day, therefore, it was one of her second-best brollies that Miss Seeton took with her as she hurried up The Street to catch the post. The wind seemed to have died down a little as she clicked shut her gate and headed north from her cottage to the red letter-box in Mr. Stillman's wall. Clouds, grey and gust-ripped into shreds, were moving across the sky with rather more decorum than before; when a glimmer of autumn sunlight eventually peeped through, it managed to gleam for several minutes before being smothered again from sight. Stepping out more briskly than the wind was now blowing, Miss Seeton made for the post office, with her letters in the bag over one arm, her brolly over the other . . .

And with both hands, of necessity, in just the wrong position to make an upward grab when a sudden, sneaky gust of wind snatched her black felt hat from her head, and sent it bowling, skipping, curvetting up The Street . . .

With Miss Seeton, after one little cry of startled vexation, in hot pursuit not very far behind.

CHAPTER 4

Mrs. Blaine forgot that she was barely on speaking terms with Miss Nuttel.

"Oh, Eric, do come quick! Just look," commanded Norah Blaine, "out of the window. It's really too ridiculous, at her age, making a spectacle of herself in front of the whole village."

Miss Nuttel peered out through the white net curtains to the world beyond. "Undignified," she agreed, at the sight of Miss Seeton sprinting, bag and brolly bouncing as she ran, after her errant headpiece. "Sets a bad example."

"You mean the schoolchildren, of course." Miss Maynard and Mr. Jessyp had dismissed their pupils for the day, and a giggling, chattering, shrill-voiced crowd could be heard approaching from the north as it made its way in the direction of one or other of the Plummergen shops selling sweets, crisps, and fizzy drinks.

"I've never understood," continued Mrs. Blaine crossly, "how Mr. Jessyp can possibly believe That Woman is fit to teach such very impressionable youngsters whenever Miss Maynard's away. One would suppose he'd know better by now, with all the *peculiar* things that happen when-

ever she's around, but he doesn't seem to. It's too strange.
Suspicious, even.''

The shrill giggles had turned suddenly to squeals of excitement, accompanied by the thunderous patter of fifty
pairs of feet as the children rushed to Miss Seeton's aid.
They hurled themselves in gleeful pursuit after the wayward, wind-tossed hat, and ignored her cries of warning lest
her young helpers should, in the heat of the moment, forget
all about their Kerb Drill and leap out into the road under
the wheels of some passing car.

"Lady Colveden," Miss Nuttel reminded her. "Board of
governors. Different if any of *them* had children there, of
course, but they haven't.''

"Oh, Eric, you're so right. One would have supposed
that Lady Colveden—not that Sir George is exactly the
squire, too old-fashioned and forelock-tugging, but somehow one does still expect them to set a good example, and
not to go encouraging people who . . . ''

"Ought to know better," supplied Miss Nuttel, as Norah
Blaine drifted to a halt. She had just remembered that she
wasn't talking to Eric, and was feeling a little embarrassed
about having been the one to initiate the conversation.

She accordingly uttered only the faintest of murmurs in
response to Miss Nuttel's remark, and stared even harder
through the window at the frenzied scene without. The ca-
pricious breeze, which had bowled Miss Seeton's hat in
tantalising fits and starts all the way up The Street just a
few yards in front of her eager hands, had allowed itself a
short breather, sufficient to drop the hat almost to the
ground at the feet of the foremost child: but it had then
changed its mind again and sent the by now battered bonnet
in a high-flying parabola right across The Street to rest, its
proud feathers crumpled, its crown covered with dust, on
the striped canvas awning over Mr. Stillman's window.

"Oh, dear," breathed Miss Seeton, as the canvas
bounced and bulged beneath the unexpected weight. Mr.
Stillman, she feared, was not going to be pleased. The awn-

ing was new, a replacement for the curved brown-and-orange canopy which had shielded the post office window from the sun since the heady days of the Best Kept Village Competition, in which Plummergen had come second. With thoughts even now turning to next year's contest, Mr. Stillman had recently exchanged autumnal stripes for mock Tudor black and white, with a smartly scalloped border . . .

And nobody could call crumpled feathers and dusty crown—midnight sable, overpowered by dingy grey—any great improvement on the original intent.

"Oh, dear . . . Children—do take care!" Miss Seeton, still lamenting the unorthodox resting-place of her hat even as she patted her hair automatically back into shape, caught her breath in a sudden gasp at the sight of the fifty Junior Mixed Infants who from time to time came under her pedagogic sway running pell-mell across The Street, crying that they would throw stones or jump up to bring the fugitive feathers down.

"Children—no, please . . . "

But by the time Miss Seeton, looking carefully to right, left, and right again before setting even one foot on the metalled surface of the road, had reached the post office pavement, the area under the awning had become a mass of laughing, leaping figures swinging satchels upwards on their leather straps to bump against the canvas, attempting to jab pointing fingers and optimistic fists into the underside of the hat to slide it over the edge and into their waiting hands . . . And from inside the shop, Mr. Stillman's customers stood and stared, astounded.

Miss Seeton, blushing, raised her voice above the cries of "Out the way, Henry!" and "My turn now!" to request—to insist—that the children, grateful though she was for their assistance, should stop, and allow her to think the problem through. Recognising the voice of command, they duly stopped; but the effort of stopping them, hard upon the exertion of the chase, had left their commander too frazzled even to start thinking what she should do next.

Giggling, shuffling, digging one another in the ribs, Plummergen's youth watched Miss Seeton ponder, her anxious eyes upturned to the dark, circular shadow visible among the stripes. Whispers of "Dare you, Helen!" and "Go on, Katy, you thought of it first" did not reach her worry-deafened ears, and in the depths of her concentration she failed to observe the curious crowd pressing against the glass of the post office window.

At last: "Use yer brolly, Miss!" came the advice from the school's recognised wag, dared by his friends and with his position to maintain. Leader of the Bigguns, he was already as tall as Miss Seeton, though by more than half a century her junior. "Do it for you, shall I?"

"Ooh yes, Miss!"

"Hold yer satchel while you jump?"

"Betcher don't do it first time!"

The clamour seemed to rouse Miss Seeton from her contemplative trance. She blinked, shook her head, and, sighing with relief, smiled kindly on her young gallant.

"I don't think it will be necessary for anyone to jump, thank you. Mr. Stillman, as I now recall, has a set of aluminium steps behind the grocery counter, so that he may more easily reach items on the higher shelves. I am sure that, once I explain, he will let me borrow them—the steps, that is—and then, with my umbrella, as you suggested, it should be an easy enough matter to . . . "

It was a sadly dilapidated headpiece which was at last tumbled from the striped awning by Miss Seeton, standing tip-toe atop the borrowed steps, poking and prodding with her umbrella. She had refused Mr. Stillman's kind offer of assistance, saying that it was her own fault for having forgotten a hatpin; she had poked and prodded, and had at last achieved success. Fifty pairs of grubby young hands reached out to grab as the battered bonnet tumbled to earth; more feathers fell off in the subsequent scrimmage. Miss Seeton, blessing the yoga which, taken up over seven years earlier for the benefit of her knees, had endowed her with remarkable agility and an excellent sense of balance, hopped sadly to the ground to retrieve her handbag from one child, and her hat—after some confusion—from the midst of a scrabbling horde of the child's companions.

"Reckon it's had it, Miss," someone said, as Miss Seeton surveyed the sorry wreckage of her property, and sighed.

"I rather fear you may be right." She sighed again: one could do—one regularly did—one's best with trimming and decoration, but there was a limit beyond which even the most skilful needle—which she acknowledged that hers was not—was unable to renew the old, restore the ruined. "It is," said Miss Seeton again, "nobody's fault but mine, for having neglected, in my hurry to catch the post, to use a pin to secure my hat, in such very windy weather—which," she added, "is a lesson from which we might all learn. More haste, children, means less speed, in the end."

Fifty small, serious faces nodded their understanding, then hid smiles as Miss Seeton, realising what she'd just said, dropped the hat on the ground and opened her bag to begin fumbling inside for her letters. As some bent to retrieve, yet again, the peripatetic headpiece, others cocked their heads on one side, listening. In the distance, an approaching diesel whine . . .

"Miss, hurry up!"

"Here comes Bert!"

And Miss Seeton slipped her letters through the official scarlet slot just ten seconds before red-haired Bert, Plummergen's expatriate Cockney postman, pulled up in his van outside the letter-box, and prepared to unload its contents into his brown hessian sack.

"Well!" was the general opinion within the post office, as Bert in his van rattled at last on his way and Miss Seeton, having once more thanked the children, trotted off on hers, bearing the sad remains of her windblown hat in her hands.

"Well," somebody promptly enlarged, "if that ain't just what you'd expect o' Miss Seeton, egging on the kiddies to mischief—and her supposed to set them a good example!''

"As good as pulled Mr. Stillman's new awning down on top o' their heads with that brolly of hers—the poor little mites," chimed in someone else, having checked that none of the children was present to overhear this unusually fond turn of phrase. "As if any of us'd ever dream o' doing such a thing! I've allus said," she added, "as there's summat *strange* about Miss Seeton."

"Which ain't to say," said Mrs. Flax, "as she's the only strange one around these parts." The Wise Woman, perennially jealous of Miss Seeton's reputation against her own, steered the conversation artfully away from her rival, and back to the topic previously under discussion. "If there's anyone here," said Mrs. Flax, in challenging accents, "as can tell me what cause Miss Nuttel's got to go buying *cheesewire,* of all things, them Nuts being vegetarian, or so they've allus said, then I'd like to know what it is."

"*And* a fishing reel," said Mrs. Skinner.

"Not to mention snare wire," said Mrs. Henderson.

They stared at each other, astonished that their thought processes should be running so plainly in parallel. It was too much, of course, to suppose that parallel lines could ever meet: but both ladies felt a certain frisson as they hastily averted their eyes, and gazed anywhere but at the face opposite.

"And Mrs. Blaine," said Mrs. Spice, "a-barging in here not ten minutes after, for a breadboard—as if anyone needs two breadboards! Not as if you'd wear 'em out, is it? Take a powerful thick crust on a loaf for a knife to cut through to the surface."

"An *ordinary* knife," said Mrs. Flax, and put her finger to her lips, looking over her shoulder and lowering her voice. "It's not so long since Halloween, remember—as who should know better than me?" She cleared her throat, preparing for gnomic utterance, and everyone held horrified breath, and waited in gleeful expectation.

Expectation was not in vain.

"There's kitchen steel," Mrs. Flax, in thrilling tones, reminded her audience, "and there's *cold iron* . . ."

And as pent-up breath was released in an ecstatic sigh, a shiver ran down the spine of everyone within earshot.

Next morning's first lesson was History, and Miss Maynard knew that, in the first week of November, there could be no choice as to the historical event covered.

"The Gunpowder Plot," announced Miss Maynard, writing on the blackboard as she spoke. "Which was also known as the Gunpowder Treason. I'm sure you all know the rhyme," she added, as twenty small hands waved in the air, and twenty treble voices begged to recite.

"Remember, remember the fifth of November—
The Gunpowder Treason and Plot.
I see no reason why Gunpowder Treason
Should ever be forgot!"

came the full-throated response, in an excited chorus. Miss Maynard smiled.

"And what is so special about November the fifth?"

"Guy Fawkes Night!" roared the chorus, more excited still. Miss Maynard smiled again, and nodded.

"And who was Guy Fawkes? Doesn't anyone know?" as there was silence. "Come on, think. Try to remember," she coaxed those who had been in her class the previous year.

"Burn 'im on the bonfire," offered someone at last, to the accompaniment of sniggers from everyone else, who knew this very well, and said so.

"Indeed we do, in effigy—that means," said Miss Maynard, "as a model, a representation. But Guy Fawkes was a real person. The bonfire and fireworks we have each year on Guy Fawkes Night commemorate the explosion Guy and the other conspirators—the Gunpowder Plotters—hoped to cause when they tried to blow up the Houses of Parliament when the King was going to be there . . . ''

Miss Maynard proceeded to narrate the thrilling story of how Robert Catesby, with fellow Roman Catholics Thomas Percy and Thomas Winter, headed a deadly conspiracy to murder the Protestant King James I when he came, with his Lords and the ordinary Members of Parliament, to open the new session in the House of Lords on the fifth of November, 1605.

Catesby and his friends hoped to seize the king's nine-year-old daughter, the Princess Elizabeth, and put her on the throne in his place as a puppet, pro-Catholic queen: Sir Everard Digby, Ambrose Rookwood, and John Grant were brought in to oversee her capture from the house where she was staying at the time, many miles from London.

"Some of them," said Miss Maynard, "would have preferred to take the young Duke of York prisoner instead, but then they heard that he would probably be accompanying his father to the State Opening of Parliament, so they had to choose the princess. The Duke of York," she added, "in fact was destined to become King Charles the First . . . ''

The plotters found other people to join them. Thomas Winter recruited his brother Robert; Thomas Percy brought in his brother-in-law, John Wright. Robert Keyes was given the job of keeping watch on Catesby's house in London, where the gunpowder was stored, and to arrange the boat trip when it was to be ferried across the Thames from Lambeth to the Palace of Westminster . . .

"Thirty-six barrels of gunpowder," said Miss Maynard, "would make a tremendous bang, once they blew up. The man chosen to light the fuse was Guy Fawkes . . . ''

The conspirators, having acquired their gunpowder—and that, said Miss Maynard, was as difficult then as collecting thirty-six machine guns would be nowadays—began to dig a tunnel from the house of a man called John Whynniard. This man lived—he was the official Keeper of the Ward-

robe—within the precincts of the actual Parliament building, as you could still do, in those far-off days when people
were not so security-minded. Whynniard was happy to rent
out his house, and the finished tunnel ran from there to a
coal-cellar owned by a merchant called Bright—a cellar
which was directly under the chamber where King James
would attend the State Opening. The plan was to cram the
cellar full of gunpowder, and to time the explosion for the
exact moment when most of the country's rulers would be
above it.

"But they had made a big mistake," said Miss Maynard.
"Between them, they completely misjudged the sincerity
and commitment of one of the newer conspirators, Francis
Tresham. Nobody quite knows why, but Tresham betrayed
the Plot to his brother-in-law, Lord Monteagle. Lord Monteagle told the authorities what he had learned, and a small
party went to check the cellar.

"And there," said Miss Maynard, "instead of coal as
they might have expected, they found piles of wood, ready
for burning—and they found a man who called himself
Johnson, who was really Guy Fawkes. But he sounded so
plausible that they moved on, and left him in peace—only
the next day, November the Fifth, another group of men
came, and one of them was a magistrate. And when the
magistrate told them to search the cellar, they found the
barrels of gunpowder, and they arrested Guy Fawkes . . . "

The lantern-light searching of the Parliament cellars
(Miss Maynard told her pupils) still takes place every year
in commemoration of the saving of the King, his Lords,
and his Commons. A scarlet-and-gold detachment of the
Yeomen of the Guard is sent for this purpose from the
Tower of London, and not a single square inch of ground
is missed. Only when the Yeomen pronounce the vaults and
basement empty of any bomb or infernal device is it
thought safe for Parliament to be opened: there must be no
repetition of the narrow escape of 1605, when Guy Fawkes,
tortured, revealed the hideous plot against the throne, and

betrayed the names of his fellow conspirators. After his betrayal, some were taken alive, some died in the fighting—these last being, said Miss Maynard, probably better off, in the long run, for those who were taken were tortured, and stood trial, and were found guilty; and were executed in a public and very horrible manner.

"They may have been cowards," said Miss Maynard, "in the cold-blooded way they tried to kill innocent people when they themselves were nowhere nearby—but they showed the courage of their convictions in the brave way they met their deaths. They were drawn on hurdles, head-down, through the streets of London to the scaffold, and people threw things at them, and insulted them. But Ambrose Rookwood asked his captors to tell him when they passed the place where his poor wife was waiting, so that he could smile at her just once more, and ask her to remember him in her prayers. Guy Fawkes was the last to be executed, and because he had been so badly tortured he was too weak to climb the scaffold without help . . . "

King James and his Parliament, thankful for their escape, ruled that, from then on, the Fifth of November should be celebrated as a holiday, with bells ringing, cannon firing, and special services in church; and (as Miss Maynard said in conclusion) with parties, and with bonfires. The fireworks came later . . .

"But nobody wants to blow up the Queen now, Miss?" asked one youngster, whose imagination had been caught by the tale, and who was of a naturally anxious cast of thought. "And they don't want to—to go around stealing princesses, or putting gunpowder in places, or—or bombs?"

Miss Maynard smiled kindly as Sally's friends sniggered. "You needn't worry, Sally. It was all a long time ago, more than three hundred and fifty years— besides, as I told you, they search the cellars in the Houses of Parliament for bombs very carefully, every year."

"And," ventured someone, "you said it was treason,

Miss. Which ain't treason against the law?''

"Indeed it is,'' said Miss Maynard. "Treason is a crime, a very serious crime against the government and the Queen—the Sovereign, or the Sovereign's family. And it's so very serious that nobody would ever dream of committing treason, because nobody would want to go to prison . . . ''

But small Sally did not look altogether convinced.

CHAPTER 5

Inspector Harry Furneux of Rye was not a happy man.

There were, of course, times when the Fiery Furnace could be the most genial of men: but this was not one of them. The telephone wires between Rye (in Sussex) and Ashford (across the border, in Kent) were red-hot proof of his misery. He had spent the previous fifteen minutes moaning without pause to his colleague and county neighbour Superintendent Brinton; and Brinton—who could sympathise only too well—was growing restless. Old Brimstone would have liked an opportunity to let off some of his own head of steam. Even a few words would have done, they'd be better than nothing; but the Furnace was roaring away at full throttle, and all Brinton could do on the other end of the line was nod sympathetically, and suck peppermints, and roll despairing eyes at the ceiling.

"You seriously think *you've* got problems? With just one lousy royal visit?"

The suffering superintendent groaned. Inspector Furneux had now come full circle for the seventh time, but he still didn't seem to realise that Brinton might want to indulge in a spot of moaning on his own account.

"One half-pint princess," snarled Harry Furneux, "that's all *you've* got to worry about—*and* you get help, which is a damned sight more than I do—"

"Only a couple of toughs from MI5," Brinton—to his eternal surprise—managed to chip in. "And the odd bod or two from Special Branch, but—"

Furneux ignored him. "You've got it made, believe me! What've *you* got to worry about? You know as well as I do, the build-up that young woman's had since she smashed her first bottle of fizz against a battleship's backside, if a bloke so much as harmed a hair of her royal head he'd have the whole damned country down on him like twenty tons of brick. It's a waste of public money—my blasted taxes, and yours—sending more than a lady-in-waiting, if you ask me. Our Georgy Girl doesn't need sharpshooters and body armour and sniffer dogs on the hunt for bombs—"

"Glurp!" Brinton was so horrified at this suggestion that a peppermint tried to go down backwards.

Harry Furneux again ignored his friend, though the sounds coming along the wire from Ashford were alarming, to say the least. "Oh, no, she just flutters those blue eyes of hers and flips her curls, and all the chummies go weak at the knees and say, 'Terribly sorry, but we promise to go straight from now on, and Gawd bless yer for being so forgiving, marm,' and the next thing you know the blighters're handing out tracts and free meals to—"

"Mam!" cried Brinton, goaded beyond endurance, spitting the wayward mint into his handkerchief. "Mam, dammit!"

"What?" The interruption had been so loud, and so sudden, that the Furnace applied an automatic damper. "Sorry, sir," simmering down, "I didn't quite catch what you said. Something about jam?"

"Mam," said Brinton, in more measured tones, after he'd cleared his throat once or twice. "We've had the briefing from Buck House, plus HRH's private secretary.

Snowed under with memos, we've been. Reams of bumf—
young Foxon's made paper darts out of half of it—but one
thing they said was that the first time, you call her 'Your
Royal Highness,' then it's 'Ma'am' to rhyme with jam, not
smarm, the rest of the time.''

''Ma'am,'' said Furneux, experimentally.

''That's right.''

''Oh.'' Furneux brooded briefly, and Brinton was about
to seize his chance when his colleague added:

''Tell you how to curtsey as well, do they?''

''For the women police officers,'' said Brinton primly,
''yes, they do. Maggie Laver's been practising her one
foot-behind-the-other-and-bob bit for days now.''

''D'you have to buy your own Union Jacks for waving,
or is there a sort of central store of the things they send
ahead and you send back once it's all over?''

''I wish,'' said Brinton, now the chance had come round
again, ''it *was* all over.'' Glumly, he tried with a dampened
finger to rub fluff from the peppermint's surface: it didn't
look so appetising now. ''I'm the old-fashioned type, I am.
Give me solid fuel any day—coal, or gas, or even oil, if
you can afford it the way the price keeps going up—but
the idea of neutrons and electrons and heaven-knows-what
bumping about together inside a hunk of uranium gives me
a nasty feeling, Harry. Someone drops a match or a fag-
end in the wrong place, and you've got something'll make
Hiroshima look like the Teddy Bears' Picnic—and not
twenty miles from here, so it'd be right on my patch. Yours
as well, come to that, except there'd be nothing much of
either left once that power station'd gone up in smoke and
a helluva lot worse—''

''Young Georgina doesn't smoke,'' broke in Furneux, so
appalled by this grim scenario that he temporarily forgot
his own woes. ''Never been known to drink, come to that,
and you can bet the lady-in-waiting won't if Georgy
doesn't. Anyway, I've been on a tour of the place—well,
not this new one, but Dungeness A, it's the same design,

another Magnox reactor—and they're a pretty careful bunch, these nuclear generating types. Got to be, of course—but there're great No Smoking notices up almost before you're through the first lot of gates, and—''

"Gates!" groaned Brinton. "What use'd gates be if some terrorist or other got the idea of planting a bomb and lighting a fuse and skedaddling before the place went up? Or turned suicidal and thought he'd chuck a grenade into the reactor, or whatever it's called—and don't tell me," hearing Furneux clear his throat, suspecting a lecture was about to begin. "I don't want to know. Chain reaction? Nuclear pile? I've seen *Dr No* like everyone else—*and*," grimly, "*Dr Strangelove,* so you needn't think I don't know what I'm worried about, because I damned well do."

"If you say so." Furneux sounded almost cheerful now: he knew very well that his friend's misery was not so much caused by fear of some maniac-begotten cataclysm as by anticipation of the horrendous traffic problems likely to attend so public an event as the official opening of a new centre of local employment by a young, pretty, and popular princess.

"And another thing," growled Brinton, making the most of it now the younger man seemed to have given up for a while, "why D, I'd like to know?"

"Wye Dee?" echoed Furneux, puzzled. "The rivers, you mean? Or is there some sinister oriental element in all this you haven't told me about before?"

"Why," enlarged Brinton, through gritted teeth, "is this one D, if the other bally thing's called A? I thought your average egghead types were meant to be logical! There's precious little logic if you go missing out B—or even C, dammit. Why's it D?"

"Haven't the faintest idea, I'm afraid. You could try," suggested Furneux, with a quiver in his voice, "ringing the Central Electricity Generating Board to ask them—or maybe if you unfold some of young Foxon's paper planes you'll find the stuff from Buckingham Palace tells you.

They brief their stars pretty thoroughly, I gather.''

"Ha! We'll be seeing stars, all right, if anyone puts a match to that damned Dungeness construction. Talk about Guy Fawkes Night—it'd be the whole blasted three hundred and seventy years rolled into one, and that's just for starters, because—''

"It'll be more the end of everything, rather than the start,'' interposed Furneux swiftly. "At least it'd stop you worrying, because there'd be nothing left to worry *about*. But when it comes to Guy Fawkes Night, well, you should have *my* worries for a bit and then you'd know what worry really means . . . ''

And Harry Furneux was off on the old, old story for—to Brinton's irritation—the eighth time, which had to be a record. Most years, he'd managed to shut him up around the fifth or sixth run-through. By now, he could recite it from memory, though he still couldn't see how the Bonfire Boys of Rye—dragging their boat through the streets of the little town, tearing down official notices of prohibition as they went, escorted by a selection of Guys in every shape and size, assembling for a gigantic bonfire on the Town Salts with the products of their riotous journey—could compare in the anxiety stakes with a royal visit. Traffic congestion? Furneux didn't know the meaning of the word. A few bob more on the rates to pay for replacing the No Parking signs? Peanuts. A handful of drunks in the cells, the odd window smashed? Worse had happened when the local football team went on the rampage after a win.

" . . . dead from the blast, then it'd be the radiation, and if that or the fallout didn't get you then the nuclear winter pretty soon would,'' Furneux was saying, as Brinton reluctantly tuned back into the miserable monologue. "Now, if you were to tell me anyone'd been monkeying around with shrapnel, I might just think you'd got a point. An ounce or two of big-bang mixture in a metal box—weedkiller, sugar, easy enough to find—pack a few nuts and bolts round it and light a fuse—yes, that's nasty. Or clockwork,'' he added, as Brinton, grinding his teeth on peppermint, bit his tongue and was rendered speechless. "Yes, if anyone tries a trick like *that* anywhere around young Georgina, I agree you've got problems—but they won't," said Furneux, firmly. "She's everyone's favourite girl, and they'd be lynched if they so much as hinted at hurting her. You've got nothing to worry about, sir, believe me. Everything," said Harry Furneux, "will be fine . . . "

The Brettenden bus had left Plummergen with Miss Nuttel, but with no Mrs. Blaine, on board.

This unwonted nuxial schism thrilled the entire village, both on the bus and off it. Those who stayed behind felt in duty bound to maintain surveillance on Bunny; those who went with Eric to Brettenden knew they faced a harder task, but, in the true Plummergen spirit, faced that task undaunted. It might be thought difficult, if not impossible, to remain unobtrusive when following someone into an ironmonger's: yet a small and determined detachment managed somehow to achieve this laudable end, thereby encouraging others to emulate their achievement in the hardware shop and, shortly after, in the electrician's.

The three groups found it more than frustrating that they were unable to discuss the matter with their friends on the return journey. Miss Nuttel, brown-paper-parcelled to the eyebrows, was, inevitably, their fellow traveller; for which reason, on their arrival in Plummergen, they repaired at once to the sanctuary of the post office. Having seen Miss Nuttel stalk up Lilikot's garden path and enter the house through a grudgingly-opened (and viciously-closed) door, everyone heaved heartfelt sighs of relief. Only now could they present their report to the Home Front, demanding in exchange the full details of Mrs. Blaine's activities during the absence of Miss Nuttel . . .

"Not seen hide nor hair of her all day," said young Mrs. Newport, with a sigh.

"Popped out once for a new washing-up bowl," young

Mrs. Scillicough volunteered, then flushed at the look of scorn on her sister's face. "Well, at least I *saw* her— not to speak to, though. Regular Hot Cross Bun today, she was, and no mistake—you ask Emmy," turning to Miss Putts on Groceries. "Hardly a civil word did she say, and nothing else did she buy beyond the bowl—eh, Em?"

"That's right." Emmy Putts was pink with pleasure at being the centre of attention, even though, with little to tell, she knew it couldn't last long. "Not even a tin o' them mock meatballs they're so fond of—and very brisk about it she was, too."

In fact, Norah Blaine had almost bitten Emmy's head off when the shop assistant had in all innocence expressed the view that Mrs. Blaine might risk breaking her glass and fine china washing up, and wouldn't a plastic bowl be better than enamel. "Told me," said Emmy, "as I oughter be ashamed of meself encouraging folk to—to deplete the world's natural resources, plastic bein' made of petrol or summat, she said. And off she went in a huff, and not seen since beyond shaking a duster out of the landing window," concluded Emmy, who had been fortunate enough to witness this exciting episode when popping home for her midday meal.

Public opinion did not take long to decide that washing-up bowls, whether plastic or enamel, lacked the glamour and intrigue of what Miss Nuttel had bought in the ironmonger's, the electrician's, and the hardware shop. Plummergen understood the necessity to clean crockery, cutlery, and glass, to wash dirtied dishes and kitchen utensils . . .

But it had—even after much racking of its collective brain—absolutely no idea why Miss Nuttel should wish to purchase (among other items) three yards of triple five-amp cable, three feet of bare copper earth wire, a conduit box, a sewing-machine belt (when everyone knew it was Mrs. Blaine as did all the needlework in that house!), ten sheets of asbestos board, a length of asbestos rope, eight steel angle joints, eight Jubilee clips, and a large selection of nuts, bolts, nails, screws, and metal washers.

After considerable discussion, it fell to Mrs. Flax to summarise the general opinion.

"Well," said the Wise Woman, "if you ask me, she's Up To Summat . . . "

And there, for the present, the matter had to rest.

Miss Seeton was busy in her kitchen with a fork, a bowl, and a waiting slab of rich, golden butter. Scrambled eggs, she had decided, were on the menu for tonight's supper. After all, since one had one's own chickens, and thanks to dear Stan these always laid so well . . .

When Cousin Flora had left her house and all her worldly goods to her grateful god-daughter Emily, she left also the perhaps more valuable bequest of Stan and Martha Bloomer; or rather (lest it be supposed that the old lady had approved the unwholesome practice of slavery) the bequest of their skilled horticultural and domestic services. Farmhand Stan had for some years past tended the gardens, both front and back—flowers, fruit, vegetables—of Sweetbriars, Old Mrs. Bannet's, now Miss Seeton's, cottage at the southernmost end of The Street, on the corner where it divides sharply in a right-angled bend to form Marsh Road, running west towards Rye, and narrowing to run between high brick walls down to the bridge over the Royal Military Canal.

One of these bridge-bound brick walls belongs to Sweetbriars, for the garden is of considerable length. As Flora Bannet, long widowed, increasingly deaf, and depressingly arthritic, was beginning to feel overwhelmed by the size of her responsibilities, Stan Bloomer, who lived in a cottage in the shadow of the Sweetbriars wall, made the providential suggestion that he should take over caring for the entire outside area of the property, Mrs. Bannet to select the pick of such crops as it produced, himself to sell the remainder at a profit, such profit to be in lieu of wages.

As for the inside as worrited her so much, well, there was his wife, London born and sharp as a needle, more than willing to come twice a week to cook and clean and do aught else the old lady might require, not just for the money but because they were neighbours, good as family living so close—and Miss Emily, popping down from Town to visit every now and then, like family as well, and no denying. Martha and him, they'd take a pleasure and more in looking after the place and the folk as belonged to it . . .

The folk belonging being in turn Mrs. Bannet and, for the past seven years, Miss Emily Dorothea Seeton.

Miss Seeton, blissfully contemplating, as she so often did, her great good fortune, sighed with mingled pleasure and regret as she prepared her supper. Pleasure as she pondered the sweet, smooth curves of the speckled shells; regret, as she destroyed their mellow brown perfection by cracking them, one at a time, into the glass bowl. She set the empty shells aside to be crushed for the compost heap, then whisked with an energetic fork until yolks and whites had combined in a froth of late summer sunshine. Pepper, a sprinkle: but no salt until later, for salt before scrambling made eggs sadly tough.

A dab of butter in the heavy metal pan; an aromatic sizzling. Miss Seeton's nose twitched. She picked up the bowl, preparing to tip its contents into the skillet—

"Bother." She set the bowl down again. Could one ignore the doorbell? Even at supper-time it would be, she supposed, discourteous. Whoever it was must know, from the kitchen light reflected on the wall at the side of the house, that one was at home. Besides, the matter might be one of some importance, even if one's friends, on these darker evenings, were given more to telephoning first than to turning up on the doorstep . . .

The bell pealed a second time. Miss Seeton clicked her tongue for her tardiness, pulled off her apron, dropped it neatly over a chair, hurried down the hall; heard strange scuffling sounds outside as she turned the handle, and the door swung slowly open.

"Evening, Miss."

" 'Lo, Miss."

A clustering giggle of children stood on the mat, nudging one another as they piped their youthful courtesies before falling into an awkward silence.

Miss Seeton, smiling, greeted her visitors in reply, her eye drifting momentarily over their heads as it was caught by further scuffling and giggling at the end of the garden, where more children hovered by the gate.

Miss Seeton was normally the most prompt of hostesses to invite her guests into her home. Her guests, however, were seldom so many in number, or so young, or in so obviously mischievous a mood—which one recognised, of course, from one's years in teaching. Children—mused Miss Seeton—as this particular group continued to giggle without utterance, did so enjoy laughter, which was, of course, so good for them. For anyone, indeed, especially after practical jokes, which—always provided they were not of a malicious or unpleasant nature—could often amuse even the adult mind, and certainly helped them to let off steam. The children, that was to say, not the adults, although dear Sir George and Lady Colveden had sometimes spoken in most, well, eloquent terms of the antics of dear Nigel and his cronies from the Young Farmers . . .

Miss Seeton's kindly smile grew wider as she thought of the aristocratic owners of Rytham Hall, for they were among her closest friends. She smiled; and the leader of the little giggling group on her doorstep was emboldened, with nudging elbows his support and prompt, to clear his throat.

"Er—Miss . . . "

Miss Seeton smiled on him as he fell silent again, and nodded encouragement. Evidently it had been proposed that she, as one sympathetic to the needs of the young—and,

without being immodest, perhaps in some ways better qualified than others in the village to be their recipient—should,
well, receive them. Or it. The joke, or jokes, not the children, or their needs. As guests, because although one tried
to be hospitable, one's cottage was hardly . . .

"Er, Miss," came the second attempt, forced out of the
speaker by a nimble prod in the small of his back. "Miss,
the other day, when it was so windy . . ."

Miss Seeton nodded again. "I remember, yes."

"We was wondering . . . with it bin a rare old mess on
account o' dust, and tumbling about, and us having to catch
it afore it blew away again . . ."

Miss Seeton blinked.

"Please, Miss, could we have your hat?"

CHAPTER 6

Miss Seeton blinked again.

"With it bin," went on the small petitioner, warming to his explanation, "not so long to go now, Miss—an' us've collected the sacks, an' the straw—"

"An' made the notice, too," chimed in someone else, with obvious proprietorial pride in this achievement.

"An' made the notice." The first speaker scowled at his companion. "An' got most of the clothes, Miss, as folks was happy to throw out—all of 'em save the hat, Miss, acksherly. So—well, we was wondering . . . "

Miss Seeton looked a little startled: but then, after a pause, as realisation dawned, smiled once more. Waste not, want not. Of course. An admirable precept—and with so many applications, although it was remarkable how many of these were not necessarily convenient to one's immediate purpose. Remarkable, for instance, how frequently what would at first glance appear to be the exact article required could not be used for that purpose because there was still good wear in it: which surely explained why—having asked, one assumed, their parents—they had come to her. Naturally—one's small part to play in village life—one was pleased to be able to help; flattered, in some ways, to have been asked, to have so won their confidence and trust that they had turned next to one who was, on occasion, their teacher. One could not—indeed should not—suppress their creative urges, though one had certainly never expected that one might be so—one could hardly call it *complimented* . . . yet the opposite—which would be, if deliberate, an insult—was far from their minds, as was any spirit of mockery, she was sure . . .

Miss Seeton twinkled down at the eager faces raised in anxious anticipation to her own. "I believe," she said slowly, "that I may well be able to help you. I had, you know, intended to try a few repairs—but really, when I come to consider the matter, I have had several years' wear out of it. And though one is not, I trust, a slave to current fashion, the wind was, as you rightly point out, very strong the other day. And it would perhaps be a trifle selfish of me to refuse when I do, after all, have others." She uttered a small sigh. "Indeed, I suspect that even if I had remembered my hat-pin it would have been unable to hold it on, or at least not without being rather uncomfortable. If you would wait there for just one moment . . ."

Miss Seeton—blessing her yoga-nimble knees—trod lightly up the stairs and into her bedroom, where she quickly retrieved from her mending basket the battered black felt with its woebegone feather trimmings. Clicking her tongue, she shook her head one last time for the loss of a Monica Mary creation. The celebrated Brettenden milliner would not, she hoped, be offended at such an unusual fate, should she hear of it, for the child of her imagination . . .

Miss Seeton blushed at herself in the glass for so very fanciful a notion, then hurried out of the room and back down the stairs to her front door. Here, she found that the original daring few had been joined by their less courageous companions from the gate.

Miss Seeton smiled on them all. The young: so full of

energy, and such a sense of fun, if only one could channel it correctly. Their undoubted energy. *Constructive play* she believed was the term she'd heard mentioned . . .

"But remember," warned Miss Seeton, as her offering was received with squeals and grateful giggles into the grubby, eager hands, "I expect to see something—something special, when the time comes. Something more than a little out of the ordinary, you know. This is, after all, a Monica Mary hat." Her twinkle was disarming, her tone amused, and the youngsters found themselves twinkling back as she went on:

"If you come back tomorrow after school, I might have found some more feathers to replace these—but not now," as further squeals suggested that tomorrow was a long way away. "The chickens, you know, have been put inside for the night, and I've no wish to disturb them by taking a torch down to the hen-house in the dark. Tomorrow, after school, and we will see what can be done."

"Ooooh, Miss," came the obedient chorus. "Thank you very much, Miss!"

"Um—pins, Miss," said the leader, made even more bold now the trophy was safe in his hands. "Allus have 'em on hats, do they?"

Warily, Miss Seeton confirmed that many persons did, but added the swift rider that many others did not. Pinning (or an absence of pins) was partly a matter of personal preference, and partly dependant on the style of hat; no, she wouldn't say there was any hard and fast rule about it, and certainly not *always*. And, of course, on the availability of the right sort of pin. No, she wouldn't call them *rare,* exactly, though she would certainly agree that there weren't as many around as there had been some years ago . . .

Miss Seeton's wariness increased. Service to one's community was all very well: one was only too happy—indeed, proud—to play one's modest part: but surely one was not expected to play it to such an extent that one was required to sacrifice one's prized personal possessions? Dear Cousin

Flora, old-fashioned though some might call her—not that her god-daughter would ever dream of such a thing—had left many charming and unusual items of jewellery—though not valuable, of course—to her heir; and Miss Seeton took a pride in wearing them on suitable occasions, enjoying the memories which the wearing brought to mind as well as the aesthetic pleasure it gave. A hat-pin, of course, could not be considered in the same class as the quaint glass necklace with its yellow beads, or the tiny silver brooch in the shape of a flying swallow, but . . .

"If there *was* a lot of 'em around, Miss, then you could wear more'n one at once," suggested he of the hat. "Couldn't you? A bit prickly, but more—more prongs, Miss, to hold it on. Like a fork."

"Or just one big one, Miss," ventured somebody else, when it was clear Miss didn't mind folk saying things. "Bigger 'n' thicker, I mean, like a—like a skewer, 'cept you'd have to take care of hurting yer head, but it'd be stronger by far nor any old fork in a wind like that . . ."

"Let us hope," said Miss Seeton, hiding a smile for the curious—and gratifying; one's teaching was perhaps bearing a little fruit—imaginative powers of her pupils—"that it will not be so windy again for a very long while. Fresh air is like so many things, acceptable in moderation but—"

She broke off. Fresh air? She sniffed. Sniffed again, nose twitching. "The scrambled eggs!" she cried; and, with a hurried farewell, closed the door on her young visitors before turning to trot, as fast as she could, down the hall to the kitchen, from which ominous curls of smoke were starting to drift.

Miss Seeton gasped, snatched her apron from the chair, wrapped it around her hand, and dragged the pan from the heat to rest on the coolness of the tiled kitchen table. Seized tea towels from the rack and threw them with a smothering motion over the sizzling skillet, then wrenched the red-and-white striped hand towel from its wall-mounted roller and added it to the rest. She darted to the cooker and switched off the ring; she turned back to the table, holding her breath. With a spitting, spattering, hissing sound, a vicious, roaring sigh, the danger seemed at last to be over.

Miss Seeton released her breath, inhaled too deeply with relief; coughed. She moved on trembling legs to the window, and threw it open. She breathed again, feeling the welcome draught. Her next cough was less hacking. Perhaps, thought Miss Seeton, she could now relax.

Except that one could hardly relax when, thanks to one's carelessness, the house had very nearly burned down about one's ears. It could be no excuse that the children at the door had been a distraction: perhaps one was, for all one's high hopes of the yoga, starting to feel—and, worse, to act—one's age. One's memory, concentration, clarity of judgement seemed to have been woefully at fault . . .

Or maybe—Miss Seeton brightened at the thought—one was just a little tired; though memory added that the day had, in all conscience, hardly been exhausting. A little gardening—deadheading, some light pruning, half-an-hour's gentle hoeing between rows of over-wintering vegetables . . . And one could not deny that one was not—well, not quite as young as before. Perhaps, before starting a second attempt at supper, a few of one's favourite postures—it was always best, as the book said and as Miss Seeton had learned by experience, to perform these on an empty stomach—for the alleviation of fatigue would improve matters . . .

The Headstand or *Sirsasana* was the most beneficial, she knew, to the brain and thought-processes, to the pineal and pituitary glands which, the author of *Yoga and Younger Every Day* explained to his readers at some length, controlled the growth and mental health of one's body. Seven years ago, one would never have dreamed of attempting such control: but seven years had made an amazing difference to far more than one's knees. Starting from the *Salamba Sarvangasana,* or Shoulder Stand, one could move up smoothly to the Headstand, to hold it for as long as comfortable before tipping slowly over into the *Halasana,* or Plough Posture, all the while doing one's deep breathing. Ten or fifteen minutes' practice, Miss Seeton hoped, would work wonders. She would slip upstairs now, and see how she felt after a brief workout followed by five minutes in the restful *Savasana,* or Dead Pose.

She had to admit that she felt better: refreshed, one could almost say. Miss Seeton opened her eyes, stretched, and rolled over on the travelling rug to arch her spine before rising nimbly to her feet. Refreshed, indeed: but she had somehow lost her appetite for scrambled eggs, normally one of her favourite dishes. The very idea of whisking eggs in a bowl with a fork made her fingers tingle, made them twitch and fidget in a most peculiar way . . .

Or maybe not so peculiar, after all. As if on automatic pilot, Miss Seeton adjusted her clothing, folded away the fringed tartan blanket, and made her way back downstairs. She found herself ignoring the kitchen, heading for the sitting room, for her bureau; for the drawer in which she kept her sketching implements . . .

With a swift pencil, Miss Seeton sketched a hat: but no ordinary hat. This was a black, broad-brimmed hat, high in the crown, almost as if the traditional witch's headgear had been lopped off halfway. A wide band decorated the crown, an enormous buckle decorated the band, and a tall, curling feather stood proudly at one side . . .

Miss Seeton blinked. This was not her hat, the hat she had given the children: this was—good gracious . . .

Smiling to herself, Miss Seeton drew a face beneath the hat: a man's face, dark, saturnine, intense of gaze, with some suggestion of the Spaniard; more than a suggestion of the fanatic in the set, the stare of the eyes. A short, trim beard on the determined chin. The hint of a collar about the neck: then more than a hint, as Miss Seeton grew inspired with her creation, enlarging it to show strong, clothclad shoulders . . . from which, to her surprise, sprang arms, not of flesh and blood under fabric, but arms of cold, cruel metal—straight, firm, gleaming; and ending not in fingers, but in sharp, curved, predatory prongs. A muscled body invisible within a belted tunic, close buckled on wide leather; legs, like arms, not of flesh and blood and bone, but of pronged metal, fourfold. Four limbs, four prongs on each: not fingers and toes, but tines.

Not arms and legs, but forks.

Guy Fawkes.

Miss Seeton, recognising the face if not the remainder of the personage, the suggestion of seventeenth-century costume, nodded. The woodcut of Guy, otherwise Guido, Fawkes was well known to those with any interest in history, and even to those who had little or none. Every November found that face reproduced on countless boxes of fireworks, on advertisements for Grand Public Displays, on posters warning children to take care when playing with matches and—even in this small way—with gunpowder. Guy Fawkes. Forks. Her cast-off hat—the children—her promise of feathers for tomorrow . . .

And the coils of smoke which wreathed about his head were, of course, only because of her carelessness with the skillet of hot fat. One must be thankful one had not gone so far as to add the eggs. A little longer for the air to clear, and maybe one might venture a second attempt. Just long enough, perhaps, to try a more, well, serious approach to a portrait of the nation's most famous, although one ought really to say infamous, terrorist . . .

The hat, the face, the beard and costume were much as Miss Seeton had drawn them in her first sketch. And surely it could not be so very unrealistic to have shown him with a dark lantern in one hand? There had been no pocket flashlights, no electricity, in the time of King James the First— as one was hardly able to forget, when the annual basement searching of the Houses of Parliament by the Yeoman of the Guard, in their renowned—although, one believed, misnamed—Beefeater uniforms, was always carried out using candle lanterns. Guy Fawkes: with coils of smoke again around his head . . . but that was no egg, dark-shelled, in his other hand. It was much darker, rounder; spherical. That was no string of albumen trailing from one side, but . . .

"Oh, dear."

A fuse.

A bomb.

And the fuse already alight . . .

"Melodramatic self-indulgence," Miss Seeton scolded herself, even as she sketched sparks and flames spurting from the fuse to the distant piles of . . . of what, she wasn't able to decide, since the explosion which had destroyed it— or them—had enveloped the entire background in smoke, and in further flame: which was foolish. Guy Fawkes had *not* (she knew very well) succeeded in his wicked intention of blowing up the Houses of Parliament, of murdering King James and his ministers. Why should she suppose that she, Emily Dorothea Seeton, had the power—even on best-quality cartridge paper—to re-write, or rather re-draw, history? The King and Parliament had all been saved, and nobody could have wished it otherwise—not even those who, for one reason or another, had little faith in politicians: which one could in some ways understand, even if one knew one's knowledge of the finer points of politics to be, well, limited. One voted, of course, but . . .

But so few of them appeared to talk sense, at least not for very long; though it certainly could not be denied that they *talked*. Indeed, most of the politicians one saw on the television, or heard on the wireless, seemed to be so fond of the sound of their own voices it was the only thing they ever did—talk—which meant they were so desperate to keep talking they often ran out of good ideas, and didn't. Talk sense. Or if they did it was far too wrapped up in rhetoric and—and "Flapdoodle," said Miss Seeton, out loud.

She smiled, sighed; frowned. One had to have politicians,

of course, to pass laws and govern the country and—she sighed again—to put up taxes—one couldn't remember the last time they'd come down—but, though one could not wish to return to the bad old days of King John, before the Magna Carta, or of Henry the Seventh and his Star Chamber, there had been, she supposed, something to be said for the system whereby the monarch—always provided that he or she had courage and kindness and wisdom, mercy and common sense—did not merely reign, but ruled. Exercising a benevolent, not a despotic, power . . .

"Off with his head," murmured Miss Seeton, doodling a tiny playing-card in one corner of her second sketch, thinking of *Alice* and the Queen of Hearts. Queen of Hearts. Did not Queen Elizabeth the Second, so dear to the hearts of her people with her obvious common sense, her great love of her country, with her family about her to help and support—the Queen Mother in London throughout the Blitz; Prince Philip with his Royal Navy training—make an excellent ruler? Nobody would ever wish to harm Her Majesty, Miss Seeton felt sure: she would never do anything foolish enough to deserve such harm. Neither (she felt equally sure) would anybody distress Her Majesty by harming those close to her. The Prince of Wales, an admirable heir—though not to inherit, one most fervently hoped, for many years. The Queen must be so proud of the way her young relatives had grown up to take their places in the public eye. Good training, firm principles. No wonder they were so popular. There was no chance of a modern Guy Fawkes with a Royal Family like this. Violence, revolution, anarchy . . .

"Not nowadays, thank goodness," said Miss Seeton. "Not in England."

And, tunelessly humming "God Save the Queen" to herself, she packed away her sketch-block and pencils with fingers that no longer twitched or tingled; and headed happily back to the kitchen, and her supper, having dismissed all thought of violence completely from her mind.

CHAPTER 7

"Hedging and ditching," said Nigel Colveden, receiving the loaded plate from his mother with a nod of acknowledgement. "And jolly tiring it can be, too. Hundreds of calories, I should think I've used up today."

With a gentle sliding motion, he insinuated the plate underneath the pages of *British Beekeeping,* which rustled at the table's top end in the hands of one the knowledgeable onlooker must have assumed to be Major-General Sir George Colveden, KCB, DSO, JP. "And me still a growing lad," went on the baronet's only son, a mere—albeit lusty—infant in his middle twenties. "Could I have another couple of spuds on that, please?"

"I do think it's unfair." Lady Colveden spooned two more potatoes from the dish to her son's plate, handed it across, and enviously watched him pour gravy in a thick, rich, fattening flood. "How you manage to eat so much without putting on weight, I really don't know. You certainly didn't inherit it from my side of the family. Even in summer, with salads and things . . . "

She sighed. Nigel grinned. "Mayonnaise," he murmured, just loud enough for her to hear. "Come out with us,'' he invited, more loudly, ''tomorrow, and work some of it off. I'm sure we could find you a set of overalls and a spare hedge-trimmer. Heaving one of those around for an hour or so must be easily as good as a keep-fit class—if not better. And a great deal more productive.''

Her ladyship wrinkled her nose. ''I hope I'm not one of those silly squeamish females, but I have to admit I don't care too much for the smell of petrol. Besides, I thought our hedges were all billhooks, and saws, and things like that, bent over and woven.''

''Rather sharp and prickly,'' suggested Nigel, ''though undoubtedly good for training the muscles . . . Cut and bend and weave first,'' he hastily agreed, as his mother frowned at him for such frivolity. ''Trim the line afterwards—it encourages thicker growth. Or you could drive an excavator, if you'd prefer.''

''No, thank you.'' In response to her son's gesturing fork, Lady Colveden passed the potato dish, and watched him cheerfully spear the largest. ''Potatoes—that reminds me, George.'' She raised her voice. *British Beekeeping* rustled again as her husband turned a page. ''George? George!''

''Plenty, thanks,'' came an absent voice from the head of the family. ''Let Nigel finish them.'' He coughed. ''Growing lad, remember.''

''There,'' said his wife, as his son spluttered, ''I knew you were listening all the time. I wasn't asking whether you wanted any more to eat, because there wouldn't be much point. Nigel's scoffed the lot. I was talking about next week's bonfire.''

This blatant distortion of the truth made Nigel drop his knife. He bent at once to retrieve it, and was a long time coming up for air. *British Beekeeping* scrunched down on the table to reveal the glittering eyes and shaking shoulders of a pink-faced Sir George.

''There's no need,'' said her ladyship loftily, ''for the pair of you to be so silly. You know very well that what I meant was that potatoes reminded me of Guy Fawkes.''

"Naturally," said Nigel, "they would." His shoulders, as he sat upright once more, were—like those of his father—shaking, and his face was red where Sir George had been pink: though this could have been due to his lengthy bending in search of the elusive cutlery.

Lady Colveden cut a thick slice of treacle sponge, and kept it defiantly for herself. Two smaller portions were passed to her grinning menfolk, and the custard was slow to follow. "Because," said Lady Colveden, "of having them for supper afterwards. In their jackets. Honestly—you two! Roasting them," as grins turned to outright laughter, "in the ashes, as I'm sure you knew as well as I did. Know, I mean. And do.''

"Sorry, m'dear." Sir George's toothbrush moustache quivered with apparent remorse.

His son's remorse was less immediate. Nigel had been all too enchanted by a sudden vision of newly-dug potatoes, their eyes bright, dressed in dinner jackets and—a loud guffaw erupted, hands shook, inundating sponge with custard—frilled shirts, complete with cummerbunds, cufflinks, and black bow ties.

"I simply feel," said Lady Colveden, on her dignity, "that it wouldn't be such a terribly good idea for us—for the village—to build our bonfire too soon in advance. And that anybody who has . . . well, any influence over them ought to say something before they do. Or ought to do something about it if they've done it already—not that I noticed anything when I drove past this afternoon," as her husband and son stared at her in some bewilderment, "but you know how Murreystone are sure to try to spoil things if they can. After the Best Kept Village Competition, and the Conker Contest and everything—not," came the voice of the temptress, "that I'm suggesting for one moment anyone should revive the Night Watch Men . . . ''

"Oh no," said her son at once, in decisive tones. "No! Not just to keep watch over a heap of woodworm-riddled

chairs''—his father stifled a groan—''and the odd tree-
trunk worth about fourpence ha'penny the lot, including
tax. You'd never dream of suggesting any such thing,
would you, Mother darling?''

His darling mother hid a smile as his father, forgetting
to groan, began to huff gently through his moustache.
Young Mr. Colveden, however, paid no attention to either
parent as he pressed on with his excuses.

''Oh, I'll admit that in theory things are reasonably quiet
at this time of year, but there's *always* something to do on
a farm—which is where pretty well everyone in the Village
Watch works. And we like our beauty sleep,'' he added,
with great firmness. ''Especially when the nights are so
long—and so cold.'' He shuddered, elaborately. ''My vote
goes for fluffy blankets and my eiderdown every time,
when I have to be up at the crack of dawn next day, every
blessed day of the week—and you can bet everyone else
you ask is going to say the same.''

''Week?'' echoed his mother, wide-eyed and innocent.
''But Guy Fawkes Night's only four days away, for goodness' sake. And Murreystone,'' she pointed out, ''are *five
miles* away at the most . . . ''

Nigel sighed. ''I had no idea, Mother darling, that you
had so great a thirst for violence.'' Gently, he fingered the
eye which had been blackened during the most recent inter-
village fracas, on the occasion of the Conker Contest; then
he found himself automatically clenching his fists at the
memory, and frowned. ''On the other hand . . . ''

Sir George cleared his throat. ''Shouldn't think they'd
risk another punch-up quite so soon. Taught 'em a thing or
two, I'd say. Need to get in training before they tackle us
again.'' His use of the first person plural was instinctive,
even though his part in the proceedings had been limited
to that of umpire, referee, and—on the stage of the village
hall, with PC Potter and the admiral beside him—overseer.
''Still, your mother could be right, m'boy. About *some*
things, that is.''

Lady Colveden wasn't going to argue one point when she seemed on the verge of winning another. "I do wish you didn't sound quite so—so grudging about it, George. You know very well I'm right—and I'm not"—unable to resist the temptation—"talking about your armchair now, though you know I'm right about that, too. But Murreystone are always . . . unreliable."

Despite himself, Sir George emitted a bark of laughter. "Can think of better words, m'dear—but, well, after that business in the spring—the arson—putting ideas in their blasted heads . . . "

"Please, Dad," Nigel stopped laughing, and looked pained. "Vandalism is one thing—anyone half decent'd want to put a stop to people digging up cricket squares or pinching garden ornaments—but when it's just a bonfire—"

"Burn it down," said Sir George, as Nigel broke off in despair, "and there'd be nothing left, dammit." The potential loss of his favourite armchair was as nothing to the idea of Murreystone victorious. "Can hardly waste decent coal to build another, or go using green wood—don't want the place riddled with sparks when it's alight, setting fire to people's clothes. And as for the smoke . . . "

"Got it!" Nigel's eyes were bright. "Don't let's build the bonfire at all! Not yet, I mean," as his parents looked startled. "I quite agree we shouldn't let Murreystone get away with anything, whatever it might be, but I fail to see why my nights should be permanently disrupted just so somebody can keep an eye on the blighters when they're in"—he grinned at his mother, winked at his father—"an unreliable mood. And they're bound to be unreliable after the Conker business, of course. Give 'em half a chance, and they'll be sneaking down here in the middle of the night to use up our entire stock of dry fuel in one fell swoop . . . but they'll only be able to sneak *if they know where it is.*"

"But how," enquired his mother, "could they *not* know?

The bonfire isn't exactly small—at least, it hasn't been in previous years, and I don't see why this year should be any different. And then, if it *is* built small, on purpose, wouldn't that be—be giving in to Murreystone?'' Her ladyship shook her head. ''That isn't how we won the War, Nigel. I really can't see that sort of—of spineless behaviour being very popular with anyone in the village, not even Constable Potter, just for the sake of peace and quiet.''

''The Colvedens,'' protested her ladyship's husband at once, ''aren't cowards, Meg.'' Sir George seldom spoke of the events which had led to the winning of his Distinguished Service Order, but the citation had left no doubt as to the baronet's courage in battle. ''Boy has a plan, if you ask me—right, Nigel?''

''Right.'' Nigel nodded vigorously. ''Thanks for the vote of confidence, Dad. I'm wounded beyond belief that my own mother should think her son would propose anything so—so dashed cowardly. Cunning, not cowardice, is the strategy applied by the Colvedens in moments of crisis—I say, that was rather good, wasn't it?''

''A cunning plan. Good show. Thought as much,'' said his father, as his mother begged her son's pardon, and pressed him for further details.

Nigel shrugged. ''Easy, really. Each person stores his or her own hunks of wood or bits of rickety furniture''—he shot a sympathetic look in the direction of his father—''or tatty old tea-chests *in their own garden shed*—and we don't bring them out until the afternoon of November the fourth. Then we go hell-for-leather building the bonfire, and set a round-the-clock guard until the Fifth, and all the fun. We can do without sleep for a few hours for one night, heaven knows, if we work the rota right. It's just the—the constant patrolling I object to. I mean, Plummergen's our own village, yet if you stop to think about it we're practically under siege half the time from those Murreystone blighters across the marsh.''

''Not a bad idea,'' said Sir George. ''Well done, Nigel.''

The old war-horse paid compliment. "Should have thought of it m'self—still, near enough. Keep it in the family. Fox those beggars thoroughly, I should think. Er—want me to give Jessyp a ring, or will you?"

Headmaster Martin Jessyp was renowned as Plummergen's finest paper-shuffler. The school timetable, the cricket team batting order, and the Christmas pantomime rehearsal schedule were no mystery to his methodical mind, even if Sir George, with his army experience, could not be faulted on overall organisational ability.

"Me? Good Lord, no. The cricket reshuffle when poor old Bert was stung by that bee was bad enough, thanks very much." Nigel turned pale at the memory, though the events to which he referred had taken place all of two months before, when postman Bert had tried, with unfortunate results, to deliver a parcel at the house of Admiral Leighton. Had the guilty admiral, a last-minute stand-in, not proved to be a master of the googly—the sneaky sideways-curving ball which caught batsmen on the hop—the result of the Murreystone needle match would have been very different . . .

"Ring him m'self, if you like. Ahem! Later, though." Sir George, like his son, had been put in mind of Admiral Bernard "Buzzard" Leighton, not only a brilliant bowler, but also Plummergen's resident apiarist. Pushing away his empty pudding-plate with a contented sigh, the baronet returned to the irresistible pages of *British Beekeeping*'s most recent issue. He and the Buzzard, who had lent him this invaluable periodical, planned to go into partnership next spring; Sir George was dreaming now of dessert sponges sweetened, not with treacle, but with the finest honey . . .

"And there's the hedgehogs, too," said her ladyship, as she and Nigel began to clear the table. "Only think how much better for them, poor things. I'm sure you didn't mean it that way at the time, Nigel, but it was rather clever of you. Maybe we should do the same thing every year."

With the gravy-boat in one hand, the jug of cold custard

in the other, her son gazed in bewilderment at his innocent parent, piling plate upon plate to slide them through the hatch, beaming at him with approval. He shot a wary look in the direction of *British Beekeeping,* but could see only the top of his father's head. Unable, with his hands full, to scratch his own pate in a parody of perplexity, he ambled across to the hatch, divested himself of his burden, mimed his confusion with an expressive shrug, and said:

"For the cricket? Alice in Wonderland played croquet, as I recall, with hedgehogs—but she used flamingoes, which are a bit thin on the ground around here. Would, um, herons be an admissible substitute? Hedgehog and Heron Cricket." He grinned. "Unusual, I grant you. Perhaps a little uncomfortable for the animals involved, but—"

"Nigel, don't be tiresome. Come and do the pans while I load the washer—you know perfectly well it was hibernation I was talking about. They creep," said her ladyship, kneeling before the open, rubber-sealed door, "into corners, and cover themselves with leaves, and sleep right through until the spring . . . "

"Sometimes wish I could, slaving away as hard as I do." Nigel scraped absently at a burned patch. "You wouldn't see me for six months—then, the first warm day and there I'd be, sitting in the sun doing nothing at all, just resting."

His mother rose, slamming the dishwasher door. "You'd be bored in a minute, you know you would. Just as you know," switching on, "that hedgehogs hibernate, and sleep so deeply they don't notice they've crawled into the middle of a bonfire, and when it's time to light it . . . Such a horrid idea, and I think you've been very clever, Nigel. We should have thought of it ages ago. They're so good for the garden—eating slugs and things, and you don't have to give them bread-and-milk to encourage them. They're rather fond of tinned catfood, apparently."

"Apparently," echoed Nigel, rinsing his final saucepan under the tap, "you've had a talk on hedgehogs at one of your meetings. What, as a matter of interest, did they say about fleas?''

''Not the same sort as dogs and cats,'' returned his mother at once. ''So Mrs. Ongar said, anyway—you know, Miss Seeton's friend from the bird sanctuary in Rye—oh, yes. That reminds me, I didn't want to say anything to them until I'd asked her, but . . . ''

''Wounded Wings,'' murmured Nigel, giving the sanctuary its full title. ''It only shows how you learn something new every day. I, er, never realised hedgehogs could fly.''

His mother ignored him. ''I do hope she won't be offended, although I'm sure they didn't mean it that way—they'd never dare,'' with a little giggle. ''They're much too—not scared, exactly—but wary, perhaps. You know how some of their parents are silly enough to say she's a witch. That's why they always behave themselves whenever she teaches them, of course. I would have said she had far too much common sense to take it as an insult, because they really have made rather a good job of it—one can't say *him,* in the circumstances, though I suppose one should, logically, or at least *historically.* And I know I said they didn't mean it that way, but it still feels a bit uncomfortable saying *she,* even if she *did* give them one of her old hats, or something that looks remarkably like one, anyway. And if she did, she must have known what it was for, or at least guessed—and Miss Seeton,'' concluded her ladyship, ''surely would have refused, if she thought it was meant as an insult. But I'd feel so much happier having heard her say so herself . . . ''

CHAPTER 8

"Penny for the guy, Miss?"

Miss Seeton, emerging from the draper's, found her attention being addressed by a huddle of her sometime pupils outside the post office, diagonally opposite. With a nod and a smile, she responded to their waving hands and shrill cries; she raised her umbrella in acknowledgement of their further salute, then carefully, looking first to the right, then to the left, then to the right once more—one should never assume that children, even in so quiet a place as Plummergen, would remember their Kerb Drill on all occasions without a good example having been set by responsible adults—crossed from one side of The Street to the other.

In the light from Mr. Stillman's window, the vociferous huddle was more plainly to be seen amid the gloom of a late autumn afternoon. Giggling, shuffling, nudging one another, the children moved aside to display their handiwork to best advantage.

Miss Seeton looked; smiled, politely; looked again; seemed, though she tried to hide it, disappointed. Offended? Possibly. On the paved footpath at her feet, gigantic arms and legs akimbo, sporting a shapeless smock, denim pantaloons, and a black felt hat with a once-proud feather cockscomb, sprawled a sacking form that was larger than life, or at least larger than any member of the enthusiastic bodyguard who now begged Miss Seeton again for the modest sum required by the tradition of almost four hundred years.

"Penny for the guy, Miss?" Eager hands pointed to the straggle-lettered sign, to the sprinkling of coins in the cardboard box beneath.

One should, of course, encourage them; but . . .

"The hat, naturally, I recognise." Miss Seeton's eyes twinkled. "And I must commend the effort which has gone into the body, and the limbs, though I do hope that none of your parents will prove to have been especially attached to any particular item of clothing . . . "

As she hesitated—honesty was the best policy, yet one did not wish to discourage them—someone said:

"Funny face though, ain't it, Miss?"

Miss Seeton's sigh of relief drowned out the furious retorts of those who had struggled with the features of the straw-stuffed figure on the pavement. One did not, after all, have to prevaricate. "Well," began Miss Seeton; then stopped. The tip of her umbrella touched in turn the blank button eyes, the smudged nose, the lipstick gash of mouth. "I'm sure you must have worked very hard," said Miss Seeton, gently. "But . . . the difficulties of working on such coarse material, of course . . . perhaps a paper mask, when you are all children who can, as I know very well, produce such splendid work in class . . . "

"Dunno what he looked like, Miss."

The admission was echoed by the rest of the little band. Miss Seeton frowned.

"But surely—on the boxes of fireworks . . . "

"Not allowed to buy 'em."

Of course: only parents, or those organising displays. So very wise of Mr. Stillman and the rest, though it was now, she believed, also a matter of law that children below a certain age should not be permitted to buy fireworks. There were, regrettably, some who could not be trusted to behave in a sensible manner with squibs and jumping-jacks . . . Yet this was no excuse.

"There are boxes in shop windows," said Miss Seeton, "if you only take the trouble to look. And to see," she added, sounding by turns stern and regretful. It was Miss Seeton's firm opinion that everyone should learn—should be taught—to see as clearly as possible. Her evident lack of success in this respect . . .

Sighing for her failure, with her umbrella she indicated Mr. Stillman's window display.

"Can't draw beards," she was promptly informed by an excited, and hopeful, chorus as it turned severally to look over its shoulder. "Nor hats, neither—nor make 'em. Nor—nor lend, like trousers . . . "

"Lend? You mean borrow?" The teacher's attempt at enlightenment faltered. Had tradition, then, changed so much? "You mean you aren't going to burn this guy on the bonfire after all? You intend to give everything back?"

Misinterpreting the guilty grins on the faces before her— the children's concept of borrowing differed considerably from that of most of the adults of their acquaintance—Miss Seeton smiled in sympathy. "Oh, I assure you the hat and feathers are of no further use to me. On the other hand," she added, "if your parents . . . "

With the tip of her brolly, she prodded doubtfully at the straw-stuffed hessian Gargantua, at its assortment of strange attire. One could hardly, of course, say anything against the tastes of others; but these were not, in Miss Seeton's eyes, clothes she could imagine anyone lamenting unduly if they were not, after all, given back once the business of collecting money to buy fireworks—or to hand to an adult to buy fireworks on one's behalf—had been accomplished. Besides, the children had clearly worked hard, even on that apology for a face. While the sacking might bulge, it had not burst: it did not leak. "Someone," said Miss Seeton with approval, "has spent a great deal of time stitching this together—and very neatly, too. How much money have you collected so far?"

The chorus, much gratified, told her. People in cars, it said, had stopped to look: not but what they couldn't do with more, to buy an even bigger box, like. Anxious feet nudged the cardboard collecting-tray still closer. "Get a whole heap more bangers," ventured one brave soul, "iffen we was just t'have a proper face on it . . . "

Miss Seeton hid a smile. No doubt this was what they had intended all along, but had been too shy to ask. Would it be churlish to refuse if one felt, as in fact one did, that they could perhaps have made a little more of an effort for themselves? Although . . . A slight twinge of disappointment, of guilt, made Miss Seeton sigh again. Her failure, her fault . . . Yet a guy—even one which was not, or so it seemed, to be burned—ought surely to be the work of the children to whom it belonged. Not that one would be so foolish as to call it cheating: there was no pressure to pass an examination, no spirit of competition . . . there was, instead, or ought to be, an element of fun, the pleasure of creation. And they had, one assumed, chosen to make the guy in their free, not their school, time, which they must have regarded as fun, because children didn't do things out of school unless they wanted to do them. And their failure to see the face under their very noses was of course far more the fault of their teacher than of her pupils . . .

Miss Seeton stared at the display in Mr. Stillman's window, memorising the bearded face and fanatical gaze of the figure on the firework boxes. "I can promise nothing," she said, "but I will see what can be done—if you, too, will promise to try again. We will exchange notes," she said, with another twinkle. "And, in the meantime, you may have not one, but ten, pennies for the guy . . . "

Amid a grateful hubbub, she opened her handbag, took out her purse, and popped two small silvery coins into the waiting cardboard box. "I suppose," she added, "that you can all tell me who Guy Fawkes was, and what he did, or rather tried to do?''

And the hubbub erupted once more as the children, in unison, told her.

Four times the heavy door had creaked open; had whispered shut behind each of the conspirators in turn. The blinds were drawn, the one central light casting a dull, yellow gleam on the faces round the table in the darkened room.

Breaking the pregnant silence came the sudden sounds of a clearing throat, the tapping of expectant fingers on age-hardened wood. There was no real need for Catesby to call the meeting to order: already subdued, the conspirators had long since conceded their leader's authority. But it could do no harm to reinforce that authority whenever the chance should present itself . . .

''We are all here.''

Even Winter, the light-hearted, did not smile at the self-evidence of this remark. Matters were too serious now for laughter. Three heads nodded gravely; voices murmured low acknowledgement of the universal presence.

''To business, then.'' Catesby, already sitting upright, seemed at once even taller. Cold grey eyes surveyed others which, uneasy, could not meet that steely gaze, and fell to the table-top, to their clasped and anxious hands.

''She is coming,'' said Catesby. ''There has been no last-minute cancellation: there has been no substitution of one who would be less . . . less useful to us.''

Again, this was something they already knew: but nobody cared to point this out.

''The *Beacon*,'' volunteered Keyes, ''has just announced the winner of the competition.''

Catesby looked a question. Keyes shook his head. ''As you know, we tried . . . a little pressure, but we couldn't risk being too . . . obvious, in this particular instance. We had, in the end, no influence over the eventual choice.''

''A pity, in some ways—but not an insuperable problem,'' said Catesby, frowning. "We have at least managed to exert our influence in . . . other areas.''

The others nodded. Keyes said, slowly:

"Everyone has their price—or almost everyone,'' as Winter stirred on his chair. "There are always secrets to discover—pressures to be applied. If only everything goes according to plan . . . ''

"But we didn't plan for a child from Plummergen, of all places.'' Rookwood, trying not to sound anxious, sounded instead almost too calm. "There will, however, be a large local presence as . . . compensation.''

"As large as possible, I trust,'' Catesby said. "The larger the crowd, the greater the confusion. The greater the confusion, the better for our purpose.''

Winter looked up. "Plummergen. Isn't that where that old girl with the umbrella comes from? The one the papers call the Battling Brolly—you know, Scotland Yard's tame art consultant they never mention by name any more.''

Catesby frowned again: it was Rookwood who replied, as Keyes sighed softly, a look of concern in his eyes.

"Yes.'' His voice was as calm as ever. "Yes, it is.''

Winter nodded. "Thought so. They used to write her up rather a lot a few years ago, didn't they? But she's obviously someone with clout—or else she's got friends who can lean on the editors—that's why I wasn't sure.'' He shrugged. "I can't remember her name. Sort of dropped out of the public eye a bit now, hasn't she? Unless you live near her, I suppose,'' he added, venturing a sideways look in the direction of Catesby.

He did not need to enlarge the point. Catesby, still frowning, clasped white-knuckled hands on the table. "There is no need to worry about this woman, whoever she is. It is simply a coincidence that it is a child from her village who has won: I see no reason why this . . . ''

"Beeton,'' supplied Rookwood, as the grey eyes searched for inspiration. "Something like that, anyway.''

"I see no reason why this Mrs. Beeton,'' continued

Catesby, "should hinder us in our plans. She might, indeed, be of use, if even half of what the papers have said about her is true. As I said, the greater the confusion, the better for our purpose."

"And according to the papers," said Winter, "this Brolly woman—I think it may have been Beeston—doesn't half let everyone in for confusion once she gets going."

"Beecham?" ventured Keyes. Winter, despite the gravity of the situation, grinned.

"Sargent," he suggested. "Boult? Or maybe even von Karajan?"

Catesby's eyes narrowed. "Winter, this is no time for your infantile jokes! Nor is this the place to flaunt your knowledge of orchestral music, or its conductors. The only interest you, or any of us, should have in music at present is knowing exactly what will happen from the instant the National Anthem has been played . . . "

"Sorry." Winter's apology sounded forced: at the bleak look in Catesby's eyes, he tried again. "I'm sorry. Though I'm not sure what the anthem's got to do with anything. Surely it—it all starts happening . . . some time after the girl's cut the ribbon and made her speech? After the Plummergen brat has handed over the flowers?"

Catesby, through gritted teeth, spoke in a tone so controlled that Winter quailed. "From the instant the anthem has been played, I said—and that is what I meant. Everything depends on accurate timing, on knowing her movements and those of . . . others. On knowing where everyone will be . . . and when. Among 'everyone,' of course, I include our . . . agents. Willing," came the grim qualification, "or . . . less so. There is no room for mistakes. Is that clear?"

And, as on every previous occasion, there came murmurs of uneasy, but resigned, acquiescence as the other three bowed to the will of the conspirator called Catesby.

*   *   *

Plummergen seethed with excitement. The teaching of Miss Maynard, of Mr. Jessyp, had paid off: a local child—a girl, fortunately, because of having a best frock already, while a boy'd mean a new suit and trying to get away with a borrowed tie, not to mention no Plummergen boy but secretly thought bowing over the hand of a lady a sissy notion—had beaten all competition to win the glory of presenting the bouquet to Her Royal Highness Princess Georgina. Young Sally was the envy of her friends, while her mother was the object of much behind-the-back remarks in the post office and other village emporia.

"It's not so much to say as three of 'em," announced Mrs. Scillicough, "wouldn't've looked a treat together, because the paper did say *school age*—only I can't help but think, even if it did keep 'em out in the normal run o' things, an exception might've bin made on account of three together being so out o' the ordinary. When there's that Sally just the one— and her mum'll've helped her write it, I don't doubt," she added. "Which, if it was accepted as fair, I'm sure I don't know as other mums couldn't've done just as well, if they'd've bin given the chance."

Mrs. Newport nodded vigorously at her sister's side. Mrs. Newport's quartet of under-fives was far better behaved than their triplet cousins, and Mrs. Newport herself—in her own opinion, at any rate, she having passed *O* Level English (Grade 6) while her sister only managed CSE—was far better able to write an essay on Nuclear (or any other type of) Power than anyone else in the family. Why couldn't Alice Maynard (demanded Mrs. Newport) have given lessons to any as asked? Open to everyone, such a competition did by rights ought to have bin, with everyone wanting the chance to meet a real live princess, and Georgy Girl so popular and pretty, though with no kids to look after and no real worries t'weren't no surprise . . .

"She'll be wed and worrited soon enough, poor lamb," said Mrs. Spice. "*And* brought to bed within the year, knowing her duty as the whole family's raised to do. Let her have her fun while she's able, the pretty dear, that's what I say. She'll be stuck with him for life, whoever he turns out to be, them not holding with divorce, and the kiddies when she's had 'em hardly her own, with bin so close in line to the throne, and—and national treasures,'' she concluded, quoting a recent article in that much-read (and occasionally accurate) periodical, *Anyone's*.

Heads were nodded gravely as Mrs. Spice, sighing, reached her rather wistful conclusion. Even Emmy Putts, on whose imagination the royal lifestyle had inflicted daydreams more bizarrely optimistic than her wont, had to admit, with some regret, that the life of a princess wasn't everything it was cracked up to be. Fun, did Mrs. Spice say? For all that she wore beautiful clothes, and jewels, and was for ever having her photograph took, well, it wasn't what anyone'd call private, was it? Not ever. And being dragged off—or sent, which came to the same thing—visiting all manner o' places you could be sure she'd never really wanted to see—that was hard on her, and no mistake. Never any freedom for the poor girl; never the chance to choose. And if anyone thought Emmeline Putts could be talked into traipsing over Nuclear Power Stations day after day, well, they'd got another think coming, on account of you could never be sure what it mightn't do if someone was to drop a match, and blow the place to smithereens . . .

''They won't,'' said Mrs. Stillman, sternly. ''Neither ask you, nor blow the place up—so you just stop your nonsense, young Emmy.''

Emmy tossed her head, and sniffed. Mrs. Skinner was even more outspoken than the postmaster's wife. ''The very idea of you being curtseyed to—it's downright blasphemous, Emmy Putts!''

''Treacherous, you mean.'' Mrs. Henderson, gleeful, was quick to correct her rival. ''Pretending to be royalty, why, that's treason. Torture you in the Tower o' London if you don't watch your tongue, they will!''

Emmy sniffed again. ''What's wrong with a curtsey? They say Maggie Laver over t'Ashford's had 'em a-curtseying to her all around the station, and not in the Tower yet. And young Sal's bin practising to Alice Maynard, I heard tell, ready to meet the princess . . . ''

''Which she'd better get right,'' someone said, ''or else we know what'll happen if she doesn't. Don't we?''

A long, penetrating stare raked the horrified assembly, which let out its breath in a shuddering sigh. There was no doubt of what would happen if young Sally let them down: the local paper had printed the name and address of the runner-up, winner of the second prize.

The runner-up who hailed from Murreystone . . .

CHAPTER 9

The road between Plummergen and Dungeness is almost level over the entire distance. On normal occasions there are those with a bent for natural history who often bicycle in a south-easterly direction across the marsh to go fishing, or to study the many varieties of bird-life—gulls, terns, grebes, shelduck, mallard, and many more—which frequent the flint-grey, pebbly peninsula.

On this particularly momentous occasion, however, it was considered neither practical nor dignified for even the most devoted cyclists to travel from the village to the Official Opening under their own power. Car owners with unoccupied seats offered lifts to their pedalling—and pedestrian—friends; Crabbe's Garage laid on both the regular bus, and the spare.

Crabbes have been mechanics for four generations. Old Crabbe (whose son, Young Crabbe, died in the last War) is well advanced in years, and has been forbidden by his family to drive either of the buses, much as he would relish the challenge. A distant connection of Daniel Eggleden, most recent in the line of village blacksmiths, Old Crabbe moved to Plummergen at the request of a previous Cousin

Eggleden around the turn of the century, when the coming of the internal combustion engine could no longer be ignored. Though trained as a smith, Old Crabbe (as he soon became) felt more at home with the petrol-driven beast than he ever had with any number of hay-eating horses.

Old Eggleden, Dan's grandfather, accordingly agreed with his Cousin Crabbe to divide responsibility for local transport between the two establishments; and thus it remains to this day. The bus, taxi, and hire car services are run from the garage on the eastern side of The Street; the farrier's and smithy stands where it always did, its double doors freshly painted in a rich grass-green, farther down on the western side, near Miss Wicks's little cottage with the wrought-iron balustrade which is one of Dan Eggleden's finest creations.

Very Young Crabbe, Young Crabbe's son, drove what might be termed the civilian bus: pensioners (including his grandfather, grumbling loudly), car-owners unwilling to lay out good money on petrol, and non-car-owners unable to obtain a lift. His son Jack had the arguably more important task of driving the bus which carried Plummergen's fifty-odd Junior Mixed Infants (including young Sally and—a concession which irritated every other parent in the village— her mother) with their three teachers: Mr. Martin C. Jessyp, Miss Alice Maynard, and Miss Emily Dorothea Seeton.

"I think it's very sensible of Mr. Jessyp to invite Miss Seeton to go with them on the bus," said Lady Colveden, as she tidied her wavy brown hair beneath her hat, a beautiful and costly Monica Mary original from the renowned Brettenden milliner. "Goodness, how one feels constricted, dressed like this—but it's only for an afternoon, thank heavens, and rather fun, once in a while. Naturally, I'd planned that we should offer her a lift, but he'd already spoken to her, as she's really very good at keeping them on their best behaviour. Only think how awful it would be if HRH saw them the way they can sometimes be. She rang

earlier, you know, to ask me what to wear,'' she added,
tucking a final mischievous curl in place.

"Georgy Girl?'' enquired Nigel. "I should've thought
she had enough advisers at Buck House, without having to
phone all the way to Plummergen for help.'' He loomed
over the top of his mother's head, checking the knot of his
tie in the hall mirror. "Perhaps I'd better do it again—what
do you think?''

"I think you're trying to annoy me. You know very well
I meant Miss Seeton. She's a teacher, after all, even if it is
only part time—and it would be like a lady-in-waiting,
wouldn't it? So HRH will understand. Poor Sally—she's
as jumpy as anything, even though Miss Maynard's re-
hearsed her for simply ages. And so's she—and her mother
is, too.''

"I would've thought,'' said Nigel, "that if Mrs. Maynard's been curtseying all over the place she'd be more than
jumpy, she'd be crippled. The number of times that poor
woman's been stuck in bed with her back, with her daughter rushing off to look after her . . . Hence Miss Seeton's
part-timing, of course, which saves us taking another car,
as Dad's not coming and the two of us can easily fit in the
MG.''

Lady Colveden sighed. "Such a shame he had a sitting
today, of all days—but justice has to be done, and someone
has to do it.'' She frowned. "Dispense it? Anyway, you'll
never make a magistrate, Nigel, while you have such a
dreadful sense of humour. I meant that Miss Maynard is
jumpy, and so is Sally's mother. Miss Seeton is always so
wonderfully calm, she'll do them a tremendous amount of
good, especially now she doesn't have to worry about her
clothes.''

Nigel, thoughtfully knotting his tie, spluttered. "Life
classes are one thing, Mother, but surely even Miss Seeton
can't propose to attend an Official Opening in the nude.
The imagination boggles—sorry.''

But his grin did not suggest undue repentance, and

his mother shook her head at her undutiful son, and sighed.

Miss Seeton shook her head, and sighed. The mirror—not always, she felt, an entirely reliable guide. Lady Colveden had said that the sort of clothes one had worn to the Royal Garden Party at Buckingham Palace would do very well— but, as one would have expected her ladyship to recall, that had been in the middle of summer: this was November. At least the forecast was neither for fog, nor for rain—which meant that a warm suit should suffice, being mostly, as one understood, indoors, rather than standing about in the open air. Lady Colveden—intending, no doubt, to be helpful— had added *but warmer, of course*. Perhaps one should, after all, wear over one's suit the Parisian coat which, when reversed, was so sensible a shade of gaberdine, but which was an undoubtedly smart, if a trifle flamboyant, red-and-black check on the other side. It did not exactly match the suit, but that would hardly matter, since it was unlikely to require unbuttoning in so short a time . . .

The suit: a discreet and reassuring tweed, with a sensible blouse. One's yellow beads—dear Cousin Flora! A hat? Naturally. Even on normal occasions, it was seldom that one cared to venture forth with one's head uncovered: but with what to cover it now? The red felt with its cheerful cockscomb would be an exact colour match, but perhaps somewhat too . . . spritely, for a teacher there in her official capacity. On the other hand, to reverse the coat to gaberdine would mean a hat in fawn or grey, which by itself, as a contrast, would do, but which with an entire coat would be—for royalty always wore such gay colours—imperial purple, royal blue—not only a little dull, but also, perhaps, disrespectful.

Miss Seeton bobbed a hurried curtsey at the very idea, and continued planning her wardrobe. Gloves, of course. Not white, which was a summer colour, as one's neat straw had been a summer hat: but leather, black and soft, with those three neat lines along the back. Court shoes, despite the suitability of the name, were perhaps a trifle lightweight for a royal occasion in November: luckily, one had a pair of walking shoes in grey which, at a pinch—except that they in fact fitted very well—would do. A new handbag; and, naturally, no other umbrella but the black silk, with the gold handle. Dear Mr. Delphick! What, wondered Miss Seeton idly as she began to button and zip herself at last into her chosen attire, was he doing now?

In Scotland Yard, Chief Superintendent Delphick had turned from his mid-morning perusal of the *Daily Negative* to gaze with some amusement at his long-time sidekick, the enormous Detective Sergeant Ranger.

"*What* did you say?"

Bob coughed. "Sorry, sir, I'd forgotten all about it. You know how busy we've been recently with . . . Sorry, sir." He coughed again. "We heard a day or so ago, when Anne's mother rang." Bob's wife, the former Miss Knight, had before her marriage lived in Plummergen, where her parents still ran the local nursing home. "It was only when you mentioned Dungeness just now that I remembered."

"Remembered," prompted Delphick, "what?"

"That one of the, er, Plummergen kids has won some newspaper competition for the job of handing a bunch of flowers to Princess Georgina, sir, when she goes to open the blessed thing." It had been Delphick's heartfelt comments on the probable traffic and security problems attendant upon the princess's visit, and his gratitude that the Yard, for once, was spared such problems, which had jogged Bob's memory. "Mrs. Knight says most of the village seems to be going to watch the fun, sir, even poor old Miss Wicks, with her arthritis: and half the, er, ambulatory patients"—Bob shot a look at his superior: jargon didn't always impress the Oracle—"are cadging lifts on one of the buses."

"And who, might one ask, goes on the other?"

"The, er, school, sir. All fifty of the kids, with the, er, teachers." Bob shot another, more wary look in Delphick's direction. "All three of them, sir."

There was a long, thoughtful pause.

Delphick ended it. "Wherever Royalty goes, police officers and members of the security forces—MI5, MI6, and, for all I know, MI one-hundred-and-thirty-seven—go with it: before, behind, between, above, below. Done, as one might say"—he permitted himself a brief smirk, though the joke was lost on Bob—"to a turn. There will—or at least there should—be a copper on every corner, directing errant cars and buses to their appointed place; there should be plainclothes men and women mingling with the crowds, their eyes watchful for the least hint of trouble. Given the, ah, combustible nature of this particular occasion . . .

"I wonder," he murmured, "how many of them have been deputed to keep an eye on Miss Seeton?"

Miss Seeton, with Miss Maynard and Mr. Jessyp, was too busy keeping an eye on her fifty small charges to notice whether anyone else might be keeping an eye upon herself. It would have interested Chief Superintendent Delphick to know that there was, in fact, no such curious, overseeing eye. Moreover, had there been, and had Miss Seeton noticed it, she would have considered this attention on the part of the security forces to be quite unnecessary on her own account. Miss Seeton, as has already been mentioned, does not—cannot—accept that she leads on occasion a life of incident, of drama, of criminal connection deserving of official concern: her involvement in such occasions, she believes, has ever been a matter of mere passing chance, and is in no circumstances anything over which she—or anyone else—need feel the slightest concern.

As Crabbe's coach pulled into the car park at Dungeness D, Miss Seeton's immediate concern was for the health and safety of those who had been entrusted to her particular care. The journey from Plummergen may have been short—no more than a dozen miles, along level marshland roads—but it had been crowded with incident. Children, wildly waving Union Flags, had prodded other children in various soft portions of the anatomy. Umbrage had been taken, insults hurled, challenges issued. A fully-fledged fencing duel had been fought up and down the central aisle before anyone could prevent it. The juvenile jousters had been forcibly parted by Mr. Jessyp just as they closed, their broken weapons discarded, in hand-to-hand combat on the floor; their supporters, leaping and squealing on either side, had contrived to sit on their packed lunches, to the detriment of the sandwich fillings, the seat covers, and the children's nether garments.

Several infants had succumbed to the first stages of motion sickness, and now drooped, pale and glassy-eyed, across the armrests overlooking the aisle, their heads bumped by other children, more robust, rushing (despite every stricture from Mr. Jessyp and—striving valiantly against her own nausea—Miss Maynard) to and fro as they sought the best view of the tall, brooding shape of the power station which loomed at them out of the distance.

Amid all the chaos, Miss Seeton's seat was a haven of calm. No riot or upheaval, no duelling or fisticuffs dared approach the place where she sat with young Sally and her mother, chatting brightly, reminiscing about her attendance at the Buckingham Palace Garden Party and the graciousness of Her Majesty the Queen, assuring her charge that curtseys would come easily, especially after so much coaching, since she herself—the yoga, of course, but Sally was so very much younger—had managed without any coaching at all . . .

Sally and her mother held out until Jack Crabbe pulled on the brake and switched off the engine. Forty-nine shrill voices were raised in a clamour to be first off the bus; one sad pipe addressed itself to Miss Seeton's ear.

''Please Miss, Mum—I don't feel well.''

''It's only natural you should be a little excited,'' said

Miss Seeton, after a quick look at the girl's mother had shown that such comfort as the child required must be offered by herself alone. "A short walk, you know, in the fresh air will work wonders."

Miss Seeton hopped nimbly up from her seat, and twitched her umbrella down from the overhead rack. Holding it like a baton, she brandished the brolly before the startled noses of the other forty-nine children, and made it plain that the first to leave the bus should be herself, young Sally, and—as pale, now, as her daughter—Sally's mother.

Jack Crabbe caught her eye, and pressed a lever to open the door with a hiss, and a rubbery thud.

The little procession descended the steps into the cool, windswept landscape of the shingle flatlands which comprise the unique promontory of Dungeness, the headland at the tip of Denge Marsh. Overhead, seagulls swooped and wheeled, screaming; higher still, clouds scudded across a slate-grey sky. The air felt damp against the skin, and there was a sudden taste of sea-salt on the lips.

Sally shivered. "Miss, I really don't feel—"

"A short walk," said Miss Seeton firmly, deciding with regret that the girl's mother, quaking and speechless at her side, must fend for herself. The second coach had pulled in next-but-one to their own, decanting older friends who could administer rather more brisk assistance than Miss Seeton—the child's teacher, but to the mother merely an acquaintance—felt would be acceptable.

"Come with me," Miss Seeton instructed the junior star of the forthcoming ceremony. Sally trotted meekly in the little figure's wake, taking deep breaths as Miss told her, counting the red-and-black squares on her coat, and maybe not feeling quite so queer as she'd thought she felt, five minutes ago . . .

"Look at the lighthouse, Sally." The umbrella pointed to the solitary structure, tall and weatherbeaten, almost at the water's edge. "Try to guess how far away it is. Could you draw it, do you think? What colours would you use?"

"Oh, Miss, everything's cold, and grey, and horrid!"
The complaint came loud and clear. Miss Seeton smiled to
herself: her prescription had worked. "Can't we go back
now, where it's warm? Mum 'n' the rest'll be wondering
where we've gone."

The roses had returned to the child's cheeks; and there
was sure to be one last rehearsal for her to attend. Miss
Seeton nodded, turned, and headed back towards the power
station entrance. There would, no doubt, be some official
at the gate who could advise her where she should deliver
her young charge for the final run-through . . .

Peak-capped security guards issued directions; smiled at
Sally, patting her on the head; paid compliment to her appearance as they checked lists, then stamped and handed
out those cardboard oblongs which granted access to the
less public parts of the building. An escort would, of
course, be provided for such a pretty young lady. She and
Princess Georgina together would be a sight for sore eyes.
Just wait for the pictures in the papers, on the television!

The hum of voices echoed down the third—or was it the
fourth?—corridor: they must be nearly there. Sally, however, was starting to turn pale again. Nothing more (Miss
Seeton hoped) than the contrast between the fresh autumn
breezes and the surprisingly—one had always understood
such places to be air-conditioned, for the sake of the
delicate machinery—the surprisingly stuffy atmosphere
indoors. The oppressively—one might almost say
aggressively—fresh paint, she supposed, silently wondering
how Royalty survived such atmospheres day after day, visit
upon visit. Noblesse oblige, no doubt, as well as habit: their
escort, a tall and very upright, broad-shouldered young
man, did not appear to be affected, while she herself, of
course, was long accustomed to paint, and its smell. But
one had to admit that in such large quantities, and in these
windowless passages . . .

"Miss," came small Sally's even smaller voice, as the
trio rounded the last corner to confront the waiting crowd,

to see the anxious faces; to hear the hurried footsteps of an unknown dignitary as their arrival was greeted with sighs of relief. "Miss, I think I feel—I don't feel well, Miss, please." A tug on Miss Seeton's sleeve, the voice, still small, rising to a pitiful wail.

"Miss, please—I got to go!"

CHAPTER 10

In such moments of juvenile crisis, the experienced teacher well understands that there is no time at all to be lost. As the young man with the shoulders, audibly gulping, could only gaze at Sally in mute alarm and begin to edge away, Miss Seeton glanced rapidly about her. Observing nearby a female figure in a discreet check overall, she recognised with relief the uniform worn by the waitresses in Bretten-den's Cosie Tea Rooms.

It did not occur to Miss Seeton that aprons and caps of this design were so convenient for catering personnel that they were popular among many other establishments besides that run by Miss Enden. Miss Enden's staff were renowned for their courtesy, promptness, and willingness to help: and, at that particular moment, courteous promptitude was precisely what was needed.

"Excuse me." Miss Seeton, standing on tiptoe, waved her umbrella to catch the discreetly-checked young woman's full attention. "Excuse me!"

Drawn by the compelling force of a practised pedagogic eye, the young woman hurried over. The problem was quickly explained: the remedy less quickly found, although she spoke as quickly as anyone Miss Seeton had ever met.

The little girl wanted the toilet? Oh dear, well, she really couldn't say, having only just popped in to see the fun, with being busy over t'other side setting out the buffy for later: what the boss'd called a collation—not that it mattered, she reckoned, what fancy name they gave it for the likes of Princess Georgina, living on caviare all day long the way she did, never nothing so dull as fish and chips or beans on toast or scrambled eggs. Only the best for Georgy Girl—a brand-new toilet brought in special—no (as Miss Seeton managed to squeeze in a word), not the Portaloo lot, but local, KarriKlozzet, that was them, and with a mink-lined seat, she wouldn't wonder, and a regular crying shame she couldn't let the little girl use it first, but there it was, more than her job was worth, though if it'd bin up to her she'd have said use it, and welcome—

"Please, Miss!" Sally's face was pale with the agony of tension. The gulping young man gulped again, realising he would soon be called upon to act; then he allowed stiffened shoulders to relax as the unknown dignitary finally succeeded in making his way through the throng.

"The lavatory?" Dignity's relief, on at last seeing the missing flower-girl within a few yards of where she was supposed to have been ten minutes ago, soon changed to shocked dismay as his words boomed and echoed around the room. "The lavatory—at a time like this?"

Immediately, every head within earshot turned towards the little group. Dignity flushed purple, Shoulders scarlet, Miss Seeton demurely pink: but she did not forget her duty to young Sally, and explained, quietly but firmly, that she could not possibly allow her pupil to present the princess with her bouquet until she had first been permitted to refresh herself.

"Her Royal Highness," Dignity informed Miss Seeton in an irritated whisper, "is already drawing close to Dungeness D, I am informed. Within five minutes, I must be at the main gate to welcome her." The whisper grew more important. "And she will be making her speech, and cutting the ceremonial ribbon, within a quarter of an hour from now!"

"In which case," said Miss Seeton, in her best school-mistress tone, "there should be ample time for Sally to pay a visit to the nearest cloakroom. Moreover . . . " Really, one did not wish to sound rude, but if there was no other way of putting one's message across . . . "Moreover, if you will excuse my saying so, the longer we stand about discussing the matter, the more time is likely to be lost."

Despite clear evidence to the contrary, Dignity was so powerfully reminded by Miss Seeton's manner of his prep school headmaster's refusal to accept any excuses for the cricket ball's breaking of the gymnasium window that, within seconds, the still-blushing Shoulders had been deputed to whisk Sally and her chaperone down yet another passageway to a suitably discreet door, and to comfort.

Nigel Colveden, in company with every other male present, fell instantly in love with Her Royal Highness. Georgina's eyes were sparkling orbs of sapphire blue; her hair was a riot of rich, burnished gold, her smile a radiant ruby curve about pearl-white, regular teeth. Her photographs, Nigel decided, didn't do her justice: he doubted if anything but the reality could.

"Gosh," breathed Nigel, a devout worshipper, from that moment on, at the shrine of Royalty's youngest star. "Oh, gosh, I wish I was Miss Seeton!"

Lady Colveden had never before known her son—heir to a baronetcy, in the prime of life, tall, muscular, and (even to a mother's partial gaze) good-looking—express the desire to be metamorphosed into a small, thin, grey-haired spinster of a certain age: but her ladyship was, on this particular occasion, unsurprised at his expressing such a desire. Indeed, she had a strong suspicion that the sentiment was shared by almost everyone else, male or female, present: for Miss Seeton was nearly as close to the princess as her lady-in-waiting, and looked set to continue this closeness for the remainder of the royal Power Station Tour.

Returning young Sally, under escort, from her visit to the cloakroom, Miss Seeton had been asked by those responsible for the Presentation of the Bouquet to stay, in the regrettable absence of her pupil's parent, as moral support for that parent's child. Though the Plummergen presence was strong, it was, sadly, by one presence less strong than it had originally been. Sally's mother, overcome with emotion, had succumbed to stage fright in a bout of mild hysteria. She was being cared for (out of sight) by a posse of first aiders armed with smelling salts, burnt feathers, and sips of cool water: but the Show Must Go On, Regardless. Should anxiety about her mother prevent the child from carrying out her ceremonial duty, there was always—the sly official remarked—the competition runner-up in reserve . . .

Sally was a true daughter of her village, and resolute that nobody from Murreystone should even attempt to steal the thunder of a Plummergenite. When the time came to make her floral offering, the curtsey she swept would have turned Margot Fonteyn green with envy. She threw a beaming look of triumphant relief towards Miss Seeton, who had been so very kind; and she gasped with audible delight when Georgina, beaming back, exclaimed:

"Oh, thank you. What beautiful flowers—and such a lovely ribbon! Do you know, it almost exactly matches your frock?" So tiny was she that she hardly had to bend at all to hold the wide satin streamer against the skirt of Sally's best dress. "It does!" She laughed with sheer pleasure. "Don't you think it would make an absolutely perfect sash?" And those sparkling sapphire orbs made their appeal to the nearest person. To Miss Emily Dorothea Seeton.

Teachers of art have, of necessity, an excellent eye for colour; Miss Seeton is one of the most truthful persons in England, if not the world. This combination of circumstance made it inevitable that, thus appealed to, Miss Seeton should bob a curtsey, smile a modest smile, and agree.

"Wonderful!" Georgina straightened, plucked a single flower from the bouquet, and handed the rest, with a grateful nod, to her lady-in-waiting. "This is just for now," she said, presenting the flower to young Sally with a little bob and smile of her own. "You mustn't go too far away," she told the blushing infant, "while we all walk round, or I'll lose you in the crowd, and I shouldn't like that. And then, once we've seen everything, I'm going to let you have the ribbon to keep for your very own, if you'd like it. Would you?"

"Oh!" Sally almost dropped the flower in her excitement, and forgot all the etiquette she had ever known. "Oooh, Miss—I mean Mam—Princess—oh, yes, I would!"

"Then you mustn't let me forget. Promise?" And Georgy Girl's wink thrilled the hearts of many more than Sally.

Having been issued with regulation hard hats, the tour party moved off. Her Royal Highness, escorted by Dignity, was followed by Shoulders escorting the lady-in-waiting, who carried the bouquet—and Georgina's set of earmuffs, until these should be required. A small huddle of lesser beings from both parties, the Power Station and the Palace, walked in the rear, their helmets on their heads, their muffs in their hands; and, caught up by Royal Command in that same huddle, ahead of everyone else—Press and Plummergen and Murreystone included—walked Sally and Miss Seeton.

As they walked, hearing Dignity's running commentary in the near distance, Miss Seeton felt an overwhelming sense of power, harnessed but ready—should chance decree otherwise—to be unleashed upon an unsuspecting world. Inevitable, of course, in such a place. The air hummed, the very walls seemed alive with some huge, invisible animal presence that whined, muted, muzzled, restrained: a wild animal, capable of terrible force, of horrific destruction if once—a fanciful notion— the beast broke its fetters, and ran free. To one of Miss Seeton's generation, the names of Hiroshima and Nagasaki spoke only too clearly of just what terror and horror there could be . . .

And yet here, now, it seemed that terror and horror had— by a miracle of science she knew she could never hope to understand—given way to good. Electricity: light and heat and transport, power for industrial use, warmth and safety for people in their homes . . .

Miss Seeton looked with bewildered approval on pipes and wires and metal tanks, on dials and switches, on rows of knobs and buttons, on ranks of television screens. She blinked at wall-mounted cabinets containing, so Dignity's boom informed all within earshot, potassium iodate tablets; she smiled with the rest as Princess Georgina made fun of herself in huge earmuffs, and led the way, laughing, up narrow concrete stairs and through the huge Steam Turbine Hall, where the ever-present whine of the beast was drowned out by the roar of its even more monstrous parent, water-driven.

Dignity, earmuffs now removed, spoke in learned tones of boron steel and concrete shielding, of refuelling gantries and access pits. The princess heard that a tenth of London's entire electricity supply would come from here. Red lights—the eyes of the beast—glowed as the party passed by; its warm breath blew from ducts and internal vents on the exposed faces of the intruders as they passed changing-rooms filled with white overalls, free from dust and contamination.

Tiled floors, ceilings, walls. Desks covered in paperwork; swivel chairs, the seats of power in more ways than one. From staircase windows, a glimpse of the cooling ponds outside; talk of band-screen-filtered salt water siphonically discharged, of local fishermen happy to eat, or to sell, what they had caught. Georgina made a little joke about sea-trout and salmon; with chuckles her words were repeated, ripples spreading across the whole company.

Before leaving the controlled area for the next part of
the tour came the Radiation Check. "Do you think I'll light
up in the dark?" enquired Georgina, thrusting her hands
happily into the spring-rubber slots of the cream enamelled
metal box, huge and floor-standing, with its winking eyes
of dull red, clear green. Smiling, she twirled in a slow pir-
ouette, arms outstretched, as Dignity took it upon himself
to run the scanning beam of the monitor, microphone-
shaped, from head to dainty foot over her royal person, and
pronounced her radiation-free.

The others followed in turn: Dignity, ministered to by
Shoulders; the lady-in-waiting, scanned by—at her own
regal request—Her Royal Highness Princess Georgina, after instruction from a proudly blushing Shoulders. Not a
man in the party but would willingly have changed places
with him as Georgina, allowing Lady Vaudine to pass on
a steady green light, blew him a quick kiss of gratitude for
having let her share the fun.

The second rankers came next, watched with much interest by Her Royal Highness, reluctant to rejoin Dignity
and her bouquet as the queue snaked slowly on its way.
She would love, she said, to try again. A brief, silent consultation, and she was permitted to operate the scanner upon
the portly form of the Chief Physicist, the slender shape of
the Electrical Engineer. "What would happen," asked Her
Royal Highness, "if there *had* been a leak?"

The crush, the chaos in the monitoring lobby grew
greater as the rest of the tour—lesser beings, slower walk-
ers—gradually arrived. Those waiting to be let pass outside
milled about, crowding; those already outside pressed
closer for their first glimpse of the princess. Sally and Miss
Seeton, mindful of royal command, tried not to be swept
aside: there were many taller, heavier, more self-important
than they to make their importance known, and Sally
uttered a little cry of vexation as the crowd surged past
them.

Miss Seeton—indignant not for her own sake, but for

Sally's disappointment—took the child's hand in hers, used her brolly as a pathfinder, and edged her way to the monitoring station, where a white-coated figure demonstrated the rubber slots, the cream-and-silver microphone.

"Hold my rose, please, Miss?"

Small Sally, on tiptoe, felt rubber clamp gently about her hands, saw green lights gleam. The microphone wafted up and down her infant frame, and she danced aside.

Miss Seeton handed back the rose, slipped her umbrella up her arm, and imitated Sally and the rest with the placing of her hands. Green, silent permission was granted.

The silver microphone sniffed the soles of the shoes one by one, trailed in a swooping zigzag up the stockinged legs, the tweed checks of the coat; swerved around the buckled belt, the neatly-buttoned breast—

And came screaming, whooping, clanging to a sudden halt just as it reached Miss Seeton's face.

Everyone leaped as lights flashed, bells pealed, gongs deafened the ears. Every head turned to Miss Seeton where she stood, wide-eyed with dismay, trembling for the clamour she had wrought. With a clatter inaudible above the sound of the alarm, her umbrella slipped to the tiled floor and lay there, its golden handle seeming to blink as the redness above flickered on and off, on and off, on and off.

Dignity rushed to the rescue. "Switch it off at once!" Without waiting for the white coat to obey, he pressed levers down with shaking hands. The clamour was stilled, the red eyes dulled. "You—you must have done it wrong." Dignity mopped his brow: he did not dare—nobody dared—to glance in the direction of Georgina. "Let's hope it isn't . . . you haven't broken it. Try again. And carefully, this time!"

All eyes watched the monitor once more weave its upward, swooping path; all ears prepared for the clamour to begin again, though none believed that it would . . .

It did.

"Oh, no," breathed Miss Seeton: but nobody heard her.

Dignity, now deathly pale instead of purple, kicked aside
the umbrella, snatched the silver microphone from the
white-sleeved hand, and turned it upon himself, first clicking the switches off, then on again.

Nothing.

Nothing, until it was held again to the collar of Miss
Seeton's red-and-black checked coat. Some, with less self-
control than others, already had their fingers in their ears
against the racket which ensued.

"Take your coat off, woman!" Dignity, overwrought,
had no time to spare for the social niceties. Obediently,
Miss Seeton began with trembling fingers to undo her buttons.

Dignity pressed the switch for silence, then beckoned to
another minion. "The Geiger counter," he commanded;
and it was brought. Dignity gestured towards Miss Seeton
as she stood revealed in her light tweed suit and discreet
blouse, with her favourite yellow beads about her neck, her
neat felt hat—even the proud cockscomb looked embarrassed—on her head, her leather gloves and bag invisible
under sleeves which had slipped down her arms as the coat
swung open.

Tick. Tick. Tick. Tick, tick, tick, tick tick tick tick tick-
tickticktickticktick . . .

"The necklace!" Dignity pushed aside the second white-
coated assistant to spin Miss Seeton bodily round on the
spot, fumbling with the catch of her necklace as the Geiger
counter rattled out its warning. "The necklace . . ."

With Cousin Flora's beads well out of range, the Geiger
counter was held once again to Miss Seeton's neck.

Nothing.

"I've—I've never heard of such a thing in my life."
Indignant Dignity tossed the beads to one of the minions
with instructions to measure their output properly.

"Great heavens!" He ordered a second measuring. He—
everyone within sight—gaped.

"Great heavens—madam," recalling his manners with

an effort. "Do you realise that you have been walking about with two and a half thousand becquerels of radioactivity around your neck?"

"Good gracious," was Miss Seeton's weak, bewildered, and utterly helpless reply. "I'm—I'm really very sorry. Is it serious?"

Dignity rolled his eyes in speechless despair. It was one of the white-coated minions who replied. "Let's say you shouldn't wear those beads of yours for too long at any one time, Miss. The glass they're made of is coloured with uranium salts—those yellow streaks, you see. There was quite a vogue for that sort of thing back in the Twenties, when folk didn't realise how dangerous the stuff could be. You gave us quite a shock, I must say."

"Good gracious," gasped Miss Seeton again. "Oh, dear, I really must . . . " And she began to explain that Cousin Flora had left her, as well as her dear cottage and a modest sum of money, the contents of that cottage, these including her personal possessions and, of course, her jewellery, which she only kept for best, and, naturally, in honour of the princess's visit—

"Great heavens!" Dignity again went white. Never mind the confusion caused by this untoward occurrence; one could not with impunity ignore one's guest of honour—especially one whose blood was of the bluest, and whose influence on those responsible for compiling the Honours List could be considerable.

"I must humbly beg your pardon, Your Royal Highness, for the interruption." He thrust Miss Seeton and her apologies aside as he began to make his way back to where Georgina waited.

"But everything is now under control, Ma'am, and . . . "

To where she was not waiting.

"Ma'am?"

Attention snapped away from Miss Seeton, darted about the room. The lady-in-waiting uttered a little squeak, then began to turn pale.

''Ma'am?''

Heads turned, searching back and forth. Was Georgina playing—the nation's darling was surely not so foolish—a practical joke?

Surely not!

''Ma'am . . . ''

Dignity was pleading now. Lady Vaudine's white lips parted in a whisper. Other voices, low at first, then louder, took up the cry.

There came, no matter how loud the crying, no reply.

No reply at all.

Her Royal Highness Princess Georgina had completely disappeared.

CHAPTER 11

"She—she can't have disappeared!" Dignity cast a frantic look at the lady-in-waiting. "She—she must be playing some—some trick on us . . . "

For all the tension of the moment, Lady Vaudine Elliot visibly winced. "Her Royal Highness," she said, with icy scorn, "does not"—her lip curled—"play tricks." After her first white, stunned silence, Vaudine's aristocratic training had come swiftly to her aid. Her voice did not shake as she echoed Dignity's desperate words; and her head was high, her spine was straight as she went on: "Nor, let me assure you, is she given to—to *disappearing* whilst engaged on her official duties."

Lady Vaudine's voice did not shake—but her hands did. Dignity's gaze was irresistibly drawn to them as, despite her ladyship's air of studied calm, they writhed beneath their burden of Georgina's earmuffs and bouquet . . .

The bouquet! The child . . . and the old woman with the child—the old woman who had caused so much commotion even before the princess's arrival, and who had caused even more just before she—surely there could be no other possible word—disappeared . . .

Dignity whirled to face Miss Seeton, who, though quite as puzzled as the rest by Georgina's strange behaviour, had recovered herself sufficiently to begin the instinctive retrieval of her fallen brolly. "You!"

As he pointed a challenging finger, and uttered his one bitter syllable of blame, Miss Seeton, bending, jumped. She blinked. The umbrella clattered again from her grasp . . .

"Leave that alone!" Dignity was now in full command of himself and, he hoped, of the situation. He glanced round for the security people, and found, to his relief, that they had forestalled his next instruction. They were closing in on Miss Seeton—not one of them under six feet tall, all of them broad-shouldered, narrow-eyed, menacing—and Miss Seeton, startled by their menace, was taking a few nervous steps backwards.

She had left, as ordered, her umbrella alone. One of the security team muttered sideways to his companions and left them to continue their closing action while he veered from his course to begin a cautious approach to the sinister gold-and-black shape on the floor. Miss Seeton, surrounded, uttered one muffled squeak, then was frozen into silence by the force of the multiple slit-eyed stare directed at her from high above her head . . .

The security man neared the umbrella—held his breath—bent, warily, low . . . peered at the handle. His scrutiny passed slowly, intently, from the handle to the spike; he leaned over and squinted, frowning, at the ferrule, then seemed to have reassured himself that the rubber did not conceal the muzzle of some custom-built weapon; and moved back to the handle once more. Taking a deep breath, he thrust one hand behind him, motioning everyone away . . . while, with the other, he reached out for the exact centre of the umbrella, and picked it up. Smoothly, he rose to his feet . . .

He rotated the umbrella three times before deciding that it might be safe to examine it in yet more detail. He held it to one eye—squinted down its length; he held it in the middle and twisted the handle to and fro, aiming the fer-rule— for safety's sake—at the floor.

Nothing happened. No explosion—no bullet—no swift steel blade. It seemed there was no bomb, no gun, no sword-stick concealed in the umbrella's hollow steel shaft . . .

It seemed: but seeming was not believing. Expert knowl-edge of the ways of villains warned that the apparently harmless could even yet be something else. There was one check still to be made before the brolly's innocence could truly be believed. As there came a long, thrilling sigh from the watching crowd, the security man signalled again for continued caution, then fumbled with the fastening strap and, with a resigned grunt, slid the steel ring slowly up the shaft to its connecting notch. The spokes sprang wide apart . . . And the umbrella, in all its silken glory, was safely open.

Another sigh; murmurs of relief. It was no more than an umbrella, after all . . .

But was the old woman who had dropped it no more than an old woman?

All heads turned, as they had turned before, towards Miss Seeton. Dwarfed among her captors, she was gradually coming to the realisation that, somehow, everyone thought everything that had happened was all her fault—as, indeed, one had to confess that much of it was. Dear Cousin Flora's beads . . .

Miss Seeton saw the turning heads, the accusing eyes—and blushed.

"Oh, dear," said Miss Seeton. "I'm—I'm really very, very sorry . . . "

"I'm really very sorry, sir." Detective Constable Foxon was on his knees in front of Superintendent Brinton's desk. "If you hang on a sec, I'll just . . . "

With a further hitch of his well-pressed trousers up and over his knees to spare the crease, he flopped back on his heels, leaned forwards, and began to pick up the bright white bullets which Brinton, in an unusually exasperated moment, had hurled at him. Since cellophane bags of sweets are aerodynamically unsound, the bullets had not gone far in their flight before falling to the floor; and Foxon, who realised that he had, perhaps, himself gone rather too far on this occasion, had come rushing from his chair to the rescue. The rasp of Brinton's frenzied respiration was accompanied by a counterpoint of sharp plops as the peppermints were dropped, one by one, into the envelope Foxon held in his spare hand—the envelope which, as he saw his chief's empurpled face fade slowly to reassuring red, he moved a little farther away with each dropping. As the plops grew louder, Brinton's breathing grew calmer— or at any rate, by contrast, less noisy. Foxon, with an elaborately courteous cough, ventured to speak again.

"I'm afraid the packet's gone for a burton, sir. Burst its sides and fit for nothing—I'll bin it, shall I? But a bit of a dust-off and the mints should be okay."

"Throw away the lot," growled Brinton. "Then throw your own damfool self after 'em! It's time I traded you in for something easier on the eye, laddie—high time," as Foxon, risking a discreet grin, rose to his feet. "Why I've put up with you all these years, I'll never know . . ."

Foxon carefully readjusted the knees of his trousers to their former knife-edged elegance before folding down the flap of the envelope, crumpling the torn packet, and heading for the waste-paper basket. Its grey metal mouth yawned greedily as he held his booty directly above. "Could be the the contrast, sir," he ventured. The basket clanged. "Opposites attract, and all that. Me with my dress-sense, and you . . . well, yours is very different, sir, you've said so yourself. And there's you with all your experience of police work, sir, compared to me hardly off the bottom rung of the ladder—"

"If that's a reminder you've had thoughts about putting in for sergeant, you've picked a bad time for it." Brinton sighed, then absently pulled open the drawer of his desk to grope within. Somewhere, he knew, was his emergency packet: not that triple strength was anything like strong enough, though. Nowhere near it, when a man with his worries had worries like his . . .

"Oh, sit down and stop hovering!" His fingers had found cellophane at last, and he relaxed as he drew the packet out and tore the top open. "It's bad enough waiting for news, without having you prance about the place like some blasted grasshopper in that godawful outfit . . . "

Foxon's choice of shirt that day had been a rich emerald paisley, adorned by a burnt-orange tie striped with gold. His trousers were not only flared, but pale green; and there had been a Gala Dinner the previous night which the hapless superintendent had been obliged, in the course of his professional duties, to attend. The early-morning combination of a hangover and Foxon's spritely sense of colour had been altogether too much for the choleric Chris Brinton, though he had managed to suppress the full majesty of his wrath until the young constable had dared to tempt fate by speaking the unmentionable name . . .

But now, with peppermint soothing his savage breast, it was Brinton himself who mentioned Miss Seeton. "I should think," he said, replying to Foxon's not-so-innocent remark of ten minutes earlier, "she's having a whale of a time, if I know women. Hobnobbing with the bluest blood, best bib and tucker . . . " Then he grimaced. "With a swanky titfer to top the lot, of course. I've no idea why females *will* have a new hat whenever there's anything special going on, but they always do—and it doesn't come cheap, Foxon, believe me." Mrs Brinton, like many of the local ladies, was a frequent—their loving husbands would say far too frequent—customer of Monica Mary Brown, Brettenden's renowned, and expensive, milliner. "Thank heavens Maggie Laver's gone in uniform. I shudder to think what the bill'd've been for her to do the plainclothes bit . . . "

The words reminded him of his first sight of Detective Constable Foxon's *plain clothes*. For the second time he closed his eyes, groaned softly, and shuddered.

Foxon grinned. "Fetch you some coffee, sir, if you like." His voice was that of one wise in the ways of alcohol and its after-effects. "Black with two sugars'd do you best. Tone up your system for you nicely, that would. Give you, um, pep, sir—"

He broke off, looked at Brinton, and grinned even more broadly. "Well, it'd keep you going for an hour or so, anyway. Want some?"

"I don't want toning." Brinton's eyes were still shut. "I don't want pepping. The only *going* I want to do is home to bed, and the only *want* I have apart from that is for a nice, peaceful existence—"

The telephone's sudden jangle drowned out the rest of his wants as it woke him from his daydream. He opened his eyes, uttered a curse, and grabbed for the receiver with one hand while his other reached automatically for a pencil.

"Brinton." The telephone squawked in his ear. After no more than half-a-dozen words, the superintendent went rigid. "Dungeness? What's wrong? Don't tell me the blasted roads are snarled up and her precious Royal Highness is stuck in a jam somewhere, because—" Further, frantic squawking.

"Worse? You mean the girl's been in an accident?" His eyes darted to the large-scale map on the opposite wall, then narrowed with irritation. "Either it is, or it isn't. For heaven's sake stop babbling, girl, and answer a straight question. Is the princess all right?"

The telephone was slow to respond, then squawked in a manner that was almost hesitant. Brinton let out an exasperated snort. "What the hell d'you mean, you don't know? Call yourself a police officer when you can't make a proper statement? Once and for all, what the blue blistering blazes has happened?"

The telephone seemed to take a very deep breath. Then it told him.

"Princess?" Brinton blinked. "Disappeared?" He glared at Foxon, who had been a fascinated eavesdropper of the one-sided conversation, and clapped a furious hand to his forehead. His fury was so great that he forgot to wince. "This is no time for jokes, Laver. How the hell can the princess have *disappeared?*"

In his ear, Woman Police Constable Maggie Laver's voice rose to a wail. "I'm sorry, sir, I just don't know. But—but she has, sir. Gone, I mean. She just . . . vanished. Sir, she's c-completely disappeared . . . "

Now that Brinton had heard the worst for the second time, he was prepared to believe it. He became the epitome of professional calm to anyone who could not see him, though Foxon observed, with some alarm, that his face had already begun to turn purple. "Stop keening like that, Constable, and take a deep breath, and start again from the beginning. How long ago did this—this disappearance take place? And how"—the calm was starting to fray around the edges—"the hell did it happen?"

As Maggie Laver told him, Foxon—who'd been frozen into immobility at his chief's first words—shook himself out of his stupor and headed for the extension on his own desk. He had just reached for the receiver when he dropped it back on the cradle at Brinton's startled bellow.

"*What?*" roared the superintendent. The walls of the office thrummed. The central light began dancing on its flex. "*Miss Seeton?*"

And then, through gritted teeth, he added grimly:

"I might have known . . . "

"I don't care where he's gone, or who he's with, or how big the blasted building is." Brinton's tone left no room for argument. "Find him—and find him fast. Tell him if he's ever had an emergency to deal with, this is an emer-

gency with bells on—and no,'' as the switchboard at Scotland Yard tried a little discreet pumping, ''I'm *not* telling
you what this is all about. Just you get me Chief Superintendent Delphick on the line, pronto—and you needn't
bother,'' bitterly, ''listening in, my lad. You'll find out soon
enough, believe me.''

The switchboard recognised the voice of a superior under
considerable stress, and permitted itself only the briefest
mutter of wounded feelings before asking Brinton if he'd
mind hanging on again while various extensions were
tried—

''Can't you put out something over the public address
system? You must have one, for heaven's sake. Or send
out a search party—a dozen search parties!'' Brinton knew
how many floors there were in New Scotland Yard. He
could guess how many offices there must be, hidden behind
so many windows; and he hadn't realised, until he'd been
put through and had to suffer the long, hollow ring of an
unanswered telephone, just how much he'd counted on Delphick's being there when needed. ''Take a look in the can-
teen, for a start. Ask if anybody's ceiling's buckling under
the weight of young Ranger on the floor above—the lad's
with the Oracle more often than not. At a pinch, he'll do
instead of Delphick—but it's Delphick I really want.
Now!''

''I'll do the best I can, sir, but it may take some time.
Would you like to give me your station number, and I'll
get him to call you back when we've found him?''

Brinton spoke through gritted teeth. ''No, I wouldn't.''
Even in this moment of crisis, he had sense enough to know
that the very mention of the word *Ashford* would prompt
the question ''Middlesex, Derbyshire, Devon, or Kent?''
And the ''Kent'' reply, coupled with the urgency of his
request to speak with Delphick, would immediately alert
the most dull-witted detective—and those were pretty thin
on the ground at the Yard—that the crisis had something

to do with the Oracle's personal discovery, Miss Emily Dorothea Seeton . . .

"Chris?" It seemed an eternity later that the welcome voice appeared on the other end of the line. Brinton was moved to groan aloud in sheer relief. "Delphick here, as if you didn't know. You've been hunting for me high and low, after all: but why such heartfelt thanks to almighty powers? What's up?"

Brinton groaned again, but even now did not fully abandon caution. "Anyone with you?"

"Detective Sergeant Ranger, of course; and the assistant commissioner. We're in his office. Sir Hubert had summoned not a few of us to a meeting on the subject of terrorism, but everyone else"—did the oracular voice here quiver with faint amusement?—"has, ah, made his excuses, and run for cover. They—we—guessed that your cry for help was not unconnected with a certain, ah, lady of our acquaintance—and it seems," as for the third time Brinton groaned, "that our guess was correct. It must be pretty serious, for you to have browbeaten the switchboard into interrupting a top-flight terrorism briefing—so tell me, Chris. What's Miss Seeton done to upset you?"

In Ashford, Brinton could only gulp. He groaned; he gasped. He ran a hand around the collar of his shirt, took a deep breath—and gave up. He cast a pleading eye in the direction of Detective Constable Foxon, listening—at his chief's command—on the extension; and even the normally ebullient Foxon could only respond in the most hesitant of tones.

"It—she—it's not so much what MissEss has done to upset us, sir—well, I suppose she started it, so you could say she *has*—but it's got to be some mistake, sir," said Foxon, warming to his role as Miss Seeton's champion. He'd had a soft spot for MissEss ever since the night (as she herself was wont to say, with a twinkle in her eye) they had spent together, in a disused church,

looking for atmosphere and ending up in the middle of
a full-blown Black Mass, with a witches' coven thrown
in for good (though he supposed he ought to say bad)
measure. "It's got to be! I mean, she's not the sort to
complain, never has been, but it's bound to have upset
her, being arrested like that—not that they had any
choice, because—"

"Arrested? Miss Seeton?"

There came a series of clicks on the line as Sir Hubert
Everleigh, Assistant Commissioner (Crime), followed at
once—permission be damned—by Detective Sergeant Bob
Ranger, snatched up telephone extensions and began to fire
a volley of questions which deafened Delphick quite as
much as those listening at the Ashford end.

The babble seemed to bring Brinton to his senses.
"For the dear Lord's sake, *shut up!*" In his wildest
dreams he'd never imagined himself telling an ass.
comm. from the Yard to shut up, but what'd happened
now was one hell of a lot wilder than that, and if his
pension suffered it was just too bad. "All right, Foxon,
thanks," as everyone subsided. "Yes, Oracle, *arrested.*
Miss Seeton. And Foxon's right, there was nothing else
they could do, in the circumstances, but I agree with the
lad, there's got to be some mistake. That's why I want
you to come and sort it out, because I'm only a humble
copper, and in a case like this—when I'm damned if I
can understand the way she works, though she might
even be of some use, because God only knows what
other leads we've got to go on—"

"Chris!" Delphick's desperate cry broke into Brinton's
torrent of explanation. "Take a deep breath," he instructed,
in an unconscious echo of Brinton's earlier instructions to
Woman Police Constable Laver. "Let's start right at the
beginning. You say Miss Seeton's been arrested, and that
the arresting officers had no choice. Why not? What's the
charge?"

"You aren't going to believe this, Oracle. I can still hardly believe it myself." Brinton drew in one of the deepest breaths of his life. "The charge . . . the charge is . . . treason."

CHAPTER 12

The distance between Scotland Yard, in London, and Ashford, in Kent, is—as the crow flies—about fifty miles. The distance between Ashford and Dungeness is just under twenty: but the roads are not as good. In such circumstances, it should have come as no great surprise to Superintendent Brinton that the vehicle bearing Chief Superintendent Delphick and his sergeant should arrive in the Ashford police station car park at almost exactly the same time as that bearing the bewildered, and unhappily handcuffed, form of Miss Emily Dorothea Seeton.

The cars might have parked around the back, but—since this was November—their passengers had to come in through the front door. The rear entrance only stood open during very hot weather, when even Desk Sergeant Mutford, a staunch member of Brettenden's Holdfast Brethren, was prepared to yield Security to Comfort: open doors, although technically a potential risk, gave a through-draught which no number of electric fans could supply. Although Mutford was but seldom known to smile, a chilly day always gave him a slightly more cheerful aspect than one of scorching heat.

As the first arrivals pushed open the double doors, the sergeant looked up from the Occurrence Book, which he had been studying with the glum thoroughness of a man who always suspects the worst of his fellows, and has never yet been proved wrong.

"Ugh." Mutford nodded his recognition of the newcomers, and raised a hand in slow salute. "A good day to you, Chief Superintendent." Mere sergeants, being of equal rank with himself, did not deserve the honour of the greeting direct. Mutford simply nodded again as Bob passed by in Delphick's wake, then turned back to the Occurrence Book and resumed his pessimistic perusal of its pages.

Within fifteen seconds, the double doors clanked open again. Mutford, the gleam in his eye announcing to the initiated that he was enjoying himself as much as a Holdfast Brother would ever admit to such a thing, glared across at the noise: and froze.

"Constable Laver! What may be the meaning of this, if I might enquire?" He frowned awfully at the wrists of the hapless Miss Seeton, handcuffed in front of her. Maggie Laver had hated having to use them, but without her promise that they would remain fastened until her charge had been handed over to a higher authority, the security forces would have insisted on whisking Miss Seeton away in an armoured van to a destination unknown.

"All wickedness," said Mutford, in reproving tones, "is but little, Constable, to the wickedness of a woman. Ecclesiasticus Twenty-five, verse nineteen."

"Oh, dear," breathed Miss Seeton. "Oh, dear . . . "

WPc Laver, with a toss of her head and a muttered "Take no notice of him, dear," hurried Miss Seeton—she couldn't think of her as the prisoner—past the desk and down the corridor in the direction of Superintendent Brinton's room. Having favoured her charge with a sheepish grin, she knocked on the door, hearing at once Brinton's bellow for her to come in, and quickly, if she was Maggie Laver—and, if she wasn't, she could—

Constable Laver flung open the door before Brinton could say anything to fluster Miss Seeton any more than she'd already been flustered. "Miss Seeton, sir!" she announced, and ushered her charge gently inside.

Four pairs of masculine eyes fastened upon Miss Seeton and her uniformed escort.

"Oh, dear." Miss Seeton would have wrung her hands, but the short chain of the cuffs wouldn't let her. She lowered her gaze, her cheeks unusually pink, her brow furrowed in a look of helpless confusion. Delphick, Brinton, Foxon, and Bob couldn't think when they'd last seen her look so lost: it must, they each independently decided, be because she was, for once, without her umbrella.

"Miss Seeton." Delphick was the first to recover his wits; the first to rise from his seat to welcome her. "From what we've heard," he said, as Bob leaped to his feet to fetch a chair, and Brinton muttered to WPc Laver to take those blasted things off the poor woman's wrists before the weight of them dragged her arms out of their sockets, "you have been"—he saw her anguished expression, and smoothly changed tack—"well, you have been . . . somewhat in the thick of things today, haven't you?"

Miss Seeton was the only person in the room not to marvel at the enormity of this masterly meiosis. Still blushing, she glanced up at the chief superintendent's tone of—despite the undeniable gravity of the situation—faint amusement, and found herself relaxing, just a little, as she was coaxed towards the chair. As she sat down, Bob patted her on the shoulder, and gave her a reassuring wink out of the eye Brinton couldn't see.

Miss Seeton took heart from the encouragement of her adopted nephew, and spoke in tones less trembling than might otherwise have been the case. "I'm—I'm rather afraid I have, Mr. Delphick, and I'm really very sorry, because I'm sure I never meant to. Poor Cousin Flora!" Miss Seeton sighed. "She would have been profoundly shocked, for they were some of her favourite beads and I only wear them for best, which in the circumstances—the princess, you know—I naturally considered . . . oh, dear.'' She gulped, and looked hastily away, her cheeks reddening, her hands, now free of their fetters, writhing on her lap.

''Oh, dear, indeed.'' Yet Delphick—with some effort, admittedly—still contrived that his tone should be one of faint amusement, though from the frantic messages they'd been getting every five minutes from Buckingham Palace via the Yard and the security forces, he didn't in all honesty see how anyone could find the present circumstances in the least degree amusing.

But seven years' knowledge of Miss Seeton stood him, he believed, in excellent stead. Fluster her—browbeat and bully the poor woman, as he'd no doubt the MI5 people had done—handcuffs, indeed! If those hadn't been Security's daft idea, he'd happily surrender five years of his pension . . . worry, confuse, upset her, and goodbye to any chance he or anyone else might have of harnessing her unique abilities to assist in solving this undoubtedly unique case. While the combined constabularies of Kent and neighbouring Sussex searched for clues; while squads of hand-picked detectives and Intelligence men rushed down from London to interview known anarchists, communists, and similar subversives, he, the Oracle of Scotland Yard, watched the hands of the chief suspect dancing on her lap, and knew beyond any doubt that those hands held the key to the mystery. A key which could only be turned with great care . . .

''I do see, of course, that one cannot blame them.'' Miss Seeton's voice was almost steady, though it sounded little above a whisper. ''The—the unexpectedness, you see, of the noise, and Her Royal Highness . . . '' She faltered, blinking rapidly several times. ''They hardly do her justice, you know, when one sees her in real life. Such a—a joyful young woman, and bringing so much pleasure to so many . . . The police, that is, although Miss Laver was most kind, but one has, naturally, one's duty to perform, and I can quite understand . . . '' She sniffed, very discreetly, and her hands ceased in their aimless dancing to search for something more definite. ''My bag,'' she murmured, sniffing again, her eyes downcast. ''Oh, dear . . . ''

''Here, Miss Seeton.'' WPc Laver had argued loud and long with Security before they'd let her take the bag in the same car as its owner: nor had they let it go without giving it a very thorough check. It was emptied out on a table in front of Miss Seeton's startled, but obedient, gaze; a list was made of its contents; the power station staff were asked where there might be a convenient X-ray machine, to save ripping out the shot-silk lining. At this last, even Miss Seeton made a faint protest: but there had, fortunately, been no need to pursue the threat. While a detachment of MI5 operatives scrutinised for hidden horrors Miss Seeton's little purse, the modest sum it contained, the comb, lace-edged handkerchief, and mirror, her diary, address book, and sketchpad, the pencils, pens, and similar useful items, another group bore the bag itself away for the most rigorous of radiographic examinations. Neither party, despite the most detailed investigation, could find anything amiss. The contents were duly restored to the handbag, and the whole committed—albeit with reluctance—to Maggie Laver's care.

''I'm sorry,'' she said, ''not to have remembered before, Miss Seeton. And I'm even sorrier about—well, I'm sorry, but I did the best I could . . . '' She mimed helplessness, and Miss Seeton forced an understanding smile, though it was very shaky. Despite every argument Maggie Laver could put forward, Security had insisted on retaining, as hostages for Miss Seeton's subsequent good behaviour, her necklace of yellow glass beads . . . and her gold-handled umbrella.

''Thank you.'' Miss Seeton's whisper was barely audible, and to Delphick's keen ear it sounded as if there was more than a hint of emotion in her voice. When she took out her handkerchief and blew her nose, he was sure of it:

he didn't know when he'd ever seen her so upset.

"Miss Seeton, perhaps you'd like a cup of tea before we talk about what's happened? Chris, I think we could all do with some, to be honest."

Miss Seeton's slender frame quivered. "That would be most kind, Mr. Brinton, but please don't go to any trouble. I feel quite dreadfully to blame for—for everything . . ."

With the fingers of one hand, she crumpled her handkerchief into a damp, nervous ball, while with the other she opened and closed the metal clasp of her bag with quick, repeated snaps. Miss Seeton, it was only too obvious, was more than a little disturbed.

"I'm really sorry to press you, Miss Seeton," Delphick began, as Foxon slipped out with WPc Laver to organise tea and biscuits. "But I'm sure you appreciate the gravity of the situation. Everyone is doing all they can to help find the princess, and you, with your special talents, are bound to be of more help than most. You were, after all, an eyewitness—I'm sorry," as she flinched, and blushed again, and murmured of dear Cousin Flora, and how very dreadful it must seem, but she'd had no idea . . .

"Of course you hadn't." Delphick's mouth twisted in a wry smile. "As far as I can gather, your necklace is something rather out of the ordinary. You couldn't be expected to know that it had such . . . remarkable properties."

"No," said Miss Seeton, mouse-quiet. "I—I suppose not—except," she added, more firmly, "that dear Cousin Flora—that I had always noticed the beads, even as a child, and ought perhaps to have realised—the eye of an artist, you see . . . and she would sometimes allow me to wear them for—for fun, because they had so distinctive an appearance . . ." Reminiscence was helping her to relax. "Unique, indeed," she added, even more firmly. "Or at least, so I imagine."

"Indeed, yes, as far as we can tell. As, Miss Seeton, are you." Delphick smiled again. "Not merely as an eyewitness of—of recent events; not merely as an eyewitness who has been trained to use her eyes more than most. But as a trained eyewitness who has been retained by Scotland Yard as a consultant . . . ''

Miss Seeton winced, nodded, and slowly sat up straight. Any appeal to her sense of professional duty was bound— as Delphick didn't need to be an oracle to know—to urge her out of any mood she might be in; though he couldn't honestly blame her, on this particular occasion, for not being her normal happy, innocent, untroubled self.

"I will," said Miss Seeton, "do the very best I can, of course, Chief Superintendent, but . . . '' Her fingers danced and writhed again, fiddling with the clasp of her handbag, pleating her handkerchief, stroking the light tweed of her skirt in a quick, repetitive motion.

"But I can't—'' said Miss Seeton—"I'm so sorry, but I simply can't seem to *see* anything, Mr. Delphick . . . ''

"And she couldn't.'' Delphick sighed at Miss Seeton's would-be rescuers, who had arrived half an hour after her departure. "She did her best, as she always does, but she'd been too upset by everything to see clearly, I think.''

"Well, for heaven's sake, that's hardly surprising.'' Nigel Colveden was giving his best-ever performance as Sir Galahad. "The way everyone jumped on her—those Intelligence brutes with their beastly bullet heads and revolting slitty eyes—''

"Of course it isn't.'' Lady Colveden was every whit as indignant as her son, but was old enough to know how to temper indignation with guile; she also had no wish to be sued for slander by the security forces. "Poor Miss Seeton!'' She brandished the gold-handled umbrella under Delphick's nose. "Without this, naturally she was . . . disorientated.'' The word pleased her, if the circumstances did not. "She wasn't just worried about the princess— though, goodness knows, nobody in their right minds would dream of harming Georgina because they'd never live to tell the tale—but *you* gave her this, Chief Superintendent, and she was worried it might be . . . well, damaged—or lost—or something—"

"Whereas," supplied Delphick, as she drew breath for a further protest, "it was Miss Seeton herself, as you so rightly point out, who was, ah, lost. Without her umbrella—any umbrella . . . " He fixed her ladyship with a curious eye. "Incidentally, the last Superintendent Brinton and I heard from Woman Police Constable Laver, the MI contingent had—had received that into protective custody, and seemed highly unlikely to let it out again. How did you manage to effect its release?"

"We didn't post bail for the blessed thing, if that's what you're thinking." It was Nigel who answered: Lady Colveden was still being discreetly indignant. "We called in the cavalry. Brought in the heavy guns, as it were."

"Sir George," said Delphick at once, observing the look on her ladyship's face. "I'm not surprised—or rather, I am. That the major-general allowed things to go as far as they did before he, ah, responded, I mean—"

"George wasn't there." Indignation forgot courtesy, and interrupted briskly. "As soon as he heard, of course, he came across at once. Oh, there were interviews and things going on all over the place, and people giving statements, but he said he knew the moment he saw the umbrella that Miss Seeton must be in it somewhere—"

"And he was pretty peeved," Nigel broke in, "to find out she wasn't, any more. In it, I mean—the power station, with all the rest of us, because she'd already gone. It was only when he heard she'd be coming here, and guessed it'd be Mr. Brinton, at least, and most likely you as well, who'd be dealing with her, that he calmed down enough to start organising everyone Martin Jessyp hadn't already organised." Nigel grinned. "The village back on the bus, the schoolkids on *their* bus, the Crabbes keeping an eye on both lots, and Miss Maynard keeping an eye on young Sally and her mother . . . you can't say we didn't leave Plummergen in good hands, with Dad and Martin C. in charge."

"I would never dream of such a thing. But," Delphick enquired, "why did you? Leave, I mean. One hesitates, of course, to suggest that it was desertion in the face of the enemy. May I assume that it was more in the nature of obedience to command?"

"Got it in one." Nigel chuckled. "Dad said she'd be completely lost without her brolly, and to bring it along pronto, so we did, once he'd had a quiet word or two with the MI blokes." Nigel had no more idea than his mother what Sir George had said to influence the fate of the umbrella: but "MI" stood for Military Intelligence, and Sir George's wartime career had not been without distinction. "We'd no idea you'd, um, got rid of her quite so quickly."

"Miss Seeton," Delphick informed him, "was sent—was driven home in an unmarked police car, with the recommendation that she should make herself a strong cup of tea, and stand on her head for half an hour or so, to relax. After which—"

"After which," said Lady Colveden, "you'll expect her to start drawing, poor thing, and goodness knows what you'll see if she does, if she's been silly enough to follow your advice, which normally she wouldn't, because Miss Seeton has a great deal of common sense, in normal circumstances. Only she's so upset today she probably already has, so it's too late. With her insides swimming in tea, and then turned upside-down—she'll have nightmares, at the very least, and I can't see that they'll help you at all." She regarded the chief superintendent shrewdly. "You'll have been meaning to pop in to see her later on, of course, once you've checked into the George."

Meekly, hiding a smile, Delphick confessed that such had been his intention.

"Well, it's not very practical." Lady Colveden patted the umbrella on its gleaming handle, and sighed. "Really, although George has his good points, I sometimes think men, on the whole, are ... still, never mind. There are enough of the Security people around to keep everyone happy for tonight, aren't there? And the sooner we give this back to Miss Seeton, the better she'll feel about things in general. Just give her time to calm down, and don't arrive on her doorstep until after you've both had breakfast tomorrow. And then," said Lady Colveden, "you just see if she doesn't draw exactly the sort of drawing you want."

CHAPTER *13*

It was not Miss Seeton, but Martha Bloomer, who opened the door next morning to the pair from Scotland Yard. Her face, on seeing them, expressed a strong conflict of emotions. In the normal way, Mrs. Bloomer would be more than short in her manner towards anyone who had upset her dear Miss Emily—and there was no denying Miss Emily was still upset, even after a chance to sleep on it, with the wireless news and the papers full of nothing else but the Disappearance from Dungeness; but Martha—as did Miss Seeton herself—felt much admiration for Princess Georgina, and if Delphick and Bob were really going to find that blessed girl, they couldn't, she supposed, be blamed for coming to badger the poor soul so soon after breakfast . . .

"But you're not to go getting her in a state," came the sternly-whispered warning from the loyal domestic dragon. "In any more of a state, I mean, the way she's been already. Hardly touched a bite, then sits with her pencils and paper as miserable as if it really was her fault—which anyone with any sense knows it wasn't, no matter what she might've said yesterday, with the shock of it all being only too easy to take advantage of if it hadn't been for Sir George, bless him, and her ladyship seeing her right.''

Martha pointed to the umbrella-rack on the wall. Clipped firmly in its usual place was the gold-handled brolly of which its owner was so proud. ''Brought that back yesterday evening, and you'd've thought it'd cheer her up— which I dare say it did, a bit, but she's really not herself this morning, and no mistake.''

''We're very sorry to hear that, Martha.'' There was no doubting the sincerity in Delphick's voice, or the look of compassion in his eye. ''But you understand that we do need to see her, even though I imagine she's had more than her fill of questions from police and security people— they're off in pursuit of their own theories, and good luck to them. If they find Her Royal Highness before we do, then we'll be delighted; but something tells me things aren't going to go as smoothly as that.''

''That blessed lamb!'' Martha shook her head. ''How anyone could even think of such a thing I can't imagine, her being one of the sweetest girls you could hope to meet, they say. If only I'd been near enough to—but you want a word with Miss Emily, don't you? If there's anyone,'' said Mrs. Bloomer proudly, ''can help you, then it's her, and never you mind MI5 and Scotland Yard—begging your pardon, Mr. Delphick.'' She didn't bother apologising to Bob. Since his marriage to a daughter of the village he counted more or less as an intimate, among whom apologies for the obvious were rarely deemed necessary in Plummergen etiquette.

''Come on through,'' said Martha briskly; and led the way to the sitting-room.

They found Miss Seeton, as Mrs. Bloomer had predicted, seated at the table, with her drawing equipment spread out in front of her. On hearing the click of the opening door she started, and hastily flipped shut the cover of her sketch-pad before turning to greet her visitors.

When she recognised them, she blushed.

"Chief Superintendent," she murmured, rising from her chair to shake hands. For Bob, she forced a smile: the sergeant and his wife had long ago adopted Miss Seeton as an honorary aunt. This relationship she was more than happy to acknowledge, except that when he was in the presence of his superiors it made choosing the correct form of address a trifle awkward. A smile, Miss Seeton generally felt, was the safest solution; but she didn't feel much like smiling just now . . .

"I hope you're feeling none the worse for yesterday's little adventure," said Delphick, as they took their seats. "I'm pleased to see that you've already started work," with a nod for the sketchpad, pencils, and eraser arranged on the table. He tactfully ignored the even pinker blush which now tinged Miss Seeton's cheeks: she was always embarrassed at the creation of one of her special Drawings, and her embarrassment no longer caused him any great surprise. One had to coax her, perhaps remind her of her professional obligations if she seemed particularly bothered: he was used to it. "We know," he said, "that we can rely on you to fulfil your contract, and more than fulfil it: you've never let us down, Miss Seeton. May I see the drawing, please?"

As he smiled, and held out his hand, Miss Seeton's face flamed. Her eyes dropped to the closed cover of her sketchpad, on which her fingers twisted in a tormented knot, as if protecting—withholding—the sketch from Delphick's sight. She murmured something the chief superintendent didn't quite catch, and her hands moved suddenly apart as if to wrench and tear the sketchpad in two.

"Miss Seeton!" Delphick glanced at Bob, who shook his head, bewildered. "This isn't like you, Miss Seeton. You mustn't even think of destroying your picture, no matter what you think of its—its artistic merits. Scotland Yard owns the copyright, you know." And once more he held out his hand.

"Oh . . . " Miss Seeton, still pink-cheeked, raised her eyes to meet Delphick's firm but kindly gaze. "So—so very . . . disloyal . . . '' she gulped. "T-treas-treason . . . "

"Not," said Delphick, "if you give it to me now, without further delay. I'm a servant of the Crown, remember, and my duty, quite as much as yours, will be called into question if I fail to follow up every possible clue in this case. No matter how obscure or," and he smiled, "unusual. Please?"

He reached again for the sketchpad. Reluctantly—as reluctant as they'd ever seen her—Miss Seeton allowed him to take it; then she pushed back her chair and jumped up from the table before he could inspect her work. "I'll—I'll just see if Martha is making a cup of tea," she said; and fled.

Delphick looked again at Bob. "Entirely natural, of course, that she should be less than her normal happy self, but I can't help wondering whether the shocks of yesterday haven't, after all, been too much for her. We've grown so used to her bouncing back from her numerous trials and tribulations that we tend to forget she is, alas, not as young as—great heavens!"

As he spoke, Delphick had opened the stiff paper cover of the sketchpad. The exclamation had come the moment his brain had advised him that what his eyes had seen really was what Miss Seeton had drawn. "Great heaven and earth . . . "

There was a long, fraught silence. Bob, who had craned his head across to look at the sketch, had frozen in midlook, too startled even to whistle.

"No wonder," said Delphick at last, "that she spoke of treason . . . "

Miss Seeton had drawn a woodland glade in high summer, surrounded by leafy trees, carpeted with luxuriant grasses. In the middle of the glade, taking their ease on the grass, were three figures: one man, one woman, and one of indeterminate gender, who sprawled, leaning on one elbow, to the right of the little group with the other arm outstretched, the hand holding a bottle. The figure's face was shaded; the hand and bottle were sharply defined. The middle figure—like the first, decorously clad in jacket and trousers, but with a tie rather than (as the first) a frilled cravat—leaned rather than sprawled away from his companion, as if conversing privately with the third member of the trio.

This was a young woman, petite but shapely, her hair a mass of bright curls, crowned with a jewelled tiara. The young woman's face was instantly recogniseable as that of Her Royal Highness Princess Georgina; her body—with one knee bent up, one arm resting to conceal her bosom—was discreetly, but completely, nude.

Bob stared, blinked, and gulped. He was speechless. He stared again: there could be no doubt. The naked young woman was indeed Georgy Girl, the darling of the nation.

"Tastefully done," said Delphick at last. "No artful wisps of gauze or similar abominations—not that she needs them, of course. The pose, in itself, is quite unexceptionable—if somewhat surprising, given the subject."

"I'll say," muttered Bob. "I know she's used to nudity—Aunt Em, I mean—life classes and all that—but . . . "

As words seemed to fail his subordinate, Delphick said: "But you appear to have paid rather less attention to the foreground of the picture. The hamper, the tablecloth, the food waiting to be eaten—the wine . . . "

The hamper, tablecloth, and food were more impressions than definite shapes. The bottle of wine, however, elegant and slim, was so sharply drawn that Bob almost felt he could read the letters on the label; and the glasses beside the bottle were diamond-bright crystal, not feeble flickers of light and shade. The wine . . .

Bob looked at Delphick. "That's twice she's made a—a feature of the booze, sir, with this, er, chap here holding the other bottle—but surely she can't be trying to tell us young Georgy's an alcoholic!"

"I think not." Delphick smiled. "I think not, indeed—though she is, of course, trying to tell us *something*—and

I will hazard a guess as to what that something might be. Tell me, do you recognise this picture?''

"You mean it's a copy of a—a real picture, sir? Then I can't say I do. Sorry.''

"The, ah, real picture is itself, in a way, a copy—of an engraving by Raimondi, after Raphael. *The Judgement of Paris*—in the Metropolitan in New York, I believe. But the copy, as it were, is, unless I'm very much mistaken, Edouard Manet's *Dejeuner sur l'Herbe*.''

"Oh,'' said Bob, who felt he ought to say something, even if he'd forgotten most of the French he ever knew. "Er breakfast?'' he hazarded and Delphick did not smile.

"That's *petit dejeuner,* Bob: literally, 'small luncheon.' A good guess, though, since some people have large breakfasts, others have small luncheons: people's appetites, as you should know more than most, vary enormously.''

He smiled as he said this, and Bob had to grin. Anne often teased him that she cooked for three and ate for half, while he—more than twice her size—had the rest.

"The original title would translate as *Luncheon on the Grass,*'' said Delphick kindly. "Not that I imagine it's so much the sylvan setting as the more casual nature of the meal which has caught Miss Seeton's interest.'' He sat up, his eyes bright. "The buffet, Bob—the dining arrangements laid on for the aftermath of Georgina's visit. That's where we must start our investigations, I fancy . . .''

Bob frowned. He couldn't exactly see it himself—but then he wasn't the Yard's Seeton expert the way the chief super was. Even the assistant commissioner, who kept trying to sneak Aunt Em's originals out of the files to add to his private collection, could never make much sense of them while a case was still going on. But once the Oracle had—had . . . Bob frowned again, groping for the right word; then thought of breakfast and luncheon, and had to grin. Once the Oracle had translated the Drawings . . .

"You find my theory, I gather, attractive.'' Delphick was observing his subordinate in some amusement. "I'm glad it meets with your approval, Sergeant. It now remains for me to obtain Miss Seeton's approval, or perhaps I should say permission, for the use of her telephone. As a member of the family, do you think you could slip along to the kitchen and ask her?''

Two minutes later, he was standing, with a curious Bob at his side, in the hall, holding the telephone receiver in one hand while the fingers of the other beat an impatient tattoo on the table. ''Come on, Chris—Foxon—anyone, just answer this damned phone!''

The station switchboard broke in. ''Sorry, sir, there's no answer from Superintendent Brinton.'' Delphick resisted, with a considerable effort, the impulse to retort that he knew this very well. ''Would anyone else do instead?''

''No, thank you.'' The idea of explaining to a stranger how a doodled bottle or two of wine had inspired a Scotland Yard ace to demand a detailed investigation of the catering firm hired by the Central Electricity Generating Board did not appeal. ''Couldn't someone run a spot-check around the station? Today, of all days, I can't credit that he isn't on the premises—and my call has some bearing on the matter of Her Royal Highness's disappearance, which means it's more than urgent.''

''I'll put you through to the front desk, sir. Sergeant Mutford's more likely than most to know where Mr. Brinton's gone—if he's gone anywhere, that is.''

Delphick acknowledged the worth of this suggestion; he knew Mutford of old. The Holdfast Brethren maintained the most strict adherence to rules, regulations, and biblical law of any sect he knew: for a Brother to allow a telephone to go unanswered when his job was to answer it would be a serious lapse in observance.

It came, therefore, as some surprise when the telephone, yet again, went unanswered, though the switchboard let it ring for over a minute before breaking in to enquire whether the chief superintendent wanted to hang on, or whether he was quite sure nobody else would do.

"Try Mr. Brinton's office again, please. Even if he's not back, perhaps young Foxon could take a message—and I can't," he said, aside to Bob, as the connection was made, "stand much more of this. We're wasting valuable time here while—hello? Hello!"

"Hello," came the cautious response on the other end of the line.

"Chris, is that you?"

"Who wants to know?"

"Chris, stop playing games. You have a serious case on your hands, and there isn't time to—"

"Oracle!" The relief in Brinton's voice was obvious. "Thank the Lord for that. I've only just escaped with my life from a crowd of reporters out the front—Mutford and his gang are doing the Horatius-at-the-Bridge bit while Foxon and I made a run for it—and I was afraid you were another of the blighters who didn't believe that No Comment was honestly all I had to say right now."

"Reporters," said Delphick, momentarily sidetracked by memories of his own suffering at journalistic hands. "Yes, I can well imagine the sort of thing you've had to put up with. It's a great pity that Mel Forby and Thrudd Banner are still, as far as I know, out of the country—they tend to have a civilising influence, of sorts, on their more importunate colleagues."

The pair to whom he referred—Amelita Forby of the *Daily Negative,* and her close friend Thrudd Banner of World Wide Press—were acquaintances of long standing. They had severally entered the Oracle's ken by becoming involved in one or other of Miss Seeton's many adventures, and—being as fond of Miss Seeton as they were of headline exclusives—had succeeded in persuading Fleet Street and the news broadcasters that it was in everyone's interests to keep Miss Seeton's name, if not her adventures, out of the public eye. Nobody quite knew how they had managed to achieve this, but achieve it, on the whole, they had: for which Delphick and the rest of Miss Seeton's friends were more than grateful to them . . . and for which Miss Seeton was not in the least grateful, since in the first place she remained unable to conceive that her adventures were adventures at all—and, even if they were, she would suppose them to be the business of nobody but herself and (because they paid the retainer for her sketches) the police.

If anyone could make life at a press conference easier for Superintendent Brinton, it would have been Mel and Thrudd: but they were both, as Delphick had thought, out of the country. Thrudd had recently achieved a spectacular Drugs Scandal scoop, involving high-ranking officers in the Swiss Navy and an eminent pharmaceutical conglomerate. The supplying of substandard seasickness pills to Helvetian matelots had been only the first step on the downward path of corruption which Thrudd, with his usual brilliance, had excavated. His World Wide employers had given him worldwide coverage—and a bonus, which he had summoned Mel to the fleshpots of Geneva to assist him in spending.

"Importunate," spluttered Brinton, "be damned! All they *said* they wanted was a statement, to begin with—and then once they'd got me there the blighters were firing questions at me left, right, and centre. How many times does a bloke have to say he doesn't know before Fleet Street starts to believe the poor devil?"

"I sympathise," said Delphick, who certainly did, "but I have a notion that I may be able to increase your knowledge somewhat. You may have gathered that I am speaking from a—a village not a million miles from Ashford—"

A weary groan interrupted this circumlocution, followed by a thud as—or so Delphick deduced—the superintendent dropped heavily into his chair. "Don't tell me," begged Brinton. "You-know-who's been sketching again!"

"She has." The time for circumlocution was past. "And something she's sketched suggests to me that it might well be worth your while investigating the firm of caterers who supplied the food and drink—especially the drink—for yesterday's beanfeast. In depth,'' he added, as there came a long silence from the other end of the wire.

"Bragbury's,'' said Brinton at last. "Bragbury's Banquet and Buffet Service: they did the lot. They're a family firm—the electricity people like to support local industry as far as possible—and how the hell,'' he cried, "did Miss Seeton know? Though I ought to be over letting her surprise me, after all these years . . . ''

"Know what?'' Delphick tried to suppress his excitement. "You mean she's on to something—confirmed something—you already knew?''

"In a roundabout way I suppose you could say that, but there's a good few checks I'm going to arrange right now before I'll say she's hit the nail exactly on the head—''

"For heaven's sake, Chris!''

"Sorry. It's just that it isn't my case, as such, with Georgina on my plate enough for any man—not that I'd be likely to handle an ordinary RTA anyway, at my rank—''

"A road traffic accident?'' Delphick's response was swift. "And one of the Bragbury crowd was involved?''

"The father,'' said Brinton. "He and one daughter were both there yesterday, mum and sister stayed home to cook for other orders and do the washing up. Daughter and another girl were waitressing—silver service to impress the nobs with how well they could dish out the smoked salmon patties; dad drove the van, helped set the stuff out, hung around in a bow tie and swish jacket looking lofty. Quite a performance. They've done one or two of our police bashes, and they know—knew—their stuff, all right.''

"Past tense,'' said Delphick, thoughtfully. "I see.''

"For the father, yes. Car came off the road last night, went into a tree, and bingo. Dammit, Oracle, it seemed like a straightforward accident! The chap was known to be a fast driver, except in the van—Traffic've given him more tickets than he's given them hot dinners. Nobody was surprised to hear he'd finally written himself off. But now . . . ''

"Now," advised the Oracle, "you'd better have what's left of that car checked and doubled-checked, Chris. There is the distinct possibility that it was a third party who did the writing, in this particular instance—and, if so, it would be of the greatest help in recovering Georgina if we could only find out who that party might be."

CHAPTER *14*

Delphick and Bob thanked Miss Seeton for the use of her telephone, caught Martha's eye, and drank a hasty cup of tea. Then, making their excuses, they were gone.

By the time they had driven to Ashford, a distance of fifteen miles at most, official inspection of the Bragbury car was well under way.

"Good, you've made it in time." They might have expected rather more by way of salutation, but Superintendent Brinton was never one for the niceties when there was work to be done. Before either Bob or Delphick could blink, he had whisked them along to the garage where a team of experts was subjecting to rigorous examination the wreckage of the vehicle in which Donald Bragbury, founding father of the catering firm, had died the previous night.

They watched, and waited. Mechanics in oil-stained overalls crawled underneath the ruined car, and peered knowledgeably inside it. People wandered about with spanners and wrenches, looking important. Notes were jotted on pads of paper clipped to boards, measurements were taken; and taken again, as photographs were consulted.

"Then she was right—as if we couldn't have guessed."

Brinton's tone was resigned as he read the report rushed to him by the leader of the expert team, and discussed over a brief, private huddle. "Driving that route, he'd never have stood a chance, the way he always used to motor on the first clear stretch of road . . . "

"May I?" Delphick, unable to bear the suspense, took the clipboard from his colleague's hands, and studied it as if the mysteries of the internal combustion engine and its working were to him no mystery at all. "Ah, yes."

Without a word, he handed the clipboard to Bob, who received it with a faint grin. Brainy though the Oracle undoubtedly was, that brain had its limitations. Understanding what went on under the bonnet of a car was one of them—especially if what went on was anything at all out of the ordinary. Come to that, Bob didn't go much for custom motoring, either . . .

"Track rod ends," he said, having reached the relevant passage. This, at least, Sergeant Ranger understood, even if he had his suspicions that the Oracle didn't. As a loyal subordinate, he'd better help the old man out. "You mean somebody mucked about with the poor devil's steering?"

"Looks like it." Brinton, like Bob ignoring Delphick's little sigh of relief, jerked a head in the direction of the wrecked car. "From what you said on the phone about wine bottles, I might've wondered if he wasn't drunk, or'd had somebody slip him a Mickey Finn—and I suppose the autopsy could well show something-or-other on top of the rest—but it was the steering. Lucky it didn't catch fire in the crash, because it was easy enough to find the evidence, once MissEss'd put us on the right track—and that's a laugh." He wasn't laughing. "Talk about tracks, that's what chummie did—loosened the lock-nut on the track rod end, then knew he only had to wait for Bragbury to try taking a sharp bend. *Try* being the operative word, of course. Go in a straight line, and he was perfectly safe. Take one corner, and . . . "

"And the tree he hit," said Delphick, "is, I assume, on

the first corner he would reach after leaving home?''

Brinton rolled his eyes. "Give you three guesses."

"Top marks to Miss Seeton, then." Delphick nodded to Bob, who passed the clipboard back to his superior without a word. "There seems little doubt," murmured the chief superintendent, "that someone wished to take advantage of Donald Bragbury's known propensity for speed . . . Do we know yet why he was on that particular route at that particular time?''

"Have a heart." Brinton sounded hurt. "We've only this minute found out he was murdered, never mind a blow-by-blow timetable of his movements for the past twenty-four hours—but if you'd like to bring your young giant along to take notes, I think we should be able to remedy the situation before very much longer."

There were no obvious signs of mourning at the Bragbury home: no curtained windows, no black-ribboned hatchment on the gatepost, no procession of callers to the front door bearing condolences and flowers—food, of course, in such a circumstance would have seemed, perhaps, tactless.

When Brinton rang the bell, it clanged, unmuffled, in the hall. Hurrying feet soon came to answer it.

"Yes?" Mavis Bragbury, a massive white apron around her ample form, frowned at the three tall men on her doorstep. They gazed at her with some interest: here were no swollen eyes, no tear-stained cheeks, no haggard look of a sleepless night. "Yes? You looking for me?''

"Er," said Brinton, recovering himself, and producing his identity card. "Mrs. Bragbury, we're police officers. We're extremely sorry to have to disturb you again at a time like this, but—''

"Whatever it is you're about, it'd better not take too long." Mavis took the offered card and peered at it, then sighed as she handed it back. "I suppose you'd best come in—but we're very busy today, you know.''

"I can imagine," said Brinton, in his most sympathetic

tones, as Mavis led the way into a chilly parlour, papered in muted tones of beige, grey, and a peculiar green which matched the ugly pattern of the carpet. The only sign of frivolity in the entire room was the flock of plaster ducks winging their mournful way across the wall opposite the net-curtained window—the window through which, since it faced north, no sun could ever shine to lighten the gloom.

"Can you, indeed?" Mavis sniffed. "I very much doubt it—not unless *you've* ever been expected to cater a sit-down meal for sixty people forty miles off with nobody to drive the van. Have to pay someone, I will, even if I can find 'em at such short notice, which'll mean double wages, in any case. Can you *imagine* a way round that?"

Brinton goggled. "Well, er . . . "

"You are a courageous woman, Mrs. Bragbury." Delphick came promptly to the rescue of his floundering colleague. "To be able to sublimate your grief in your work—your late husband would, I am sure, have been very proud of you."

Mavis favoured the chief superintendent with a sour look. "Satan's never found *mine* a pair of idle hands, nor any in this house, believe me—and I've no patience with them as'd rather be passengers than crew. We've our living to earn, whether Donald's here or not, and never a minute to waste in earning it." She looked pointedly in the direction of the sad-faced clock on the marble shelf above the empty grate, and sniffed again.

"Then we'll try to waste no more of your time before we let you get back to work," said Delphick, as Brinton, at his side, still gaped in stunned amazement. "We have reason to suspect, Mrs. Bragbury, that your husband's accident was not, in fact, an accident. We think that someone tampered with the steering of his car, and—"

"Not an accident?" Mavis went pale. Her voice rose to a squeal. "The car's bin tampered with? Oh, that's wicked lies! I won't—I don't believe you!"

"Please try not to distress yourself too much, Mrs. Bragbury. This must be hard for you, I know, but there is the strongest evidence—''

''Evidence?'' Her eyes widened in horrified dismay. ''You mean it's true—it weren't an accident?'' She saw his nod, and turned white. She gulped. ''But—but that means the insurance mightn't cover it!''

It was Delphick's turn to goggle, though he recovered himself more speedily than had Brinton. ''I really couldn't say about that, I'm afraid. Perhaps your financial adviser will be able to—''

''Financial adviser? There's another thing!'' Mavis was growing red faced now, and her eyes were angry. ''Donald it was kept the books for the business, with me not seeing why we should pay good money for someone outside the family to do what anyone with a bit o' gumption could be doing for us for free—and now that'll mean more money down the drain, neither me nor the girls being much inclined to sums, and busy with the cooking, what's more. And now here you come telling me the insurance won't pay out on the car—and nothing to get on his life, most like, if what you say about tampering's true . . . ''

As even her indignant breath had at last to give out, Delphick leaped into the breach. ''It appears so, Mrs. Bragbury—which is why we've come to you. We've no reason to suppose this tampering was a—an episode of random spite, or casual vandalism. Did your husband, do you know, have any enemies?''

''That's libel,'' snapped Mavis, inaccurately. ''And I'll thank you not to go spreading tales o' that sort around the neighbourhood—this is a respectable family, let me tell you, and we've kept ourselves to ourselves right from the start. We don't go in for no nonsense, and that's a fact.''

''A business rival, maybe?'' Delphick wasn't going to give up easily. ''Bragbury's has an excellent reputation in these parts—and justifiably so, I'm told. It could well be in someone's interests to, ah, curtail your activities by—by reducing your workforce: especially if, as you suggest, your husband was the only one capable of handling the larger vehicles such as the delivery van.''

"Handling? Yes, and,'' said Mavis, as the grim realisation dawned, ''servicing, which is summat else we're going to have to pay for now, me and the girls not being inclined to oil and grease, never mind the taste it'd give the food, and the customers not paying to eat in the inspection pit. Oh, it's a black day for Bragbury's, and no mistake!''

Delphick, for all his training and experience, was at something of a loss over the correct response to her remark. Fortunately for his composure, however, Mavis continued to enlarge on her theme for some minutes to come, and he was able to collect his scattered wits and jump into the next conversational breach as soon as it presented itself.

"It would be the greatest possible help in our investigations if we knew why your husband was out so late last night, and where he was going. After all the excitement and upset of the princess's disappearance, I would have thought that he and your daughter, as witnesses of the event, would prefer to spend a quiet evening at home.'' And he hoped he'd be forgiven the lie: he couldn't remember when he'd last seen so unrestful a house. It didn't seem probable that any of the other rooms were more welcoming; he dreaded to think what the Bragbury daughters were like if, as so often happened, they took after their mother. Since Donald had been responsible for the service and maintenance of his car, if it was learned later that he'd tampered with the steering himself, and committed suicide, the Oracle wouldn't be in the least surprised.

"Evening at home?'' Mavis looked astounded at the very idea. "When there's business to be done? The girls were washing up—all that good food gone to waste, none o' the Dungeness lot bothering to eat it, and never thinking to put it in the cool until too late—and then helping me get ready for today, which is no more'n you'd expect, us with a business to run.'' And once again she sniffed, and stared at the clock on the overmantel; and she sighed, and wiped restless hands down the front of her apron.

"So your husband went out on a—a business matter?"
The deduction, thought Delphick, wasn't unreasonable; he
was pleased to observe Mavis's brisk nod of confirmation.
"Was this a long-standing appointment? Would an outsider
have known—could he or she have expected—him to leave
the house and drive in that particular direction at that particular hour?"

For the first time, Mrs. Bragbury's look was neither hos-
tile nor disbelieving. Her dark eyes narrowed, and her forehead creased in a frown. "You wait there," she said; and,
wheeling, marched out of the room without another word.

As she failed to close the door behind her (saving time,
each of the three policemen independently guessed), nobody dared say anything in case, on her return, she over-
heard it. Their expressions, however, were more than
eloquent as they looked at one another in a strained,
thoughtful silence.

"Here," said Mavis, marching back into the room with
an appointments diary in her hand. She slapped the book
on the table in front of Delphick, and opened it. "Read
that!"

Whatever the female Bragburys' ability with sums, nobody could fault their handwriting skills. The booking was
plain for all to see, and Delphick—after a startled gulp—
duly read it aloud.

"Eight thirty, Mr. Mountfitchet. About his daughter's
wedding." Above the gasps of Brinton and Bob, he addressed Mavis Bragbury with a note of more than urgency
in his tone.

"Mountfitchet? Do you mean *Charley* Mountfitchet—
from Plummergen?"

"That's who he said he was."

Something in her voice told Delphick what his next question should be. "You didn't believe him?"

She shrugged. "No reason why not."

"But Charley Mountfitchet's a bachelor, for heaven's

sake. He hasn't got a daughter!''

Mavis gave him an old-fashioned look. ''Not as we've heard of so far, no, but they're a funny lot over to Plummergen. No telling what he got up to in his young days a-coming home to roost now, is there?''

The landlord of the George and Dragon was a cheery, open-natured soul who delighted in helping the police with their enquiries on the least excuse. The most unlikely persons, Delphick knew, had the darkest of secrets hidden in their pasts; but Charley Mountfitchet seemed even more unlikely than most.

''So this . . . Mr. Mountfitchet telephoned to ask for some help in catering for his daughter's wedding. Did he ask for Mr. Bragbury by name?''

'' 'Twas allus Donald as did the driving and the bookings, me and the girls being busy with the preparation and the cooking. Everyone knows that.''

''Do they, indeed.'' Delphick frowned. Mavis pounced.

''They do, and if you're trying to name me a liar, I'll thank you to keep a civil tongue in your head! Me a poor lone widow-woman as I am—you oughter be downright ashamed o' yourself, and that's a fact.''

Once more, Delphick gulped. The idea of Mavis Bragbury as a grieving widow had long since passed from his memory. ''I—I apologise, Mrs. Bragbury. I'm just . . . confused, you see. Didn't it occur to you that the call from Mr. Mountfitchet might not—might not be entirely aboveboard?''

She shrugged again. ''Thought it weren't so likely he'd a daughter being wed, that's true . . . ''

''Then why did you allow your husband to go rushing off on what might well have proved to be a wild goose chase?'' Delphick restrained himself nobly from reminding her of what Donald Bragbury's errand had finally proved to be.

Mavis sighed. She answered in the voice of an exasperated adult addressing a very stupid child. ''Just acos he'd no wedding for the catering didn't mean as there weren't no cause for Charley Mountfitchet to do business with us. The George and Dragon's good enough eating, but nothing fancy—and for all I knew he was a-planning to bring in our stuff by the back door and try for a rosette in one o' they hotel guides—ah, and I'd've made sure he'd paid handsome for the privilege, and all!''

Delphick glanced at Bob, who was making a note to check with Charley the instant they returned to Plummergen. There was, he supposed, always the outside chance that the landlord hoped to go up-market: ever since the Best Kept Village Competition, and Plummergen's second prize, there were more visitors than ever before. But such a hole-and-corner way of improving the George's *cuisine,* which was good plain fare rather than particularly *haute,* was very unlike the Charley Mountfitchet they'd known for so many years . . .

''Then it never occurred to you, Mrs. Bragbury, that the message might be a hoax? You thought that Mr. Mountfitchet was about to propose to your husband some . . . some slightly dubious—ethically, if not commercially—deal?''

For the last time, Mavis shrugged. She looked at the clock with impatience; she looked at Delphick with scorn. ''And why not?'' she demanded. ''Why not? 'Twould have bin a good bit o' business coming our way, wouldn't it?''

CHAPTER 15

Catesby gazed slowly around the darkened room. The other two at the table gazed back, without speaking. Winter moved restlessly on his chair; Keyes sighed, and licked his lips. His feet shuffled on the floor; his fingers pattered on the tabletop in a nervous dance of which he seemed unaware.

Catesby frowned. "Where is Rookwood?"

"Checking on . . . on our visitor," said Keyes, stilling his fingers for no more than a moment.

"That one," volunteered Winter, now the silence had been broken, "is a bit of a handful, and then some." He winced as he rubbed his shin. "Call her the spitfire type, and I won't argue. She doesn't come across like that in public, though, does she? Quite a surprise. None of your blue-blooded stand-on-your-dignity-at-all-times nonsense about *her*. She's not going to give in easily, believe me— if she keeps on like this much longer, I vote we think about doping her rations." He ventured a grin. "Or d'you reckon that would be, um, treason?"

"Treason?" Catesby's echo was an icy hiss. "It would be closer to the truth to call it stupidity—and dangerous stupidity, at that, when not one of us would have the least idea of what we were doing. What use would she be to us . . . damaged—or dead?''

"We could ask someone," said Winter. "Or look it up in the library—just a few sleeping pills, tranquillisers, something like that. Just to keep her quiet."

"She's hardly," said Keyes, "a noisy guest."

"Noblesse oblige." Winter grinned. "Anyway, wouldn't do her much good if she *was*. Noisy, I mean, stuck out in the middle of nowhere like she is . . . ''

"Nowhere, as you call it," Catesby reminded him, "has its advantages."

Winter tried hard to give his answering shrug an air of bravado. He almost succeeded. "Did I say it hasn't? Nobody's going to complain about the—the planning of this operation. None of *us*, anyway."

Catesby's shrewd glance made him fidget again, and lower his gaze. Beside him, there was an empty chair: in the next chair to it, Keyes continued to patter his fingers on the tabletop. Suddenly, he cleared his throat.

"I—I don't know about complaining," he began. "But—well, there's been talk—"

He broke off. From outside, there had come a rattling sound, followed by a soft thud as someone opened the door. Every head turned.

"Rookwood!"

"You are late," Catesby informed him.

Rookwood, breathing hard, slipped, limping, into his seat. With a tender hand, he massaged the top of his head. "From now on," he said, "we go in twos."

"We have already agreed it is too dangerous—"

But Catesby, for once, was not allowed to finish. "In twos," insisted Rookwood, "and to hell with whether anyone notices we aren't there!" He himself did not notice that Keyes stopped his relentless finger-pattering, and winced; neither, for once, did the all-observant Catesby. "Do you know"—Rookwood sounded incredulous—

"she kicked me on the kneecap, and hit me on the head with the tray when I dropped it?" He ignored the sudden snort which burst from the listening Winter. "She'll have to go hungry tonight, and serve her right—though of course we don't want her to starve," he concluded, catching Catesby's eye, and calming down a little. "I mean, a kid like that . . ."

"A spitfire," corrected Winter, with feeling. "Sleeping pills, that's what she needs—"

"No!" Catesby slammed a forceful hand on the tabletop. "No, we might do more harm than good. If . . . if things should, by some horrible mischance, go wrong . . . if we are discovered—it will look better for us if we have treated her with . . . with the respect due to her position. As far as possible, that is. In the circumstances."

There was a long silence.

"Well, naturally, after all the trouble you—we've gone to, we don't want to be discovered," said Winter.

Keyes clasped his hands together, tightly clenching his fingers. He coughed, and blushed. "It—it wouldn't do any harm to—to think about Stage Two . . ."

Rookwood glanced at him: at the white-knuckled hands. He said nothing, but his look was eloquent.

Catesby's loss of command had lasted but a moment. A cleared throat; a darkling frown. A finger, tapping on the tabletop . . .

"Stage Two," said Catesby. Keyes looked up, silently pleading. "The day after tomorrow," Catesby went on, "not before. There must be a—a discreet distance from the Bragbury episode."

"Still a lot of cops sniffing around," said Winter, the irreverent.

"Sniffing in the wrong places," the loyal Rookwood reminded him. The rebellion had been brief, and, now that Catesby had appeared to yield, would not be repeated. "Just the way—Catesby—predicted . . ."

Keyes, once again, shifted on his chair. Catesby looked

at him, and raised an enquiring eyebrow. Keyes dropped his gaze to his clasped hands.

"There's ... talk," he mumbled, at last, when the look of enquiry had become overwhelming. "I couldn't help hearing ... they've brought a man in from Scotland Yard."

"In a case like this," Catesby reminded him, "you would expect nothing less."

"But—but he's not an ordinary Yarder." Keyes blushed again. "I mean, he's not one of the Big Four, or anything, but he's big, all right, and—"

"Once again," Catesby broke in, "we would have expected nothing less."

"Yes, I know, but ... " Keyes, hot-cheeked, thanked the shadows in the room for hiding so much of his embarrassment. "But it's that man Delphick the one they call the Oracle."

"And?" prompted Catesby, as Keyes began to cough again.

"And ... and—he's the one who's always hanging around with the Battling Brolly," brought out Keyes, at last. "And you know how she—she helps him with his cases—it's in the papers all the time ... "

"And they know," said Winter, "about that business with the Bragbury car, and the Mountfitchet phone call. So I've heard," he added, as everyone stared at him. "You know how people gossip—and there's bound to be at least some truth in what they say ... "

"There is, indeed." Catesby's lips were thin, white; as white as the knuckles on the clasped hands of Keyes. "Has anyone," demanded Catesby, "heard ... anything else?"

Winter, for once reluctant to stir up trouble, favoured Rookwood and Keyes—especially Keyes—with a meaningful, sideways stare. Rookwood looked unhappily at Catesby, and tried to speak, but failed. It was Keyes who made the great effort, and finally brought out:

"There really is ... talk—questions. Curious looks," he gabbled, "and gossip—nothing definite," as Catesby gave him a particularly curious look of his own, "but I can't help thinking—thinking that Stage Two oughtn't to wait for the day after tomorrow," he finished, bravely. "Once people start to suspect . . . "

Catesby stared at him, in silence—a silence neither Rookwood nor even Winter dared to break. The leadership of a natural leader is not readily challenged a second time in any encounter if it has already once prevailed.

"Any one questioner above another?" enquired Catesby. Keyes licked dry lips. "Well . . . "

With the silent encouragement of Rookwood and Winter, he enlarged, stumbling, on his remark; and Catesby's frown was awful. This time, the unbroken silence stretched into what seemed an eternity.

"Stage Two tomorrow, then," decreed Catesby, at last. An audible sigh of relief filled the room—to be drowned out by the final, ominous rider:

"And if gossip and suspicion are correct . . . we may have to consider amending our plans somewhat. After Stage Three, we may have to devise a Stage Four . . . "

"Posted," said Brinton, going over the evidence yet again, "in Maidstone. First class stamp, and for once it only took a day to arrive . . . not that it helps us much. If we'd only known in advance to put a twenty-four-hour watch on the busiest post office in the area, we might have spotted the blighter who popped it into the box. As it is . . . "

"As it is," said Delphick, "he, or she, could have come from anywhere—and probably did. Maidstone, unfortunately, is hardly off the beaten track—only thirty-six miles from London, around thirty from any of the Channel ports—"

"Oh, God!" Brinton was too despondent even to tear his hair. "If they've taken her abroad—"

"I don't think they have." Delphick was studying, for the umpteenth time, photocopies of the envelope and letter received that morning at Kensington Palace by the private secretary to Her Royal Highness, Princess Georgina. While copies of the documents had been rushed to all investigators concerned in the case, the originals remained in the care of the security forces, being subjected to the most detailed scrutiny. "These, Chris, unless I'm much mistaken, are not foreign typefaces." He coughed. "It was Sherlock Holmes, of course, who could instantly recognise the differences between the leaded bourgeois type of a *Times* article and the slovenly print of an evening newspaper—but I trust that our own experts do not, nowadays, lag so very far behind Holmes in their expertise. If, just by looking, a humble Yard chief super can see that these cut-out capitals are from headlines in the British tabloid press, the experts should surely be able to tell us which tabloids they are, and which their days of issue—maybe even which edition, and in which region of the country it was sold. After all, Holmes would have done no less almost a century ago."

"And he'd have done it a damned sight faster!" Brinton sighed. "How long does it take to read one of those yarns? He makes it all look so easy . . . "

Delphick had to smile. "Conan Doyle played with loaded dice, my dear Chris—as is the case with all writers of mystery fiction. They have, remember, the distinctly unfair advantage of knowing in advance how much significance is to be attached to the fact that the letter was posted in Gravesend by a man with a dirty thumb—"

"Gravesend?" Brinton gaped at him, horrified. "Are you trying to tell me they're dragging the poor girl from one side of Kent to the other just to keep us off the track?"

"Nothing," Delphick assured him, "could be further from my thoughts . . . " But then he frowned. "Unless . . . perhaps a true word, spoken in jest . . . Might there be at least an element of disguise? I don't for one moment suggest a tangled red wig or a repulsive scar, but Georgina certainly has been much photographed. Her appearance is more than well-known—her face, her hair . . . "

"Princess Petite," said Brinton, with a snort he would

never have dared to emit in the presence of his wife, for Mrs. Brinton was a devoted fan of Georgy Girl. ''Five foot nothing and curls like Shirley Temp—oh. I see what you mean. If they've got her anywhere people might spot her, they'll've had to—to camouflage her, if that's the word I want . . . No, it'd be too risky. Wouldn't it?''

Delphick did not reply. Foxon and Bob, hitherto silent participants in this discussion, looked at each other; and it was Bob who cleared his throat and ventured to speak.

''Surely they wouldn't force . . . wouldn't risk hurting her, sir? I mean—assaulting a member of the Royal Family—that'd be treason, wouldn't it? She's always seemed such a—a nice kid. It—it doesn't seem right, sir.''

''I doubt,'' said Delphick drily, ''the folk who have taken HRH are sticklers for the conventions, Sergeant Ranger. One can hardly be considered obedient to the strictest rules of etiquette when one kidnaps a princess of the Blood, takes photographs of her blindfolded, and sends them with a demand for half a million in used notes to be delivered as and when later instructions shall be received. These are not *nice*,'' crisply, ''people, Sergeant Ranger.''

Bob went red, and gazed at his boots. ''Sorry, sir . . . ''

Delphick was already shaking his head. ''No, I'm the one who should apologise, Bob. Blame it on sheer frustration, if you will. There ought to have been a multitude of clues, but whatever we've tried has come to nothing . . . ''

''Nothing.'' Brinton's echoing groan was heartfelt as he began to enumerate the dead-end leads which they had, at one time or another, pursued: which they were still, for want of anything more hopeful, still pursuing. ''The girl's *probably* not left the country—might not even have left Kent—but that's a hell of a lot of places to start looking, without a nudge or two in the right direction. Every nark in the land's been asked to keep his ears open—but nobody's heard a thing, though the blighters all worship the ground she walks on. That snap's no real help. There isn't a house in England doesn't have white sheets, and apart from young Georgina in the foreground that's all anyone can make out, no matter how they take their magnifying glasses to the thing. Every blasted chemist and photographic processor in the country's been told to sing out if he's handled snaps of a blindfold girl—and there hasn't been a murmur . . . '' He looked up, frowning. ''Wonder why they didn't use an instant camera? The amount of money we're talking about, you'd've thought they could afford a Polaroid—except, I suppose, they can't afford it till they've got the cash . . . ''

''Perhaps,'' said Delphick, very slowly, ''they wished to occasion no remark by a sudden, out-of-character purchase. Perhaps they are not, as has been suspected, the anonymous international gang beloved of mystery writers around the world, but a—a more home-grown enterprise, whose every action would run the grave risk of being observed by their friends and neighbours . . . ''

It was not, of course, to be supposed that the presence of a large portion of the Plummergen populace at the kidnapping of a princess would not occupy the greater part of local gossip for many days after the event. It occupied, in fact, the entire part of village conversation for at least twenty-four hours, fuelled and fermented by a large Press presence: in response to which presence Mr. Jessyp made it firmly known that all classes would be held, for the duration, behind shuttered windows, in case illicit close-ups of young Sally should be snatched against his (if not the child's mother's) wish. The headmaster further decreed that the additional expense incurred by the use of artificial lighting during the day should be charged, on receipt of the electricity bill, to the Press Complaints Council; and he added that anyone venturing to enter school property did so at his or her own risk. It would be nothing to do with Mr. Jessyp if, in the course of regular autumnal care for the school playing-fields, trespassers were inadvertently sprayed by tractor-driving farmers with high-octane liquid manure.

The journalists—not one of them born with mud on his boots, and all (thanks to their editors' monumental lack of foresight) without waterproof clothing—duly took the hint, and decamped to besiege the palaces of Buckingham and Kensington, with small detachments on the steps of New Scotland Yard and the headquarters of MI5.

And so Plummergen was left in peace—in relative peace, that is. Discussion of the events at Dungeness was not, naturally, abandoned: it formed, as has been explained, the greater part of local gossip: but there was room, now, for fresh subjects to be introduced, for older subjects to be revived . . .

"I still say it's summat *queer* they're about, the pair of 'em." This from Mrs. Skinner, in the post office, and at full volume, the pair in question having safely—and severally—departed.

Her words were accompanied by nods, and a general murmur of agreement from everyone—including, to her chagrin, Mrs. Henderson: but there was no denying the truth of her rival's observation. *Summat queer* was, if anything, an understatement of the position which had now been maintained by the parties under discussion for some weeks past.

"Not a word," said Mrs. Spice, "has there bin from either of 'em, save good morning and such, since long afore that business at the power station—"

"Sulking on the bus there and back," chimed in young Mrs. Newport. "Regular old misery-guts, the pair of 'em . . ."

"And what cause Miss Nuttel's got, of all people," said Mrs. Scillicough, "to go buying *an icing set* beats me, on account of it's the Hot Cross Bun does all the cooking in that house, which we've heard tell many a time."

"The Bun," Mrs. Henderson pointed out, "bought three new spatulas and a scale-pan, didn't she? You'd'a thought she'd enough o' such things already, and to spare."

"Not forgetting," added Mrs. Spice at once, "the palette-knife—which ain't to say as she couldn't sharpen that up and do someone, mentioning no names, a fair bit o' damage if she'd the inclination, which from the way they've bin a-snapping and snarling at each other'd never come as much of a surprise, would it?''

Even Mrs. Spice had to agree it would not, although the gleam in the eyes of Mrs. Henderson as she spoke of knives made her frown. But Mrs. Flax, to whom all heads turned for the definitive opinion, defused the burgeoning squabble by approving this general agreement with a ponderous nod: following which she decided that the time was ripe for adding her own scandalous—and generous—pinch to the brew of speculation and surmise now that (thanks to the hard work of everyone else) it was coming close to the boil.

Mrs. Flax drew a deep breath. She gazed slowly round upon the assembled company, and lowered her voice. Everyone flinched in horrified delight: some awful revelation, it was clear, was about to be made. Hadn't the Wise Woman's son as worked for Farmer Mulcker bin to Brettenden that very morning, for tractor spares? And hadn't Miss Nuttel nipped into town on the same bus, so quick there'd bin no time for any to follow her?

"Aah," said Mrs. Flax, ominously exhaling. "Ah, and when Miss Nuttel was fixing to buy *angle irons,* of all things," gloated Mrs. Flax, in doom-laden tones—"did she tell anyone what for she wanted 'em? She did not!"

The response to this sinister statement was all the Wise Woman could have hoped. Angle irons? Those who knew the purpose of these small metal fastening-plates paraded their knowledge with glee: those who didn't clamoured to be told more, and Mrs. Flax looked on in a smug silence as they were told. Angle irons? Why should Miss Nuttel want such contraptions? And screws, to fasten 'em? There'd bin no talk of her taking up carpentry, had there? Putting up shelves? Making boxes?

"Oh!" Mrs. Skinner's scream of realisation curdled the blood in everyone's veins, and froze their tongues in mid-wag. "Oh . . . it was *boxes* made me remember . . . when Mrs. Putts was at the admiral's asking for honey, and—and Miss Nuttel was a-digging that—that hole . . . "

She could not continue.

She did not need to.

"For a coffin," gasped the post office, with glee . . .

And then gasps turned to echoes of Mrs. Skinner's scream as there came, from outside, an explosion.

CHAPTER 16

"They pesky brats!"

Mrs. Skinner was not the only one of Mr. Stillman's customers to feel justifiably indignant. People's nerves, already frayed by intimations of Miss Nuttel's apparently sepulchral intentions, had now been stretched to their limit by the high-spirited detonation, right outside the post office, of a large firework by a small group of children begging pennies for the guy from passing motorists. The noise had not so much been loud as startling in its suddenness: and as sudden was Plummergen's response. Once everyone realised what had happened, mothers indoors rushed outside to clip their offspring (if present) about the ear, while others looked smug, and spoke loudly of the manners of the younger generation.

The latter speakers included the childless, those whose children had long since reached years of discretion, and those whose children had made a different guy, and set it up on a different pitch—these last having spent the previous few days lamenting the unfairness of life when, just because others'd got Miss Seeton to give 'em her bashed-up hat and had made the biggest guy, they'd been mean enough to stake their claim to the pavement outside the shop with the best-lit windows in the village, so that everyone driving by, strangers and all—who'd even slow their cars for a proper look, which was unfairer still—threw money in the hat, leaving nothing for t'other kids farther down The Street . . . who would never (their mothers now insisted, at virtuous full volume) dream of doing such a dreadful thing as to set off a firework just to attract the attention of a car as didn't look as if it was going to give 'em any money, their kids not being as mercenary-minded as Some They Could Mention . . .

As the outside mothers came back in, they caught the tail end of these remarks, and waxed even more indignant than they'd been before they went out. Who was being called mercenary? They'd thank Some People not to use words they most likely couldn't even spell, and even if they could were slander, in any case. Everyone knew it was the luck o' the draw each year when it came to getting a pitch for Guy Fawkes, and if Some People's kids were bad losers, well, they'd had to have learned it from somewhere, and where else but home? A pity to set kids a Bad Example, they thought, but then there were Some People as just didn't know no better, and you had to make excuses for 'em, poor souls. Besides, what else could you expect, Guy Fawkes Week and kiddies with fireworks? One or two let off early once in a while couldn't hurt . . .

And in all the flurry of insult and counterblast, the matter of Miss Nuttel's conjectural coffin-building was quite forgotten.

"Guy Fawkes Week, you expect one or two fireworks let off ahead of time," said Brinton, slowly. "Just a bit of fun, that's what anyone'd say—and mostly they'd be right, because there's no real harm done. But sometimes things go wrong . . ."

He was addressing Sid Noakes, leading fireman of the first appliance to reach the scene. The rest of Sid's crew were busy packing away their equipment; the crews from the other engines, having played their part, had already packed up, and gone. There was no sense in staying where they were no longer needed: and, indeed, there was some element of risk if they did. As Brinton had said, the week of Bonfire Night was invariably crowded with emergency calls: at any time, the fire brigade might be summoned to tackle some conflagration or other, large or small, which they could hardly do with their tenders dry, their hoses improperly coiled, their turntable ladders sticky with soot. There were all too few tenders to spare once a fire was definitely out; moreover, those there were, were manned by crews with their own lives to live.

In rural areas of England, the fire service is Retained, rather than full-time. The firemen come from every walk of life, from every town or village or hamlet within bleeper-range; a retained fireman, when on duty, is never without his radio pager, and it is not so very long ago that the old air raid sirens from World War II were finally phased out with the arrival, in most homes, of the telephone. The bleeper, a more modern invention yet, is better even than the telephone: it can be worn, and its summons heard, in the middle of a field, or the middle of the street . . .

Sid Noakes, indeed, had been in the middle of his supper when the alarm was raised: but he had, in the circumstances, small hope of being back in time to enjoy his lamb chop and peas, whether his wife left them warming in the oven or not.

"How long," Sid now enquired, glumly, "d'you reckon they lads'll be, Mr. Brinton?"

The lads to whom he referred, whose every movement he and Brinton were watching with deep concentration, did not belong to any fire crew. Though they wore uniforms, it was of a constabulary rather than conflagrationary nature, for they were under the command not of Leading Fireman Sid Noakes, but of Superintendent Chris Brinton . . .

"Sorry, Sid." Brinton shook his head. "As long as it

takes—afraid I can't say better than that. There's your statement to get as well, of course. We can't afford to cut corners when it's a question of a body . . . ''

Sid sighed. First appliance on the scene, first man among the crew: it was his responsibility to check, and his luck— whether bad or otherwise he wouldn't care to say—to have been the one who discovered the dead man in the burned-out building. At least, he'd supposed the body was that of a man: it had been much more badly burned than the build-ing, not to mention damaged by part of the roof collapsing on top—but the bits that were still visible had looked like a trousered leg, a heavily-shod foot. Still, you couldn't go jumping to conclusions in this job, any more'n you could if you were police . . .

"Know their stuff," said Sid, paying compliment as the uniformed figures searched through the rubble, warily moved beams, shifted timbers, took photographs and mea-surements, all in an efficient silence.

"So do you." Brinton returned the compliment. As soon as he found the body, Sid had banished everyone else from the immediate neighbourhood, and taken up his position as guard. He detailed one man to call the police, and sent another to fetch Dr. Wyddial from her sister's house: every-one for miles around knew the doctor's car, and by a lucky chance he'd just happened to spot it as they were hurrying to answer the nine-nine-nine call to the KarriKlozzet site.

Dr. Wyddial was not given to sloth. By the time the police arrived, she had examined what she could see of the body, pronounced it—as required by law—dead, and said she'd be only too happy to do an autopsy on the poor chap once he'd been retrieved, which she expected would take a couple of hours, at least. She'd get back to her family knees-up for now, if they didn't mind; she would apologise to her sister and leave for the mortuary in an hour or so— all right?

"Er—all right, Doc—and, er, thanks." Brinton was long accustomed to the brisk efficiency of Dr. Wyddial, but it always unnerved him slightly. "Er—sorry about the party," he added: but she'd already been out of earshot.

As Sid, still brooding on his lost supper, sighed again, there came the purposeful sound of footsteps crunching over rubble and ash and fallen timbers. Delphick, with Bob and Foxon close behind, arrived to join his colleagues as they contemplated the steady searching of the KarriKlozzet ruins by the ranks of uniformed police.

He raised an enquiring eyebrow in the direction of the leading fireman. "What do you think, Mr. Noakes?"

"Well, now . . . " And Sid frowned. He was not unduly awed by having his opinion sought by a man from Scotland Yard: it was no more than you'd expect, him being as much of an expert on fires as this Oracle was an expert on crime. Each to his own: it made good sense if you wanted to know the why and wherefore of anything. But Sid Noakes wasn't to be rushed into an opinion without first giving the matter careful thought. He rubbed the tip of his nose, and frowned again. "Well, now . . .

"Bonfire Night, o' course," he said at last, "and days not so distant either side o' the Fifth, we do tend to have a fair number o' what you might call accidents o' the high-spirited sort . . . "

"But?"

Brinton closed his eyes, and groaned softly. It wasn't as if he hadn't had his own suspicions. He prided himself he was as good a detective as anyone from the Yard, and he'd only been waiting for the preliminary report to back up what his good copper's instincts had already told him, loud and clear, before he launched into a full-scale murder investigation. Trust Delphick, though, to be the one to put it into words when they weren't absolutely sure just yet . . .

"But," said Sid, with a nod of approval. With all the fuss the papers, which everyone knew were allus out to make a story, 'd given this Oracle for being the great detective, seemed they might for once be right. "But—well, there's not just the matter of the dead'un, whoever he is, though I've my own ideas about him—but this looks to be more'n kids lobbing a cracker or a jumping-jack careless-like, if you ask me.'' He waved an expressive hand towards the wreckage, and sniffed once or twice. ''There's a queer sort o' smell t'all this—and I don't just mean they chemicals for the toilets as spilled when the drums bursted with the heat—which is what you'd expect, and dissolving stuff and disinfectant, so far as I can make out with talking to young Mr. Cuthbert—he's off home now,'' as Delphick's look made it plain he sought further information. ''Reporting to his ma, most like, if I know him.''

''Cuthbert?'' Delphick glanced about him at the ruins. ''Ah, yes, the owner of KarriKlozzet, of course.''

''Not exactly.'' Even at such a moment, Brinton couldn't help a rumble of laughter. ''Cuthbert Kelshall, that's who was here earlier—we only had a few words, with him not staying long once he'd seen what'd happened and how we were dealing with it. Sid's right, he'll have hopped off home to report to his mother. She's a tartar, that one.'' He rolled his eyes, and grinned. ''Mrs. Caroline Kelshall, she is, and don't you forget it in a hurry. Never even thought of retiring when her old man died, no idea of handing over to the younger ones—keeps as close an eye on the business as she ever did, and when she says jump, they jump. Cuthbert and Claud, of all the daft names.''

''And Cleopatra,'' put in Sid Noakes, also grinning.

''Good heavens.'' Delphick shook his head, wondering at the peculiarities of human nature. ''Some people, I fear, have far too restricted a sense of responsibility when naming their offspring.''

''Young Cleo married one of the Therfields—Peter,'' said Brinton, ''the youngest boy. They're a farming family, but he'd no taste for it. Went in with his wife's lot instead. He and Cleo have a pair of twins called Oswald and Osbert—not quite as bad as Cuthbert and Claud, but near enough. The poor little devils have been having a tough time of it at school, so I've heard.''

"I'm not surprised." Delphick shook his head again. "Irresponsibility clearly runs in the family—as does the business," he added, returning to his original muttons. "A family concern—a large, presumably influential, family. Are they," he enquired, "popular?"

Sid Noakes shifted on one large foot. He glanced at the superintendent beside him; Brinton nodded.

"Go on, Sid. Give the man the local colour."

Mr. Noakes cleared his throat, and took a deep breath. "Since you insist, Mr. Brinton—well, no, Mr. Delphick, right now I have to say they ain't. They've laid a good few folk off this past couple o' months, which jobs lost don't make them as caused 'em losing none too popular, and open to all manner of mockery, though in part 'tis the kiddies' daft names, I won't deny—and then, with talk o' yet more jobs going afore too long, I can't help but wonder . . . well, if you was to tell me there was petrol or summat o' the sort in among the chemicals, I'd not call you a liar."

Everyone sniffed. The air was heavy with the acrid tang of burned ash, moist and lingering. The firemen's hoses had spouted thousands of gallons of water to extinguish the fury of the flames, and the spillage from the burst drums of chemicals had only added to the black, muddy, reeking mess. It was hard, of course, to be sure whether the reek was simply that of cinders mixed with disinfectant: they did not all have the long experience of Leading Fireman Noakes in the aftermath of conflagration. Cuthbert Kelshall, when the matter had first been raised, remarked that a heavy smoker like himself had an impaired sense of smell, but that he could not, in any case, seriously credit that anybody would wish to harm one of the largest employers in the district, if that was what Sid and Mr. Brinton had been hinting, let alone risk harming any of the employees. It was nothing more or less than a shocking accident—some honest worker working late, whose honesty had been cruelly rewarded . . . still, if they wanted to stir up a mystery, they were welcome to go wherever they chose to look for it.

They had his permission, just as he was sure his mother would give it, if she'd been there—and, talking of his mother . . .

Cuthbert had beaten a hasty retreat, to present—as Sid Noakes (who'd voiced the first hint of mystery with his discovery of the body) and Brinton guessed—his report to Mrs. Caroline Kelshall, relict of Caradoc, and currently head of KarriKlozzet Limited, the nation's third largest supplier of portable cloakrooms for all occasions. As the slogan had it, KarriKlozzet Cared for the Convenience of the Public in Private, and with Discretion.

"So Cuthbert," said Delphick, once Sid and Brinton had brought him up to date, "doesn't believe, or shall we at least say doesn't want to believe, in a—a vendetta of any sort, recent sackings notwithstanding. Would his view, do you know, be that of the other family members? The redoubtable Caroline, in particular."

"Carrie likes to keep her finger firmly on the pulse." Brinton grinned. "That's just with one hand, of course. With the other, she holds the whip that gets cracked over the heads of the rest of the family—the rest of the firm, come to that—if they set one toe across the line she's drawn. If Cuthbert says he doesn't believe in a vendetta, then he's saying what Caroline'll say, and the rest, once we get around to asking them—he'd never dare be different. *She* probably thinks it's a downright liberty of the natives even to think of such a thing—always very lord-and-peasant style, KarriKlozzet, even while old Caradoc was alive. Hire and fire—not, mind you, that they did so much firing until recently. Noted for looking after their people, in some ways—so, well, in some ways I could almost believe our Cuthbert when he said there was nothing—nothing vindictive about what's happened. You don't turn round all of a sudden and bite the hand that's fed you for so long, do you?"

"You might," said Delphick, "if the shock of being fed no longer had sent you slightly round the bend."

Sid Noakes reminded everyone of the petrol he'd felt sure he'd smelled, and pointed out that the fire—wherever it had started, which was hard to tell, and if that weren't a suspicious circumstance then he didn't rightly know what was—did seem to have spread awful quickly, considering. Portable toilets being by nature not exactly tinder-dry, that was to say, and back to what he'd said earlier about crackers and jumping-jacks on their own not liable to cause such an inferno . . .

Delphick was frowning. "A strong suspicion of arson," he murmured. "A firm with a paternalistic style of management suddenly starting to let its dependants down . . . Chris, this *could* be a simple grudge matter. And that poor chap, whoever he turns out to be, could be dead by a dreadful mischance . . . yet it seems more than strange for someone, no matter how great the grudge for having lost his job, to ruin the chance of employment for others in the community . . . "

"Round the bend," Brinton reminded him. "You said so yourself—and you could be right. Could be the grudge got to him faster than thinking about the effect on everybody else—on everybody he worked with, I mean. He'll have been only too aware of what the effect'd be on the Kelshalls—on KarriKlozzet as a whole. They'll lose a fair bit of trade by all this, never mind whatever insurance cover they've got—there's goodwill, lost orders, that sort of thing. Could take 'em years to get back on their feet again . . . "

"If," said Delphick, "such was the intention. An ordinary, sordid business motive makes it all too easy . . . "

Brinton looked at him; at the eager, interested faces of Bob and Foxon; at the puzzled frown of honest Sid Noakes. "I'm a humble country copper," he said, slowly. "I'm not up to your big-city complications—I like my crimes nice and easy and straightforward. But I've got a very nasty feeling you're going to complicate this one for me, with bells on. Am I right?"

"I don't know." Delphick shook his head. "Maybe I'm imagining it—but the coincidence cannot, surely, have escaped your attention. We have not one, but two deaths to be investigated here. The first, of the caterer who was in attendance at Dungeness when the princess disappeared. The second—"

"Don't tell me!" Brinton almost howled the words. "Why can't it be a common-or-garden coincidence, for once? Just for once, an ordinary crime? With Guy Fawkes Night three days away, and fireworks all over the place, and if it's not yobs being careless it's their dads angry for losing their jobs . . ."

Delphick regarded his friend with some sympathy. "Maybe I'm imagining it," he said again. "Maybe. I hope, in some ways, that I am, although in others it would be helpful if I'm not—the more complex the coincidences and connections, the easier a crime can be to solve. It's always the run-of-the-mill affairs, the ones with nothing to distinguish them from a hundred other cases, which are the most difficult to bring to a satisfactory conclusion. Don't we always look for the pattern, where we can? The more bizarre the crime, the easier the pattern is to establish; and, once a pattern has been established, the solution is so much closer. It's a question of looking at the facts in the right way . . ."

He chose to ignore Brinton's horrified wince, his groan of despairing resignation. "And," he went on, "in order to look at things in the right way, it helps more than a little if one consults someone who is fortunate enough to possess the eye of the trained observer . . .

"I rather think, you know," concluded Chief Superintendent Delphick, "that I could do a great deal worse in this case than consult Miss Seeton."

CHAPTER *17*

By the time they had driven back to Plummergen, it was past supper-time—yet not (Delphick decided) too far past to pay an evening call, if the callers first took the precaution of telephoning to enquire whether or not their visit would be inconvenient. Besides (as he reminded Bob) while Charley Mountfitchet would be only too happy to rustle up a snack and a drink for his guests at whatever hour they requested them—even happier than usual on this particular occasion, since the thrill of being a suspect, however obliquely, in a murder case had delighted the landlord's enthusiastic soul—Miss Seeton might well have some of her adopted nephew's favourite gingerbread in the larder.

But Miss Seeton, it seemed, was not at home. The chief superintendent let the rhythmic "unanswered" tone ring for a count of twenty, then broke the connection.

"She might," said Bob—who'd had no thoughts of gingerbread until Delphick raised them, and who was now feeling hungrier by the minute—"be standing on her head or something, sir. You know she doesn't really like to stop in the middle of her exercises unless it's urgent. How about, er, trying again a bit later?"

"While we," murmured Delphick, "force ourselves down to the bar—there to indulge in some of Charley's excellent sandwiches, no doubt." He pondered this proposal for a few moments, then slowly nodded, as if resigned to the sacrifice of entering the saloon bar of the George, and partaking of its excellent supper menu. "It is, of course, Sergeant Ranger, in the very best interests of the investigation that the investigators should remain at all times in full possession of their health and strength. An inefficient sidekick is"—he permitted himself a quiet smile—"'something up with which no superior should have to put." He smiled once more, in a Churchillian manner, then frowned.

"I can't recall whether or not there were any lights showing in Sweetbriars as we pulled on to the forecourt of the pub. If Miss Seeton is not, in fact, standing on her head, but has gone out somewhere for the evening, it will be wasting valuable nourishment time to telephone again before we—you—eat."

Bob ignored the slur on his gourmandising. When a bloke stood six-foot-seven in his socks, he needed to keep up his strength. (Keep his strength up? Good old Churchill!) If he'd been the size of Miss Seeton, say, or young Georgina, the pair of 'em not an inch above five foot high and eating no more, he'd bet, than sparrows—well, that'd be different: but he wasn't. What he was—and he weighed seventeen stone, which he'd guess was about ten stone more than either MissEss or Georgy Girl—was *hungry*.

"Come to think of it, sir, I didn't notice any lights, either. But you know what this place is like for minding everybody else's business. If we ask downstairs where she's gone while we're having a bite to eat, fifty-to-one there'll be at least six people who can tell us."

Delphick was no more immune to the summons of the fleshpots than other men who have worked hard all day with little time, or thought, for food. He sighed. "Since you appear, Sergeant Ranger, to be growing weaker even as I look at you, it would seem that I have no alternative than to agree. We will therefore," he decreed, "take cheese-and-pickle sandwiches and a helping of gossip before another five minutes are out . . . "

Yet for once the Plummergen grapevine was unequal to the task required of it. Both the saloon and the public bars were almost empty, and the few drinkers therein did not, when asked, seem to know anything of Miss Seeton's probable whereabouts. They were rather more informative on the probable whereabouts of their (possibly) more knowledgeable friends. The Christmas Pantomime committee meeting, and the planning of the imminent Grand Firework Display, not to mention the proposed revival of the Night Watch Men in view of Murreystone's suspected sabotage of the Village Bonfire, had all taken their toll of the George's regular customers. Iffen Mr. Delphick was to come back t'ask the same question in a week or so, they didn't doubt but what they'd be able to tell him a bit more, but as for now . . .

"As for now," said Delphick, "we will address ourselves to these drinks, and this menu, and to asking Charley for an alarm call after, for once, a relatively early night. We want to be ringing Miss Seeton's doorbell before she's had time to slip off for the day."

But when they rang her bell at half-past nine next morning, it was not Miss Seeton who answered the door.

"Oh, Mr. Delphick, it's only you!" Martha Bloomer stood before them on the threshold of Sweetbriars, her eyes dark with anxiety. "Oh, dear, I made sure you must be Miss Emily come back from shopping and forgot her key and having to ring, with it being one of my days and knowing I'd be here to let her in . . . " She peered over his shoulder, past the looming form of Sergeant Ranger, northwards up The Street in the direction of the shops. "She's not usually out this early, you see, not unless she's teaching, which I know for a fact Mr. Jessyp said she needn't, with

Miss Maynard there in any case, until she'd got over all
the—well, the upset, poor soul, from the other day—but I
can't think what's happened to her. It's only half an hour,
I know, not such a time as I'd worry about normally, but
with all the upset, and no note left, and her always so careful to let me know what she's doing, even if it's just pop
out for biscuits or a jar of coffee, specially when she thinks
she mightn't be back in time to give me my wages, her not
liking to get in a muddle about money, though dear knows
I'd trust Miss Emily to pay up sooner than I'd trust most
of 'em—and of course I know if you've come straight from
the George you'll not have had much of a chance, but—
but have you seen her anywhere at all?''

Delphick glanced at his sergeant in some concern. Bob
returned the look without speaking, though in any case he
didn't need to. The same sudden presentiment had gripped
them both at exactly the same time during Martha's agitated
monologue. They remembered last night's silent telephone
calls; they knew, almost as well as Mrs. Bloomer knew it,
Miss Seeton's daily routine . . .

''I'm afraid we haven't,'' said Delphick, trying to sound
matter-of-fact about this negative response. Nothing would
be achieved by letting Martha worry herself into hysteria if
Miss Seeton should, indeed, be missing. With anyone else,
of course, there could always be the rational explanation:
pausing for a chat (but Miss Seeton didn't gossip), stopping
off to visit a friend (but Miss Seeton would never call on
anyone so early in the morning). When Miss Seeton, however, was concerned, years of experience had taught them
that it was the irrational explanation—the bizarre, the out-
landish, the recherché—the unnerving—which was, more
often than not, correct.

''There's her shopping basket still here,'' said Martha,
opening the door wide in an unspoken request for Delphick
and Bob to enter. ''And she's not in the garden, because
that was the first place I looked when she wasn't in the
house—and wherever she is, for all it's a chilly morning

she's not took her warm coat, see?''

She showed them the heavy tweed, hanging on its hook. A vision from the past flashed across Delphick's inward eye: Miss Seeton, newly returned from Switzerland via Paris, arriving at London Airport in a stylish hat and a woollen coat patterned loudly in red and black. She would keep it, she'd told him, for best. It reversed to a fawn-grey gaberdine for wet weather: might she now have decided that it looked like rain (which indeed it did) and gone out duly prepared for whatever the November clouds might send down?

The next thought was inevitable. ''Which umbrella,'' he demanded, ''did she take?''

Although this had been one of the first things Martha had seen fit to check, at Delphick's enquiry she did so again, running an experienced eye along the rack, a row of neat clips fastened to one wall with a rail underneath, holding their points above the drip-tray. ''Her best gold,'' she said, ''but it's not Lady Colveden, because I took the liberty of phoning to ask, and there's nobody there. Busy about the farm, I shouldn't wonder, and market day in Brettenden, which her ladyship always likes to pop in when she can to look at the stalls and things . . . ''

''But Miss Seeton can't have popped yet,'' Delphick said, ''because the bus''—he checked his watch—''won't be leaving for another quarter of an hour, will it? And if she'd been offered a lift by Lady Colveden, I agree with you that she would have left a message.''

Mrs. Bloomer's eyes fixed themselves on his. ''You *don't* think I'm fussed about nothing, then! Oh, dear, whatever's happened to her? Poor Miss Emily—''

''Have you looked,'' broke in Delphick, ''upstairs? What's missing from her wardrobe?''

''Perhaps,'' suggested Bob, in a warning tone, ''it would be better, sir, if—''

But he got no further. Martha had already darted off on her errand. Only as Bob groaned softly did it occur to Delphick that there could be a less sinister, though even more unfortunate, reason for Miss Seeton's apparent absence. She might well be—indeed she was—one of the fittest and most healthy old ladies of their acquaintance, but such things as strokes and heart attacks were no respecters of pers—

"Oh!" Martha's cry startled the listeners below. They did not stop to think. They headed together for the stairs, collided at the bottom, and as they tried to sort themselves out to hurry upwards, met Mrs. Bloomer hurrying down.

"I never," she gasped, "thought to look before, with her always up before I come—I just took a quick peek, and only natural I should think she'd made the bed after breakfast same as she always does, but she—she hasn't, Mr. Delphick. That bed's made, all right—but it was made yesterday, and never been slept in—you just come and see!"

"How do you know?" He didn't waste time asking if she was sure. Martha Bloomer wouldn't—couldn't—make a mistake about something like Miss Seeton's failure to sleep in her own bed: but hard evidence was always best in the case of a missing—for whatever reason—person. Even to himself, he hardly liked to use the word *abducted*—but he had a strong suspicion it would not be very long before he was forced to say it out loud . . .

"Clean sheets," said Martha. "Look!" With a flourish, she showed them her proof. She had already turned back the counterpane: now she whisked the top bedding—sheet, blankets, eiderdown—in one quick open movement halfway down the bed, revealing to their startled gaze Miss Seeton's neatly-folded nightdress resting beside a smooth white pillow on another sheet, just as smooth. Impossibly smooth . . .

"They were late," she explained, "with the deliveries this week, the laundry I mean, on account of one of the drivers catching flu and having to double up on the rounds, so the minute I heard the engine, a nasty diesel thing makes a terrible racket, I nipped across before she could do herself an injury, yoga or not, trying to turn the mattress on her own, which is what we like to do once a week, even when it wasn't one of my usual days—and this is how we left it, the two of us, yesterday afternoon. And if that sheet's been slept on I'll—I'll . . . ''

Her face began to work. She let the bedding fall from her hands. "Oh, dear, poor Miss Seeton—you know how she is, Mr. Delphick, the way things will *happen* to her, and her not noticing until it's too late. You can't help worrying about her, can you? Where on earth can she have gone?''

Delphick briefly considered, then ruled out, any idea that Miss Seeton might have suffered a brainstorm after what Martha had so tactfully referred to as *all the upset*. Miss Seeton was far too level-headed and unimaginative to allow any such a thing to happen to her.

Whatever else might happen, of course, was entirely out of her hands.

Her hands . . .

"Martha, I'd like to examine Miss Seeton's sketchbook, if I may—and I think I'd better look at the contents of her portfolio, as well. First, though, if you wouldn't mind checking in the wardrobe . . . ''

"Her Paris coat,'' said Mrs. Bloomer, after a careful search. "And her hat, the red one with the ribbon—and her leather bag she's only had a week or two, bought special for the Opening—all her smartest clothes, gone. But she's not,'' she said again, "gone off with Lady Colveden, I know she hasn't. And in any case, why would she dress up smart just for Brettenden market?''

Delphick shook his head, without speaking. Bob, patting the faithful retainer gently on the shoulder, said that Miss Seeton, she must remember, always came bouncing back in the end, didn't she? To which bromide Mrs. Bloomer, with one of her more expressive sniffs, retorted that she wished he'd sound a bit more sure of it himself, and not try to fool her he wasn't as worried as everybody else. And if Mr. Delphick thought looking at Miss Emily's pictures would help, then the sooner they stopped talking and he looked, the better it would be!

Delphick and his sergeant clattered down the stairs in Martha's wake, automatically registering their surroundings as they passed. No sign of any struggle: but that meant nothing. Wherever Miss Seeton had gone—no, be honest, wherever she'd *been taken*—she'd been tricked into going: the last thing she'd want would be to worry Martha by going off without leaving a message—and she hadn't left one, so they'd obviously hustled her away with some excuse for the hurry, and she'd swallowed it. Trickery, then, not violence—yet they weren't so confident in their tricks they'd risk letting her leave a message: another pointer to the amateurs he'd hypothesised, rather than the professionals the MI boys suspected? They wouldn't need to be professionals to trick Miss Seeton. Absolutely—almost, sometimes, painfully—truthful and law-abiding herself, MissEss must be a confidence man's dream. How she'd survived this long unscathed, he'd never know. She found it hard to believe that anyone would deliberately tell lies with intent to harm her: she would always suppose there must have been some mistake. He only hoped she'd survive this latest *mistake* as well as she'd come through all the others . . .

"Guy Forks," said Delphick, smiling despite himself at Miss Seeton's sketch of the bearded man in the broad-brimmed hat with his cutlery arms and legs. Odd: he'd never really thought of Miss Seeton as having a sense of humour—though there was, of course, that sketch she'd drawn in Paris of a lady of dubious virtue, nude, flaunting herself on top of a pile of suitcases. *Abandoned Baggage,* she'd called it—and with good reason, if his recollection was correct. They'd found the lady in question, very much deceased, inside an assortment of trunks and cases deposited at left-luggage offices all around the French capital . . .

"Oh." He stopped smiling; he stiffened. He had pulled the next sketch out of the cardboard folder: and there was Guy Fawkes, with a lantern in his hand—with a bomb in the other. In the background, smoking ruins; in the top corner, a tiny playing-card. He peered. A picture card—a female, crowned . . .

"We must advise Chris Brinton," said Delphick, "that the KarriKlozzet fire was definitely arson—probably caused by some sort of bomb. And that it's more than probably tied in with the Bragbury murder, just as we suspected—and that both are almost certainly connected with Georgina's disappearance, as witness the queen, or in Miss Seeton's version the princess, of hearts . . ."

He put the two sketches aside, and turned to the third, for which Miss Seeton had brought out her coloured pencils. "And here she is in person, bless her curly royal head —on this occasion, almost respectably attired, one might say. Although . . ." For an instant, he paused in thought; then he nodded, and smiled. "Of course—Manet, again. His version of Zola's *Nana* at her toilette . . ."

The setting was intimate: the corner of a room carpeted in red, furnished with heavy curtains, an ornate table, a velvet-covered sofa on which satin cushions were heaped. In the foreground stood the celebrated courtesan, in her underdress of cream frilled petticoat and blue satin basque, and wearing dainty black high-heeled shoes. Her body was turned towards an oval looking-glass, mounted on a slim wooden pedestal between two candles in gilded sticks; her head, the rich curls tied up with ribbon, was turned to face the onlooker—and the face was unmistakeably that of Princess Georgina. One hand sported a glittering ring, the wrist a golden bangle; the other—

"To my recollection," Delphick muttered, "that's rather different from the original. I wonder . . ."

Nana-Georgina's right hand held a powder-puff of phenomenal size, fluffy and of dazzling whiteness, the focal point of the picture.

"Yes," said Delphick, slowly. "I wonder—and there's another difference. In the original, as I recall, it's the figure of a top-hatted man in evening dress, but now . . . "

On one end of the sofa, close together, sat a little girl in frills and laces, carrying a bouquet—and, beside the girl, a small, elderly female figure in a suit, wearing a fancy hat and a necklace. And carrying an umbrella . . .

"Catharsis, perhaps." Delphick frowned, stared again at Nana, then turned to the next drawing, and sighed. "Yes, I thought as much. She's been trying to work it out of her system—and, though drawing her problems is far more in character with Miss Seeton than a course of professional psychoanalysis would be, I fear it doesn't help us as much as I hope it helped her . . . "

The scene was full of movement, of energy and urgency expressed once more in stark black and white. Two police cars, their lights flashing—you could almost hear their sirens—raced across the paper, with a fire engine, its bell being furiously rung by a burly man in oilskins and a helmet, close behind, and hotly pursued by an ambulance, its beacon ablaze. Keeping watch over the scene, its rotors awhirl, hovered a helicopter; in the background, seeming to float on a low bank of cloud, or mist, was a moated building with a drawbridge and portcullis, with turrets and towers. From the highest window in the tallest tower, a tiny Rapunzel leaned out, her tumbling locks crowned with the daintiest of tiaras . . .

"HRH in danger," said Delphick, "as if we didn't already know. And this," he went on, leafing quickly through the other sketches, "is the last of the recent batch. Not as much help as I'd hoped, I'm afraid." He looked up. "I'm sorry, Martha. We're going to have to find Miss Seeton by good old-fashioned detection—and that, unfortunately, will take time . . . "

CHAPTER 18

Miss Seeton had just finished putting away her portfolio and the rest of her sketching equipment when the doorbell rang. She glanced at the clock. It was most unlikely to be dear Martha again, since it was almost supper-time: the Bloomers, like all country-dwellers, preferred to keep regular hours. Martha would have telephoned, surely, if there had been anything of particular importance—yet she had mentioned, when she'd been so kindly helping to turn the mattress, that Stan was off to a meeting later at Rytham Hall, about the Village Watch, and the bonfire. Perhaps her visitor was dear Stan, on his way to the Hall—although if he intended asking for her advice on the matter of Murreystone, she very much feared that he would be disappointed. How could a mere teacher of art, no more than seven years a resident of the village, possibly be expected to know how to end a feud which had endured for hundreds of years?

Miss Seeton, musing sadly on the many machinations of Murreystone, clicked her tongue as the bell rang out again and she hurried down the hall, unable to stop a slight pucker of disapproval creasing her forehead as she finally opened the door.

Oh, dear. She banished the frown. A stranger: one must not appear unwelcoming. He had, she supposed, lost his way, and was seeking directions. Her eyes drifted down the front path to the car parked just outside. Although Plummergen is not furnished with street lighting, the moon was almost full that night, the sky was unusually clear for November, and there were glimmers from carelessly-curtained windows in nearby houses—and more than glimmers from the George and Dragon, diagonally opposite across the road. A dark, sleek, official-looking car . . .

"Er—Miss Seeton?"

Miss Seeton admitted her identity. The tall man fumbled in the breast pocket of his jacket, and produced a wallet, which he flipped open and held out to her. "I'm with the security services, Miss Secton." He snapped the wallet shut before she'd had time to do more than blink at it. "You can call me Rookwood, if you will." He lowered his voice. "We need your help rather urgently. May I come in?"

He seemed to be taking her agreement for granted, Miss Seeton couldn't help but think as he almost pushed his way past her into the hall. Well, perhaps not pushed—as she trotted behind him after closing the door—but he certainly was in a hurry. But then he had, of course, said that the matter was urgent: another IdentiKit, no doubt, which dear Mr. Delphick or his colleagues—hers, too, she supposed, and blushed—wished her to supply. Urgently.

"My sketching things," said Miss Seeton, conscious of the need to save every second, "are in the bureau in the sitting-room. If you would care to follow me—that is," realising that in order to lead him down the hall to the room she had just left she would have to squeeze past him, which would be—well, embarrassing, as the gentleman was a complete stranger, "if you would care to walk through—"

"Sketching things?" Mr. Rookwood didn't move: he stood with his mouth open, staring. Miss Seeton, who had taken his movement for granted, stopped in mid-step, and blessed the muscular control which years of yoga had given her. She was able to recover her original position with only the slightest of wobbles, and with no loss of dignity.

"Sketching things?" Mr. Rookwood came out of his trance, and shook his head. "Er—no, thank you, Miss Seeton, that won't be necessary. Her Royal Highness doesn't so much need her portrait painted as a—as a chaperone," he concluded, in a rush.

Now it was Miss Seeton's turn to stare. Her Royal Highness? Chaperone? "But—but surely," she enquired, with a flustered look, "her lady-in-waiting . . . "

"Is at Kensington Palace," Mr. Rookwood told her, "while you, Miss Seeton, are here. There's been no time, you see, to fetch . . . er, her ladyship from London—we've only just discovered where the princess has been kept prisoner. She—that is, her lady-in-waiting—will be informed, of course, as soon as possible—a helicopter of the Queen's Flight and she'll be here in half an hour—but for now we want someone else Her Royal Highness can . . . well, can trust, while she . . . while she's being debriefed. Someone she can relax with after her, um, ordeal—someone to reassure her, now it's over. Another woman—you know the sort of thing—so, if you wouldn't mind coming with me now . . . "

It almost seemed that he would take her by the arm: but no, she must have been mistaken. Or was she? As she looked at him, puzzled, Mr. Rookwood thrust his hands in his trouser pockets, and took a deep breath. "As quickly as possible, please," he said, in a voice which shook, just a little—from worry, no doubt. Such a grave responsibility; and here she was with her foolish objections, delaying the poor man when he'd said it was urgent—but . . .

"But surely a——a more official person than I would be the best choice to—to accompany Her Royal Highness? A policewoman, for example, since she would be trained, as I am not, even if so many years with children—not that one would consider Her Royal Highness a child, naturally,'' with a blush, ''although she is still very young, of course—but I would have thought—the uniform, so reassuring, besides being closer in age—''

''No!'' Mr. Rookwood saw the startled expression in her eyes, and laughed. It sounded, to Miss Seeton's ears, somewhat forced: but he was, she reminded herself, a young man with much on his mind. ''No, I'm sorry, Miss Seeton, but—but she has asked for you in particular. An older woman—not exactly a mother figure—'' Miss Seeton, even more startled, blushed a deep red. Mr. Rookwood coughed. ''I'm sorry, Miss Seeton, I'm expressing myself very badly, but—but, well, if you'd just like to look on this as—as being by Royal Command . . . ''

Miss Seeton paled. Would it be treason to refuse? When the poor young princess had been, one imagined, having so unpleasant a time—although surely they, whoever they were, would not have harmed her—Mr. Rookwood hadn't mentioned anything of the sort, though perhaps he was trying to spare one's feelings—but there had, of course, been one's First Aid training, even if girls fainting at school had been the limit of one's experience—and yet . . .

''Asked for me in particular?'' Even now, she couldn't quite take it all in. ''I'm sure I don't see why—''

''You met,'' broke in Mr. Rookwood—he sounded close to exasperation: the anxiety, of course—''at the Power Station Opening, remember?''

And Miss Seeton, who remembered only too well and had hoped that nobody else did, blushed again, and sighed, and murmured that if Her Royal Highness had indeed expressed a wish for Emily Dorothea Seeton, then Emily Dorothea Seeton would be only too happy to do her loyal duty.

Waiting in the hall—for one moment, she'd half expected him to insist on accompanying her upstairs—Mr. Rookwood tapped his foot with impatience at her saying she must wear, not her everyday coat, but her smart check from that very expensive—such a generous present of kind Mr. Stemkos!—shop in Paris, with her best hat, and that she would take the new handbag, which meant transferring her purse and keys and handkerchief from the one she used the rest of the time. And, of course, what other umbrella but her best, with the gold handle? When one was meeting Royalty . . .

Miss Seeton did not—could not—explain to Mr. Rookwood (she still blushed at the memory) that her sketch of Princess Georgina clothed in—well, in so informal a fashion had made her more than usually conscious of the sartorial respect due to a member of the Royal Family. *Treason* . . .

"Please hurry, Miss Seeton!" Mr. Rookwood was looking at his watch even as she trotted down the stairs, buttoning her coat. Miss Seeton, still preoccupied with thoughts of treason, trotted even faster. She did not stop at the hall stand to check her hat in the mirror; the notepad by the telephone was ignored as she snatched her umbrella from the stand, slipped the handle over her arm, and announced that she was ready.

Mr. Rookwood, who'd thought she meant it, continued to fret while Miss Seeton locked her front door, then whisked her down the path before she'd properly closed her bag on the keys, and had her buckled into the passenger seat and the car door locked—for safety, he told her—while she was still trying to recall whether there was anything she had forgotten . . .

And then, as the engine turned over and the car moved off, she realised there was nothing she could do about it, in any case.

Mr. Rookwood hadn't told her, when they set out, how far they had to go, or even where they were going, except that it was to the princess: but, although in all the hurry one hadn't thought to check the sitting-room clock, it would come as no great surprise to learn that they had already been driving around the winding, shadowed—for the moon had gone behind clouds long ago—lanes of Kent (or perhaps by now they were in Sussex) for half an hour, at least. Which naturally made one wonder—though of course they were the experts, and must understand such matters far better than a humble teacher of art—why Mr. Rookwood and his colleagues couldn't have arranged, in the time it had so far taken, for the lady-in-waiting—Lady Vaudine Elliot, as she recalled—to fly down from Kensington Palace in the helicopter. But as Mr. Rookwood was driving so fast, and seemed so very preoccupied—which must be why he had appeared to forget Lady Vaudine's name—one hardly cared to put the question to him. Or to ask why he had been driving with only his sidelights for the past few miles and not with his—Miss Seeton smiled—main beam. Dear Nigel! He was always so courteous when telling her things; it was a pleasure to ask for explanations, except that she could not, she felt, ask Mr. Rookwood in the same friendly way, in case it should appear to him not only impertinent, from a stranger, but a distraction. One knew that unless they themselves chose to open the conversation, one should never directly address the men at the wheel . . .

"Nearly there." Mr. Rookwood sighed, slowed the car, and switched off even his sidelights. Only the faint glimmer from stars and moon in a patchy sky showed where they were going. Security, Miss Seeton supposed, pleased with herself for having worked it out at last, although she hoped they would meet no other darkened cars coming in the opposite direction; and it was perhaps a little odd that one could see—except, of course, that it was dark, so that it would be more accurate to say that one could make out—no other signs of a—a security presence, as one understood from films that it should be called. Should she ask Mr. Rookwood to confirm her guess? But he seemed increasingly reluctant to talk, and in the greater dark it would be, of course, still more of a distraction if he did.

Mr. Rookwood flicked the indicator, then flicked it off again with a muttered exclamation Miss Seeton found somewhat surprising, in a man of his type. The worry, no

doubt, of so grave a responsibility as the princess's safety.
The car slowed almost to a halt, then turned through an
open gateway flanked, as far as Miss Seeton could tell, by
tall pillars; but the road ahead, which one supposed should
with greater accuracy now be called a driveway, was rutted,
and bumpy. One was too busy holding oneself steady on
the seat, despite the belt, to bother trying to see more
closely; it almost appeared that Mr. Rookwood was deliberately trying to shake his passenger from one side of the
car to the other—which was, Miss Seeton told herself
firmly, ridiculous, and showed how one's imagination—on
which one had all too seldom been able to pride oneself—
had been stimulated by the excitement of the occasion; by
the darkened, mysterious speed of this unusual journey.
Miss Seeton felt a little thrill run down her spine, and her
fingers, when not clutching at the seat for support, tingled
in the old, familiar way . . .

The car rumbled and jolted along for several hundred
yards, then stopped. Mr. Rookwood switched off the engine, and climbed out; he did not at once come round to
open Miss Seeton's door, but seemed more interested in
checking that nobody had followed them up the drive, or
was hiding behind the bushes near the house: security, of
course. Miss Seeton unbuckled herself, tried the door handle, remembered, and waited for Mr. Rookwood to release
her.

It was a pity that, in her haste, she had not had time to
transfer the torch she always carried from her everyday bag
to her best: except, of course, that one had somehow received the impression that the princess would be . . . well,
somewhere rather less isolated than this. More—more civilised. Somewhere with proper lighting; somewhere much
busier, with more people. But one had to assume that Mr.
Rookwood and the others, wherever they were, knew what
they were doing . . .

Mr. Rookwood unlocked the car door, warned of the
need for caution, and helped her out. "This way," he said,

in a voice hushed but firm—and this time he did, very definitely, take her by the arm. One might almost have said that he gripped her, hurrying her away from the car almost before she'd had time to pick up her umbrella or adjust her hat. And as for the chance to practise her curtsey, he'd given her none at all . . .

He guided—not *pushed*, surely? Not *thrust*, no matter what it felt like—Miss Seeton across to the house, up some steps, and through a darkened doorway into a shadowed hall. He seemed to know, even in the dark, exactly where he was going. "We go upstairs," he said quietly, edging her towards the steep rectangular greyness of the light from a tall window, and urging her to mount. "Careful, now . . . "

Silently lamenting the absence of her torch, Miss Seeton did her best to be careful, feeling her way with the point of the umbrella she held in her free hand. Mr. Rookwood was very like a cat, one might say, able to see in the dark, and treading so very softly and with such a sure step . . .

"Down here," he said, and led Miss Seeton towards a door at the far end of the landing: a door around the edge of which shone a narrow, golden, electric gleam, a most welcome sight in the grey, glimmering shadows . . .

"In here." He fumbled with the handle, bent, opened the door, and as he did so thrust a hand inside and switched off the light. Miss Seeton heard a rustle of movement, a little cry—and herself cried out, as she felt something—someone—push her sharply in the back, so that she lost her footing and staggered into the room . . .

And heard, to her amazement, the door slammed shut behind her, and the key turned sharply in the lock.

"Who's that? Whoever you are, keep still!"

The voice which now addressed Miss Seeton out of the anonymous dark was young, cultured, and female, and . . . not frightened, thought Miss Seeton, her hands gripping her bag and brolly for reassurance: but wary. And—judging by the accent—clearly accustomed, from birth, to command . . .

"Stay just where you are," commanded the voice, with a hint of breathlessness. "I'll put the light back on. Don't move an inch!"

The soft patter of feet sounded in Miss Seeton's ear as, despite those breathless commands, she found herself turning to track the sound around what instinct, and the accompanying echoes, told her was probably the perimeter of the room. There came a gentle, muffled scraping, and a click.

In the sudden light, Miss Seeton blinked.

And blinked again, though this time from astonishment rather than glare: for, beside the switch—with a pillow in her upraised hand and a furious gleam in her eye—stood, in a martial attitude, Her Royal Highness, Princess Georgina.

The gleam mellowed almost at once to a look of recognition—those born in the purple are raised according to the strictest principles of etiquette—and, at the same time as Miss Seeton recovered her startled wits and sank in a curtsey, the pillow, likewise, was lowered to the floor.

"We've met before," said Georgina, above Miss Seeton's murmured salutation. "At Dungeness." Miss Seeton, rising from her curtsey, blushed, and fumbled with the strap of her handbag to avoid meeting the princess's eye. Georgina nodded. "The little girl with the flowers . . . "

"My—my pupil, Your Royal Highness." Miss Seeton began to breathe a little more easily. Perhaps, after all, there would be no need to mention . . .

She relaxed too soon. Georgina had a thoughtful pucker between her brows. In normal circumstances, Royalty does not willingly cause embarrassment to its loyal subjects: in normal circumstances, the princess would never have dreamed of mentioning Miss Seeton's unfortunate encounter with the radiation alarm. But these circumstances were very far removed indeed from being normal.

"And the alarm, of course," said Her Royal Highness, fixing Miss Seeton with a brilliant blue eye. "It went off when they scanned you, and the next thing I knew I'd been grabbed—but it wasn't your fault," hastily, as Miss Seeton blushed still more, and bobbed another curtsey as she tried to frame a suitable apology.

Her mind, however, had gone blank with dismay. It was Georgina's voice which now said: "Whoever they are, they haven't said much I've been able to hear, but at least I've managed to work out that they'd planned to snatch me anyway, later in the day. Your, um, little misfortune just allowed them to bring their plans forward a bit."

"Oh, dear . . . " Miss Seeton, looking incredibly guilty, didn't know where to begin apologising. "Oh, Your Royal Highness, I do most humbly beg your pardon. My poor Cousin Flora would be so very mortified to think—"

"Don't worry about it!" Georgina ran across to give her

companion a quick hug. "I told you, it wasn't your fault—
but I thought the little girl was called Sally?"

Miss Seeton was so overwhelmed by such kindliness
from a member of the Royal House of Windsor that, in her
confusion, she dropped her umbrella. In ducking to retrieve
it, she narrowly missed bumping heads with Georgina, who
seemed to share the same automatic instinct for tidiness:
and, too startled even to blush, Miss Seeton cried:

"Oh, do be careful! Ma'am," she added, recollecting
herself hastily, and reverting to the traditional formula. "I
do most humbly beg your pardon . . . " And she essayed
yet another curtsey.

It was not, however, third time lucky. Even the agility
imparted to the knees by years of yoga cannot be equal to
a curtsey from a crouching start. Miss Seeton, wobbling,
gave a little cry, and fell over, dropping her umbrella again
as she did so. Georgina, caught unawares partly by the
wobble, partly by the handle of the brolly, likewise gasped,
and fell. The two ladies ended up side by side on the floor,
rubbing their posteriors and—after a few moments—trying,
for some reason neither could understand, not to giggle.

They tried: but failed. Miss Seeton, on the point of apologising for the umpteenth time, but too breathless with dismay for her unintentional—treasonable?—discourtesy to
do so, caught the eye of Princess Georgina. The well-
known sapphire orbs were sparkling: the ruby lips were
curving in a grin. "There—there aren't," said Georgina,
choking, "any—any bells this time, are there?"

Her laughter was infectious. Miss Seeton, relieved that
the princess didn't appear to be badly damaged, laughed
with her—chuckled, rather, and smiled; and then, quite
without thinking, reached over to pat her on the shoulder.
The poor young creature. A note, perhaps, of hysteria in
her laughter. Miss Seeton, experienced in the ways of teenage girls, patted the royal shoulder again: it was no wonder
that she seemed just a touch . . . overwrought. Anyone else,
with a less rigorous upbringing to strengthen her character,

would doubtless have given way to hysteria long ago . . .

"Come now, my dear." Miss Seeton, the years of teaching overriding all other considerations, administered one last, bracing pat, then gathered up her bag and brolly and rose gracefully to her feet. "It would be better for both of us, you know, if we were to sit comfortably on chairs, rather than on the floor."

As she dusted herself down, for the first time she did more than glance at her surroundings. She was in a bedroom of reasonable size, carpeted, and furnished with a single bed, an easy chair, a small, low table, and a bookcase with a selection of paperback volumes on its shelves. Above the bookcase was a window, thickly curtained. There was a wardrobe against one wall, and what looked like a communicating door directly opposite.

"The bathroom," said Georgina, who had recovered herself almost completely, and was contemplating her visitor with as much interest as her visitor contemplated the room. "All mod cons, I believe the saying goes. For a prison, in fact, it's rather comfortable—that's where they spilled my food the other day," she added, as Miss Seeton shuddered on noticing a large, red-brown stain on the carpet, just inside the door. Her Royal Highness giggled. "It looks awfully like a bloodstain, doesn't it? Quite horrid, but harmless, really. Tomato ketchup"—she made a face—"and gravy, I think. You see I kicked one of them on the shin, and tried to hit him over the head with the tray—but he was too quick for me, more's the pity."

Miss Seeton looked discreetly scandalized. One did not somehow expect that a princess of the Blood would be so . . . so vehement in expressing her—understandable, admittedly—indignation at—one could not, it seemed, mince one's words—at being—Miss Seeton gulped—being held captive. Not, perhaps, entirely ladylike—something rather more subtle might be more appropriate . . . except, of course, that one found it hard to envisage exactly what, in the circumstances, would—or indeed could—be considered appropriate . . .

Georgina observed Miss Seeton's expression, and was reminded of her old governess. Her giggle was apprehensive, her tone slightly aggrieved as she said:

"Oh, I suppose that sort of behaviour would send the Buck House crowd into vapours, if they knew about it—but they don't." There was a little quiver in her voice as she spoke the final words. "And—and what else could I do? The dignity of one's position is all very well in—in normal life, but you can't call . . . being kidnapped *normal*, can you?" Her voice shook again; and again she rallied. "Believe me, I've no intention of sitting about meekly waiting for a knight in shining armour to come galloping to the rescue. The Lord—and I don't mean Sir Shining Armour—helps those who help themselves, doesn't He?"

And then her face crumpled, and her eyes sparkled with something more than bravado, as Miss Seeton —whose thoughts had turned automatically to Nigel Colveden, the nearest to Sir Galahad she'd ever met—sighed, and without thinking patted her on the shoulder yet again. "Oh, dear!" gasped Georgina, and for the first time since her capture she permitted herself a few snuffles of self-pity.

Miss Seeton said gently, "There, there. You must not distress yourself, my dear—Ma'am," she added, remembering. She blushed. Should she, perhaps, curtsey? In the circumstances, it might, perhaps, be regarded as . . .

Georgina straightened, and fumbled in her pocket for a handkerchief. "Oh, please don't! You're the first friendly face I've seen since I've been here—the first face, if it comes to that, because they always wear masks—and we're in this together, aren't we?" Blowing her dainty nose, she favoured Miss Seeton with a sudden, intense look from those sparkling sapphire eyes. "Aren't we?"

Miss Seeton, her conscience—apart from the curtsey—clear, looked steadily back at her. "If it is not an impertinence on my part to say so, I suspect—indeed I fear, Ma'am, that we may be.''

Georgina sighed as she emerged from her handkerchief. ''Then I didn't imagine it? We can't—can't escape, because they . . . they have locked the door again?''

''I believe,'' said Miss Seeton, slowly—one had no wish to distress the child—the princess—further—''they did, Ma'am. That is to say, he did, Mr. Rookwood. Which came as a considerable surprise, because—''

''You know him?'' The sapphire sparkle was all interest now as Georgina—who despite her earlier words had crossed to the door to try it, just in case—glanced back over her shoulder. ''You know who they are?'' And she rattled the handle with brisk emphasis as she spoke.

Miss Seeton's brow creased with the effort of memory. ''He told me that he was a member of the—of the security forces, and from my extremely limited knowledge I have to say that he''—thoughts of the imminent Christmas Pantomime came unbidden—''he certainly looked the part, except that now I am forced to the conclusion that this could well have been a—an untruth, as he has locked the door, and there can surely be no need for such behaviour now that Your Royal Highness has been rescued. If that is in fact what has happened. And since he has locked us in, it would seem somewhat unnecessary—if a rescue has been effected, I mean, even though I explained to him that I was hardly the most suitable . . . ''

She sighed. ''He told me, you see, that''—she blushed—''Your Royal Highness had—had particularly requested my presence—which I confess I found most surprising, when they are so much better trained than I—women police officers, I mean, the full-time sort, when my—my attachment to the police, or rather my connection with them . . . ''

She blushed again, and drifted to a halt. One ought to have remembered sooner that etiquette required Royalty, not Royalty's companions, always to initiate, and thereafter to direct, any topics of conversation. Her Royal Highness had wished only to know the identity of Mr. Rookwood: should she wish to know the identity of Miss Emily Dorothea Seeton, she would, naturally, ask.

"Then who," asked Georgina, "are you? You said you were a teacher. How can you be a policewoman as well?"

"But I'm not," said Miss Seeton, forgetting etiquette in her desire for accuracy. "At least—I was, but I have been retired for some seven years now, Ma'am, although sometimes, when Miss Maynard is away . . . That is—I never have been, I assure you, Your Royal Highness."

She drew a deep breath. Had she made herself, she wondered, entirely clear? There was a puzzled furrow between Georgina's delicate brows, and a dancing light in her eyes. Miss Seeton tried again, "A teacher—of art. In Hampstead—Mrs. Benn's school, and evening classes at the Polytechnic, though I have from time to time helped out when Miss Maynard has been unable . . . But certainly not a police officer. In Plummergen, that is, not Hampstead. A retaining fee, no more—which, although in my opinion most generous, Your Royal Highness would doubtless regard as—"

"Oh, do stop!" Georgina clapped her hands to her ears, and shook her head. The golden curls bounced, the blue eyes danced still more. "As long as you're not on their side, I'm honestly not bothered—it's so lovely to see a friendly face, after all this time. Just tell me your name, and forget about the rest. It's too confusing."

"Er—Seeton, Ma'am. Emily Seeton—from Plummergen." And Miss Seeton bobbed her best curtsey yet.

Georgina glanced at Miss Seeton's left hand as it rested on the crook of her umbrella. "Miss Seeton, how do you do? And it would be too silly for me to suppose you don't know who I am—but please, you must call me Georgy, the way my family does. You've no idea how lonely . . . " The quiver was back; was gone as she continued:

"And we can't afford to be too formal, can we? When—when we could be shut in here for days—though I do hope,'' she added, blinking away a hint of further tears, ''we won't be—and then, perhaps we won't. Two heads are heaps better than one, after all. Don't you think?''

Miss Seeton smiled. The child—the princess—seemed so much more cheerful and relaxed than at the start of this rather unorthodox conversation. It was up to an older, if not necessarily a wiser, head to encourage her in her new-found optimism . . .

Besides, she did. ''Indeed yes, Ma'am, I do,'' said Miss Seeton firmly. ''Er—that is,'' as Georgina twinkled at her, and waved a warning finger, ''that is—er, yes . . . Georgy,'' in her most respectful tones.

Georgina beamed. ''That's better! That's the first kind word anyone's said to me since . . . But never mind. If we just keep going over and over it, we'll never get any-where—and we want to, don't we?'' She pulled Miss See-ton across to the bed, and made her sit beside her. ''What we want is to get out of here. Have you any ideas?''

Miss Seeton, still bemused at the turn taken by recent events, blinked. One had seen such situations many times, of course, on the television—Miss Seeton was an Old Movie fan of considerable devotion—but in real, as op-posed to black-and-white, life, it was difficult to know ex-actly how—or, indeed, where—to begin.

''Begin with what you know about where we are,'' Geor-gina promptly suggested. ''I never saw a thing while they were bringing me here, and all the windows are shuttered somehow from the outside, so that I still can't, any more than I can hear anything, either. And it's not for want of trying, either, believe me!''

Miss Seeton sighed. One disliked being the bearer of bad news, but . . . ''It was, I fear, well after dark when Mr. Rookwood came to fetch me—and he had only the side-lights on, which meant that I could see, unfortunately, very little of where we were going, since it is a cloudy night—which is a pity, as the moon is almost full at the moment. And just before we turned into the drive, he switched them off altogether——the lights, I mean.''

Georgina muttered about planning. Miss Seeton sighed again. ''Although, of course, I have ridden my bicycle on many occasions around my own neighbourhood, I have seldom ventured farther afield—if, indeed, we are. Far afield, I mean—to know now where we are, or to attempt a guess. For all I could tell to the contrary, even though we must have driven for half an hour or more, we might have been travelling in circles, and have ended up no more than a few hundred yards from my home—except, of course, that one would have expected Your Royal——er,'' as Georgina shook her head in gentle reproof, ''that one would have expected, er, you to have recognised some sounds of village life, which you say you have not. Which means that we probably aren't. There are, you see, no street lamps in Plummergen, so that sounds would be almost the only way of telling one was not in the very depths of the countryside instead.''

Georgina sighed. ''Which could mean that we really are—in the depths, I mean, miles from anywhere. So even if we managed to escape, we'd have miles to walk afterwards—not that I mind walking, of course. Grouse moors and so on . . . It's just a pity I wasn't wearing something a bit more suitable for a cross-country hike when they kidnapped me.''

The mattress lurched as she jumped off the bed to reach beneath it for her shoes—smart, dainty, thin-soled leather shoes which perfectly matched her outfit, but which could not be as comfortable as the slippers she now wore. ''Just right,'' she said cheerfully, ''for opening a power station, but not much use for the great trek, are they?''

Miss Seeton, surveying her own tiny feet in their best patent leather instead of her usual stout walking shoes, had to agree, sadly, that they were not. If only she had known what Mr. Rookwood really had in mind . . .

''Then you probably wouldn't have come,'' said Georgina. ''At least, I hope you'd have rung your friends in the

police before you did—you didn't, did you?'' with a wild
flash of hope in her eyes—a flash which soon faded as Miss
Seeton, sadly, shook her head. Why (she pointed out)
should she be supposed to think of telephoning the police
when she had been given to understand that they already
knew? That was to say Mr. Rookwood had not exactly said
as much in so many words; but it was not, she thought,
unreasonable of her to have taken him for a colleague of
dear Chief Superintendent Delphick, who did from time to
time, if Her Royal—if Georgy would not think it immodest
of her to say so, choose to—to consult her on certain matters; or even Superintendent Brinton, except that he was
from Ashford and Mr. Delphick—being from Scotland
Yard, when matters of security were always dealt with in
London, as far as she knew—might be more reasonably
thought of as being a colleague . . .

''Stop!'' cried Georgina again, quite lost in the maze of
explanation and counter-confusion. ''I'm sorry, but—but
it's all so muddling—I need to sort things out before we
even start to plan our escape. First you're a teacher, then
you've retired, then you're on friendly terms with Scotland
Yard, and superintendents from Ashford . . . ''

She shook her curly head. ''Miss Seeton—who exactly
are you?''

CHAPTER 20

"A—a teacher." Miss Seeton was somewhat perplexed. "Of art—or rather—that is . . . " She thought she had explained this once before: but it would be a shocking breach of etiquette to contradict Royalty. The princess was, no doubt, a little confused, in the circumstances: circumstances which one understood rather better, perhaps, than Her Royal—than Georgy realised . . .

Miss Seeton was herself no stranger to abduction. There had, in the past, been a red-haired young man who had popped a sack over her head—ruining, to her annoyance, a perfectly good hat—and carried her off in the back of a battered van, causing her to roll around most uncomfortably with boxes of soap flakes and bottles of ginger beer which (and one had to agree that it served him right, even if—as Mr. Delphick and the others afterwards explained—it had done the engine no good at all) she had poured into the petrol tank to stop him.

"Seven years," murmured Miss Seeton, remembering. "And then, of course, I retired . . . "

"Apart from helping out," supplied Georgina, "when Miss Maynard can't—not to mention being paid a retainer by the police, as well.'' Royalty's training is more thorough, its intellect more lively, than many outsiders ever know. ''But do please tell me—what is the retainer paid *for*? Are you some kind of chaperone for—for kidnapped girls? I can't imagine they keep you terribly busy, somehow.''

Her blue-eyed twinkle met Miss Seeton's own look of calm amusement at the very idea. Miss Seeton twinkled back, and chuckled. ''Oh no, my dear—or rather they do, from time to time, but not with chaperoning anyone. Keep me busy, that is. Really, I'm not entirely sure I would be at all the right person for such a task, despite having taught for so long, and the yoga keeping me fitter, I believe, for my age than—that is,'' for a lady did not discuss her age, even by mistake, ''with IdentiKit drawings. I am often kept very busy with those. Only the other day, indeed . . . ''

Her hands began moving to and fro along the gold umbrella on her knees: the gold umbrella which had been given to her by dear Mr. Delphick, who had so very recently asked her for another IdentiKit sketch, and she had shown him—oh, dear. Blushing, she remembered her most unusual version of *Le Dejeuner sur l'Herbe;* and she clutched in some dismay at the umbrella, then blushed all the more as Georgina looked at her with wide-eyed interest.

''My hat,'' murmured Miss Seeton, desperately trying to turn her thoughts back to less—less embarrassing matters, when the subject of her sketch was sitting right beside her quite oblivious of the dreadful—

''Guy Forks,'' said Miss Seeton, firmly. ''So very foolish,'' as Georgina's look of interest grew even more intense. Well, better appear foolish than treacherous. ''My hat,'' she enlarged hastily. ''Not the one in the sack with the soap flakes, but the other, which was blown off by the wind when I forgot to put in a hat-pin, and rolled all the way up The Street in the dust. It was quite unwearable by the time they had fetched it down from the awning. And when they came as I was scrambling eggs, I naturally said they could have it for the guy, as it was of no particular use to me any longer—not without a great deal of work, when there are several others which match quite as many of my outfits—the children, I mean. Which was where the forks came in, when I was thinking about the hat-pin. So very foolish," she said once more. "The play on words, although with it being so close to November the Fifth it is hardly surprising—the bonfire, that is. And the fireworks . . . ''

But then Miss Seeton hesitated. *Did* Royalty indulge in such rituals? Would they really wish to commemorate the remarkably narrow escape of their Jacobean forebear from the Gunpowder Plotters? Was she being—not rude, for such had certainly not been her intention—but perhaps tactless? Miss Seeton blushed again. Her fingers fluttered the full length of the furled umbrella on her knees, and came back restlessly to the handle, and, catching at it, missed. With a clatter, it tumbled again to the floor.

This time, Georgina did not bend to pick it up. A light of gleeful excitement gleamed in her eyes. "*I* know who you are!" she cried, as Miss Seeton, pink from stooping, once more retrieved her property and sat upright again. "You're the one the papers call the Battling Brolly!"

One should not, Miss Seeton reminded herself, contradict Royalty, much as one would wish to; and, of course, if there was anyone who would know how the newspapers tended to—to distort, to exaggerate, then it must surely be a member of the Royal Family. Miss Seeton, still pink— though now for a different reason than stooping—sighed, and lowered her eyes to the handle of her gold umbrella, and sighed again.

"I'm sorry," said Georgina, giving her an impulsive hug. "You must be so tired of people treating you as a celebrity, but I promise I won't ask for your autograph, or anything." She smiled. "It's so lovely, though, to meet someone for once who knows what it's like!"

Miss Seeton looked up, and smiled faintly. "It was,

of course, a long time ago," she murmured. "My poor hat . . . "

Georgina, who had not been talking so much about the shared experience of abduction as the similarly shared experience of being the darling of the newspapers, glanced at Miss Seeton's hat, and smiled; then did more than glance, as she recalled what Miss Seeton had said before.

"A hat-pin!" she cried, her eyes bright. "Are you wearing one today?"

It was not the first time since she'd met Georgina that Miss Seeton had been startled by an almost abrupt change of subject: but one had, of course, to follow wherever Royalty—even in the more informal relationship into which it had been proposed one should enter—might lead. Miss Seeton nodded. "It was, as I understood it, a special occasion," she said. "By Royal command, Mr. Rookwood told me—his idea of a joke, no doubt, since Your Royal—since you, that is, did not know I was coming, and therefore could not possibly have asked for me. Which is why I brought my very best umbrella, of course, as I had no reason to suppose that he was—was guilty of as many untruths as it now appears probable he was . . . "

Georgina seemed not to mind that Miss Seeton had let her explanation run away with her a little. She neither interrupted her, nor fidgeted with boredom: she was frowning in thought, her blue eyes moving repeatedly from Miss Seeton's hat to the door, and back again. Miss Seeton, suddenly conscious that she must be wearying her royal audience with her chatter, fell silent. Georgina still did not speak. Miss Seeton went pink; her hands plucked at the fastening of the gold umbrella. If only she had her sketching equipment . . .

She did not know she had spoken the wish aloud: but even to this unexpected remark Georgina made no reply. She was still thinking. Miss Seeton, sighing for her absent pencils and paper, continued to sit in silence, waiting.

"Yes!" Georgina came out of her trance, and clapped

her hands. "Two of us—we'll manage this time, you see
if we don't! I'm not staying here a minute more than I must,
and nor are you—and you haven't had anything to eat this
evening, have you, Miss Seeton?"

Yet another change of subject; but Miss Seeton, at once
forgetting her missing sketchpad and fearful of boring her
lively young friend, confirmed quickly that she had not; and
said nothing more.

"Goody—then they'll be back, because they aren't going to let you starve, any more than they've let me."
Georgina grinned. "As I said before, considering they're
kidnappers they're really rather, um, considerate—gosh,
that sounds silly, but you know what I mean. Proper
plumbing, and meals three times a day, except for that
once . . ." She giggled, then sobered. "But then there
was only me. With two of us now . . ." She seemed sub-
limely able to ignore the fact that neither she nor Miss
Seeton was more than five feet tall, whereas each of the
kidnappers she had encountered was a good head taller
than they, and far more solidly built.

"We must be ready the minute they arrive," she went
on, as Miss Seeton listened in a dutiful silence. "We'll hear
the car arrive- at least, I always did before, though he must
have left it farther from the house when he brought you."
With a nod, Miss Seeton confirmed that he had.

With some satisfaction, Georgina nodded back. "That's
how he managed to catch me by surprise, then. They don't
usually bother, not since they've taken to coming in pairs—
there's safety in numbers." She giggled. "Since that kicking business with the tray—but never mind. Safety in
numbers: two of them—and two of us. We must use our
wits, Miss Seeton . . ."

For the first time, a note of uncertainty entered the confident young voice. The myriad remarkable exploits of the
celebrated Battling Brolly, even as reported in the less sen-
sational newspapers read by royal households, had led
Georgina to suppose vaguely that the lady in question—

seldom, if ever, referred to by name—must be a termagant
of far more than Amazonian proportions. The sober reality—inch for inch and ounce for ounce no bigger than
Georgina herself, surprisingly smartly dressed (though far
more surprisingly hatted)—gave her pause for thought.

But not for long. One had, after all, to do *something*.
"Use our wits," repeated Georgina, firmly. "Miss Seeton,
do you think you can?"

Miss Seeton, who hated to dampen enthusiasm in anyone, young or old—and who could not help but feel they
should not remain incarcerated here for a moment longer
than necessary—nodded again.

"One carries the tray; the other keeps watch and guards
the door," said Georgina, warming to her theme. "When
they come in, you must be ready to jab your hat-pin into—
oh, some convenient piece of the one by the door—you've
taught art, so I bet you'll think of somewhere absolutely
splendid for jabbing. Anatomy, and that sort of thing—and
it will make him yell, if you jab hard enough. The one with
the tray won't drop it right away—I think there's a sort of
instinct not to, I had to positively tug and tug before he'd
let go, even though he was hopping on one leg and using
the sort of language umpty-great-grandma Victoria would
not have found amusing—but he'll be startled, which is
what we want, because I'm going to kick him again, and
trip him up, then you can grab the tray and hit the other
one with it, and they'll both be knocked off-balance while
we throw blankets over their heads and tie them up with
sheets and things, and make a run for it—and can you drive
a car?"

Miss Seeton, whose vicarious black-and-white experience of battle had never evoked in her any wish to indulge,
found herself nodding yet again at this further non sequitur,
then shaking her head. One should not, after all, forget that
there was once an occasion when a hat-pin applied to a
gunman's hand had saved the daughter of an earl from kidnap, or—Miss Seeton blushed—worse; and if one could

justify such action for an Honourable, how much more justified must it be in the case of a princess? If—she gulped—hitting people with trays and tying them up was what patriotism required of Emily Dorothea Seeton, then—she drew a deep breath—hit them and tie them she would. But as for the car . . .

"I can," said Georgina, interpreting Miss Seeton's mute signals to her own satisfaction. "Not awfully well, though, when I don't know the car—still, if it messes up their horrid gearbox, then it will just have to serve the beasts right, won't it?"

She sounded so fierce about the prospect of messed-up gears that Miss Seeton would have nodded even if she'd disagreed with her. Since, however, she was coming to feel that the kidnappers deserved every possible punishment for their act of treason—and since behind all the bravado it was not hard to see that poor (mentally, Miss Seeton braced herself) that poor Georgy had been having a bad time of it . . . she duly nodded with as much fervour as she could, and added a quiet *Yes, it will* for good measure.

Georgina did not hear her. "All we have to do is take the keys from whoever's pocket they're in, and that will be that. Freedom!" And the princess cast a most expressive look about the chamber which had been her prison for the past few days.

Miss Seeton said gently, "Both sets, of course—if you will excuse me, my dear. Keys," she enlarged, as Georgina blinked at her. "One set for the car," said Miss Seeton, "because girls are so much more practical nowadays with mechanical matters, but—though yours is an excellent plan, if we can only carry it out successfully—but should we not lock the—the gentlemen in question into this room as they have locked us? One reads so often in books, or sees on the television, or films, that it is comparatively easy to free oneself from bonds of—of an unorthodox nature, and particularly so when they have been fastened in—in something of a hurry, as these, of course, will be."

"I do know my knots," Georgina informed her, with some pride. "I was a Girl Guide—family tradition, you know—but yes, I see what you mean. You can't really tie people up so well in sheets as you could if you had proper rope, and of course there's no rope anywhere in here. They've taken care of that." She forced a laugh. "We can't have our hostage climbing out of windows and sliding down ropes, now can we? And the beastly sheets are nylon or polyester or something. You can't tear them into strips—and don't think I haven't tried—but then, there are heavy shutters across the windows, so it wouldn't have been much use even if I'd managed it."

A fleeting vision of Douglas Fairbanks flashed before Miss Seeton's inward eye, followed by a much more vivid impression of the blonde Georgina as Rapunzel: but neither sight was reassuring. Short curls, she knew, might well lengthen into gracefully-waving locks, but that would take far too long, even if—

Miss Seeton shook herself. The strain of her (or rather of Georgina's) situation was obviously affecting her common sense. How foolish even to imagine escaping down a rope of someone's hair, whether from the turret of a castle or from the bedroom—perhaps bathroom—window of a house. Far more foolish, indeed, than . . .

"Guy Forks," murmured Miss Seeton. She sighed. It seemed that—regrettable though such a step must appear to all right-thinking persons—there was no alternative for her but to obey the royal command . . .

"That's wonderful, Miss Seeton." Georgina, thinking it wise to ignore the cryptic reference to Guy Fawkes as she'd previously ignored the repeated motif of Miss Seeton's hat, chose to hear just as much of Miss Seeton's current murmuring as best suited her purpose. "You agree? I knew you would!" And the young princess threw her arms about the older woman in a heartfelt embrace. "The minute we hear the car arrive," she went on, "we'll take our places. You stand by the door—try to look helpless, won't you?—

and I'll be over here, looking miserable, but really ready to kick the tray beast just as soon as you've hat-pinned the other.''

With another sigh, Miss Seeton signalled her willingness to adopt this—unpleasant, but necessary—tactic. If only one could be sure it would succeed...

Georgina dismissed Miss Seeton's doubts with a wave of her hand. Her sparkling eyes hinted at further refinements to the plan. "Let's turn the tables on them—give them a taste of their own horrid medicine! Just before you pink the one by the door, Miss Seeton, switch off the light. And they won't be expecting it any more than I—we—did, which will give us a bigger advantage. After all, people our size need to wangle every advantage they possibly can...''

A sentiment with which Miss Seeton could not, in the circumstance, honestly disagree.

The Night Watch Men were at the other end of the village. Just one solitary passer-by was in The Street to witness the sudden extinction of the Lilikot lights, to hear the great outcry which arose immediately afterwards...

But by next morning almost all of Plummergen was speculating on the affair.

CHAPTER 21

Miss Seeton, forcing herself—in the circumstances, *forcing* was no exaggeration—to remember that a gentlewoman should, on every occasion, strive to maintain her composure, closed her eyes, and made an attempt at her most beneficial deep breathing exercises.

It was not easy.

It was, in fact, almost impossible. Such an *undignified* way to move from one place to another. And so very . . . Miss Seeton smothered a cough . . . dusty. Or rather, to be moved. Not active, but passive. Except that neither she nor Her—nor Georgy (as far as she'd been able to tell, with so much . . . excitement, one must in all honesty term it) . . . neither of them had been especially passive in their action, or rather their reaction, to the reprisals which their captors had wrought upon them after the hat-pin-kick-and-tray assault (as she'd feared from the start that it might) had—softly, she sighed—failed. The superiority of numbers . . . no, because there had been two of them, and two of *them*. But superiority, one must admit, of size. Miss Seeton sighed again, with caution. And weight. She coughed, quietly. And

then perhaps—she felt a guilty flush creep up her cheeks—
her heart, and as a consequence her energy and effort, had
never been entirely in the enterprise from the very first.
Which was understandable, since she found violence of any
kind more than distasteful, but which (she reproached herself) must also be regarded as disobedience to a Royal command—in respect of which, if Emily Dorothea Seeton,
admittedly a gentlewoman but without pretensions to noble
birth, felt so very undignified in the current situation, how
much more undignified for Her Royal Highness, Georgina
Elizabeth Mary Alexandra Edwina Victoria, Princess of the
Realm? Always assuming—and here Miss Seeton's heart
gave a horrified thump—that—

She suppressed the awful thought with a sigh of relief
as the car—or was it a van? (In the hurried darkness, they'd
had no proper chance to find out)—juddered over a bump
in the road, and a muffled squeak of indignation advised
Miss Seeton that Her Royal Highness was, like Miss Seeton
herself, in full possession of her faculties. And in a position
reassuringly near to Miss Seeton.

And in—again like Miss Secton—a sack.

Much cheered by this information, Miss Seeton breathed
too deeply the wrong way, and inhaled fibres from woven
jute. She spluttered, and coughed out loud.

Georgina at once called, "Are you all right, Miss Seeton?" And herself began to cough.

Above the stereo soprano clamour of their dust-induced
fusillade, Georgina and Miss Seeton could just make out
the frantic muttering of male voices somewhere close by:
in the confusion of the hessian dark, it was hard to tell
exactly where, but it was not—Miss Seeton was startled by
a sudden sideways thud, and was even more startled to hear
Georgina say something extremely unregal—not within
kicking range.

"Please remain calm, Your Royal Highness," said a
voice Miss Seeton recognised as belonging to Mr. Rook-

wood. "You'll do yourself no good with these heroics—
and there's no need for them, in any case. We mean you
no harm."

"You've a funny way of showing it," said Georgina,
once her coughing fit had subsided.

"Idiosyncratic," said Mr. Rookwood, in tones of the
deepest deference. "If, that is, I may venture to correct
Your Royal Highness. Eccentric, if you prefer—but never
funny. We regard this whole business in a very serious light,
Ma'am—deadly serious, indeed."

"Deadly?" Georgina wasn't going to show this kidnap-
per that she was in the least scared. "You use words like
that, and then try to tell me you don't plan to harm me?"

"I do," said Mr. Rookwood, above the sound of chang-
ing gears, "and we don't. You'll have to take my word for
it, I know—but it happens to be true. Please believe me,
Ma'am. We have no intention of harming a hair of your
head."

The car lurched, turning off the smooth asphalt road
along what felt like a rough track. The engine laboured in
bottom gear, the wheels rumbled and bounced; stones
clanged upwards against the vehicle's metal underside. Mr.
Rookwood, unable to compete, perforce fell silent.

Miss Seeton, rolled sideways by the sudden turn, was too
busy wondering at the identity of the objects—one hard
and thin and spiky, one more square and yielding—bearing
her company inside the sack to wonder why Mr. Rookwood
had been so very careful to assure Georgina, and only Georgina, that the kidnappers meant her no harm . . .

But Miss Seeton, through all her myriad adventures, had
never been able to accept that anyone, anywhere, could ever
wish harm to herself. Should harm occur, she would always
feel that it must have been a mistake: and—though on
many occasions it had been far from a mistake—her luck,
so far, had held. The harm had never been lasting . . .

But was her luck, for the first time, about to run out?

*   *   *

Delphick said, "We still haven't a clue where she's gone. We've no real idea whether she's with the princess—or even, indeed, whether she's been taken by the same people who took Georgina. If taken, of course, she has been," he added, trying as ever to keep an open mind.

"Young Georgina," growled Brinton, "there's no doubt, she has. As for MissEss, you've shown me those sketches, and I've got to say I agree with your original translation—though I can't see there's any doubt of a connection even without translating the things. Miss Seeton isn't one to be out on the tiles all night, never mind not leaving a message for Martha Bloomer—and if that doesn't mean something's happened to her, I don't know what does. If you're asking me to go along with the hunch you're not quite sure you want to put into words, I'll come right out and agree she's been snatched because she knows—if that's a term anyone can use about Miss Seeton—something in that crazy way of hers, and the snatchers —though don't ask me how— know she knows it. I'll bet my pension she's with HRH— find one, you find 'em both. And you don't need to be an Oracle to predict that when we get 'em back, MissEss'll be waving her brolly same as usual, tut-tutting and wondering why on earth we've all been so worried . . . "

Delphick said, "You're trying to reassure me, Chris, and I appreciate the attempt—but reassurance is hardly enough, is it? We need facts, and as yet we've really none to go on. We need inspira—oh." His tone changed. "What was that you just said?"

"I said MissEss is bound to turn up safe and sound as usual, waving her brolly in the air and—"

"No, before that—let me think. You said she'd been snatched because she knew something, but you didn't know how the snatchers knew she knew anything worth snatching her for . . . Chris, you could just be on to something here. Miss Seeton's identity as the setter-off of the radiation alarm has been kept out of the papers, hasn't it? The British ones, at least."

Brinton grunted. Although over the years he'd come, grudgingly, to accept that Thrudd Banner of World Wide Press and the *Daily Negative*'s Amelita Forby could be relied on to play as fair as could be expected of any scoop-hunting newshound—and though the pair had more or less persuaded their Fleet Street colleagues to mention Miss Seeton's name as seldom as possible when chronicling her adventures . . . he just didn't—couldn't—feel quite as happy about such a very informal arrangement as the Oracle evidently did. And Banner's influence on the World Wide crowd was mostly limited to the home market: Miss Seeton still hit the headlines in the foreign press . . .

"I know, Chris, I know, but I refuse to posit a sinister foreign abductor unless I absolutely must. Everyone inside that power station—everyone with access to Georgina, at any rate—was Security cleared. The nearest anyone came to having what might be called exotic connections is the head of the cleaning staff, whose husband is Welsh. And there has, I would remind you most emphatically, been not the slightest hint that the kidnapping of Her Royal Highness was carried out by Plaid Cymru."

"It's a long way to Wales," Brinton conceded. And even if the Principality had been just around the corner instead of a good couple of hundred miles away, he couldn't honestly hold the Welsh National Party responsible for the abductions of a princess and an elderly spinster: considering they were political animals—and Brinton's view of politicians was as jaundiced as any—Plaid Cymru, he thought, had far too much sense for that.

"I couldn't agree more." Delphick was inspired. "Which means that if the kidnappers are sure Miss Seeton's a threat to them, they must be local. The grapevine in these parts is more efficient than MI5 at its very best—which, Chris, means we must take another close look at Miss Seeton's sketches, for clues with a purely local emphasis. If," said the Oracle thoughtfully, "we can only work it all out, that is."

"I don't know," said Brinton grimly, "about working it out—but it's running out, all right, if you ask me. Time, I mean. Do you realise it's Guy Fawkes Night tomorrow? And if they're planning anything—anything spectacular, on top of snatching young Georgina, then fifty-to-one tomorrow's the day they'll let everyone know about it, if you ask me."

But Delphick did not ask him. Instinct had already told him that the superintendent spoke nothing but the truth.

The Night Watch Men were organised according to a highly sophisticated rota drawn up by Martin Jessyp, paper-shuffler extraordinary to the village of Plummergen. While to Sir George Colveden were due the honours of the original idea, it was Martin Jessyp who had thrashed out the finer points of a schedule which never, except around the hours of dusk and dawn, saw fewer than six men patrolling the area at any one time. These men—nearly all of them hardy sons of the soil—were as fit and muscular a band as any in Kent. Even those who were not farm workers had been selected for their ability to toss an opponent into a ditch with as little effort as their agricultural colleagues could toss a bale of hay to the top of a stack.

In the afternoon and evening of the fourth of November, most of Plummergen had turned out to assist in building the bonfire for which various logs, broken pieces of furniture, and bundles of straw had been stored, according to Nigel's suggestion, in various outhouses around the village. There is a considerable art in the construction of a bonfire. You may pile it as high and as wide as you please, but it must have a strong foundation and a supportive spine—or rather ribcage, since it is the inside which is the least strong part. As the fire burns, so it will collapse from the outside to the in, by this means sparing onlookers the risk of injury, or worse.

Everyone entered into the spirit of the occasion with as much enthusiasm as Plummergen regularly applies to any cooperative endeavour. Jack Crabbe directed traffic into the playing-field in a one-way stream, while his father ensured that departing vehicles did not collide with those bringing further bootloads of burnables to add to the collection. After school, before it grew too dark, Mr. Jessyp and Miss Maynard formed their pupils—each bearing a bundle of twigs or a small branch brought from home—into a neat queue, and sternly warned those who giggled to excess that they must behave themselves. Nigel Colveden and Daniel Eggleden—the latter, skilled in the science of the smithy, putting to good use his specialised knowledge of combustion—supervised the stacking of the heavier items, the placing of the lighter ones.

Sir George, bowing sadly to the commands of his wife, watched as his favourite armchair—its spring and horsehair stuffing gone finally to that great upholsterer's in the sky—was hoisted by brawny arms to the very top of the celebratory edifice, and Guy Fawkes, his monstrous sacking body stuffed with equal amounts of fireworks and straw, was settled in state on his throne, crowned with Miss Seeton's hat above the lopsided mask. Nobody had thought to remove the battered felt until too late, and the sight made people uneasy, though nobody quite knew why; and Mrs. Flax did not help their mood by hovering in the background, dredging up folk-memories of Napoleon, against fear of whose invasion the Royal Military Canal—not a quarter of a mile from the recreation ground—was dug, and beacons were prepared to be lit at a moment's notice.

"And never mind warnings for Boney," said Mrs. Flax, enjoying herself hugely as the more susceptible within earshot shuddered at her awful tones. "Nor fires for Guy Fawkes, neither—ah, further back we go, and further yet. Roasted in sulphur—steeped in gulfs of liquid fire—there's wend-fire, and bale-fire, the flames of Samhain and the Beltane revels, the—"

"Excuse me," broke in Nigel, who'd had quite enough of the Wise Woman's posturing. "If you wouldn't mind moving out of the way, Mrs. Flax, we can let this carload through. The ground's all churned up everywhere else. Thank you," as—grumbling, but not daring to speak out against one she couldn't help but regard as the squire's son—Mrs. Flax stepped aside.

It was not thought necessary to post a guard on the bonfire during daylight hours. Not only do two rows of council houses overlook the recreation ground, but the residence of Constable Potter and his family stands almost opposite the entrance. Even if Potter himself were out in his car on one or other of his various patrols, Mabel Potter and (after school hours) young Amelia—not to mention tabby Tibs, a cat credited by many with powers every bit as awful as those of Mrs. Flax—would be sure, for the sake of village honour, to remain vigilant as long as the sun was above the horizon.

But the sun sets, in England in early November, no later than half-past four; and people went home to their suppers, conscious of a job well done. Now it was up to the Village Watch . . .

"Been one or two cars slowing down to take a look, Jack tells me," said Sir George to Mr. Jessyp, as they checked the final arrangements for the night's vigil. "Cars he didn't recognise, that is. Wouldn't have mentioned them if he had, of course. No need. Could be perfectly harmless, mind you: idle curiosity—lost their way . . . "

"It *could*," echoed Mr. Jessyp. The echo did not ring with much conviction.

"Maybe even a few tips for their own fire," said Sir George, duty bound to give people the benefit of the doubt. A magistrate should at all times remember that people were innocent until proved guilty. "Left it a little late, though, I'd've said. Unless . . . "

"Unless," supplied Mr. Jessyp quickly—and concisely. Nothing more needed to be said. The schoolmaster and the baronet looked at each other in an understanding silence.

"Murreystone," said Sir George at last, with a nod. "It's

possible. Potter told me this morning they hadn't begun to build just yet." Murreystone was one of several villages on PC Potter's motorised beat, and his choosing to live in Plummergen was yet another source of annoyance to the rivals across the marsh.

Mr. Jessyp gave a short, barking laugh. "I imagine they must be as worried about us as we are about them—but with far less reason, of course," he added hastily. "Perhaps they'll be so busy guarding their own fire tonight they'll have no time even to think of tampering with ours . . . "

"Perhaps," replied Sir George. Once again, the echo did not ring with much conviction; there was more on his mind than just the likely machinations of Murreystone. Still no word about the little woman—either of them. Mayhem up and down The Street tomorrow night would be the final straw . . .

"Straw," he muttered, gazing at Guy Fawkes on the summit of the bonfire, his giant arms and legs akimbo, his sacking belly bulging. Well away from the pavilion, of course; safe enough for the houses, the hedge, the fence. Unlikely to be a serious accident even if—

"About tonight," said Sir George, bringing himself back to the present with a start. "How many men, d'you think?"

And the conversation thereafter became technical in the extreme.

Although the bonfire was, in the nature of things, the likely focus of any attack, the Night Watch Men were instructed to patrol the whole village. Should Murreystone employ even half the cunning attributed to them by their ancient foes they could well—while attention was focused at one end of the village—try something sneaky at the other. There was the church: never, by tradition, locked, for the healing power of prayer was not to be denied to any man, at any hour of the day or night. There were the bells, which could be stolen; there was the clock, on which sabotage could be wrought. There were, outside the church, hedges and gardens and topiary trees, garden gnomes and gatepost statuettes . . .

But it was around the bonfire that the keenest eyes and the fastest reflexes were set on guard.

The keenest eyes—and the sharpest ears. At midnight on the dot, Nigel Colveden sat up. He nudged Jack Crabbe, the best mechanic in the village. A car was approaching: a car whose engine-note Nigel didn't think he recognised . . .

And Jack Crabbe, flexing his muscles, confirmed that to him, likewise, the approaching engine was unknown.

CHAPTER 22

The engine rumbled closer. No hint of headlamps could be seen in the moonless dark: whoever was inside the car was clearly up to no good.

With a judder, the engine died. By the faint, flickering light of the stars, Jack and Nigel exchanged urgent looks with Len Hosigg, the third man sharing their bonfire vigil.

"Don't like the thound o' that," muttered Jack, lisping with slow deliberation. Youthful acquaintance with poachers had long since taught him that sibilance carries farther, by night or day, than almost anything else.

"Came from the north," murmured Nigel. Murreystone lies to the east of Plummergen; the most likely road across the marsh enters the rival village from the south, between the high brick walls which bound Miss Seeton's garden and that of the vicarage opposite. "Could be a trick, though."

"Th'right," chimed in Len, a quick learner. The three young men, united in suspicion, strained their ears to hear, their eyes to see . . .

"Over by the gate." Jack Crabbe was pointing; staring. The other two followed his gaze. Something was moving near the hedge: something dark, swift, bulky—too bulky for a fox, a badger, any other creature of the night. Any other creature save a human . . .

"Blimey!"

"Barmy!"

Definitely human. Foxes and badgers do not, as a rule, carry torches. Nor do they emit eldritch cackles as they leap up and down in full view of an audience . . .

"After him!" Jack was ready to roar off in pursuit, but Nigel grabbed him by the arm.

"No, wait! While he's over there, he can't be *here,* can he? Maybe he's not so barmy, after all."

"S'right!" At once, Len spun round to survey the bonfire behind the three whose attention had been so cunningly diverted. Beside him, Jack and Nigel did the same.

Nothing. No movement, no sound—save for the eldritch cackling on the far side of the field. Warily, they glanced back over their shoulders. The torch was still leaping—

Was extinguished.

Silence.

"Could be the Nuts," suggested Nigel, as they peered into the starlit gloom for further signs of movement. "Gone off their heads at last, I mean. You know how oddly they've been carrying on these past few weeks. The way they blew a fuse, or whatever it was, last night—maybe this is some kind of crazy light-bringing ceremony . . . "

"Could've bin a woman," conceded Jack, rubbing his chin and frowning. "A racket like that's hard to tell one way or t'other. What you reckon, Len?"

Young Hosigg was seldom given to speech when a gesture would do. He nodded, his eyes never leaving the distant hedge; then shrugged. Nigel—for whose father Len worked as farm foreman—was used to his idiosyncratic methods of communication. "Len agrees—but where does that leave us? It hardly helps, whichever it turns out to be. If it's a Murreystone male, we either jump him or let him go—and if it's a Lilikot female we've got no choice, have we? We have to let her go—imagine the fuss . . . "

Len and Jack, shuddering, imagined it. Jack said:
"But we don't have to let 'em go if they're Murreystone.
Capering about like madmen—one man, anyhow—they're
up to summat, and t'wouldn't hurt to find out what—"

"And why," said Nigel. "If it isn't just a Nutty fire-
festival, I mean. Whoever it is—"

He broke off. The cackling had begun again, the torch
was being waved—but in the opposite corner of the field
this time.

"Heading our way, or making a dash for it?" demanded
Jack, not seriously expecting a reply. The whole proceeding
made so little sense that any reply he received could only
confuse things even more.

"Could be either," said Nigel, slowly. "Suppose we—"

He never finished. With a yelp and a muffled oath, Len
Hosigg was sprinting back to the bonfire, fists flailing as
he ran. With a whoop and a yell, Jack and Nigel charged
in his wake—charged towards the three dark figures around
the base of the bonfire, who appeared to be struggling with
a fourth . . .

"The guy!" As Len waded wordlessly into the mêlée,
Jack emitted a roar of rage. "Steal our guy, would you?
Damned if we let you, you buggers!"

And then, with Nigel, he joined the fray.

Three against three were reasonable odds, on paper: and
the six were reasonably matched. Len, though the slightest
of the combatants in build, was stronger than his appearance would suggest. Years of farm work had toughened
him: he was no longer the town-bred boy who had needed
a stout stave in his hand before he could face the enemy.
He was everywhere now: leaping, dodging, punching, par-
rying.

Nigel and Jack were not to be outdone. They likewise
leaped, dodged, punched, and parried; they were themselves punched, and even kicked: but no weapons were
used by either side, and slowly it became clear that the
Plummergen trio was beginning to prevail. The Murrey-

stoners gasped, and wheezed, and faltered as they were
wrestled farther and farther from the bonfire; it seemed that
the rival village had not, on this occasion, sent a hand-
picked team of the fittest men to do its dirty work—whatever that work might have been. The attempt to kidnap the
guy had, after all, been thwarted—

Or had it? The same thought occurred to each of the
Plummergenites at the same time. The odds hadn't been
three against three, but three against four: the fourth being
that mysterious torch-waving cackler whose purpose in
drawing so much attention to himself—

They did not stop to think. Their punches flew thick and
fast as they realised they hadn't so much buffeted their
opponents away from the bonfire as been led by them out
of range of whatever mischief had been planned—

Was probably being done right now! "Let 'em run,
lads!" commanded Jack, as the vanquished foe took suddenly to its heels and began making for the gate, nearer
now than the bonfire and guy which had been the target of
its attentions. "We'll see what they've been up to, the varmints!"

Seeing was easier said than done. While combat
seethed below, the stars above had been covered in cloud:
only the faintest prickle of light now shone through the
few wispy patches which, even as Jack led the rush to the
rescue, grew ever more faint until, with a final flicker, it
vanished. The whole world now was wide and dark and
shadowed grey, a world where shapes were illusion and
senses confused . . .

But at last they found the guy. It lay some yards farther
from the fire than when they'd seen it in the hands of the
invaders; and it was almost unharmed, though its mask was
a little more lopsided, its hat jammed even lower over its
painted eyes. Apart from such minor damage, the kidnap
attempt had failed. Tomorrow's celebration was safe.

With groans of relief as their sore hands and aching muscles came into play, the Plummergen three hoisted the

straw-stuffed figure—still heavy with its internal burden of squibs and crackers—back into the old armchair on top of the bonfire. They rubbed their stiffening shoulders, and let their arms fall to their sides, and permitted themselves the luxury of a few minutes' ritual grumbling and comparing notes about how much damage each had sustained.

"Could a-bin worse," said Jack, whose left eye was, like Mr. Weller's turkey, swelling visibly. Nor was Mr. Crabbe's the only black eye; Len's right was rapidly closing, and it was doubtful whether Mr. Colveden would be as handsome next morning as he'd been the night before.

"But no serious hurt, thanks be," said Jack, a sentiment echoed by the other two. "So long's them varmints don't think of coming back, or sending their friends, that is, for I'm not so sure we could chastise 'em as well a second time, are you, boys?"

Nigel, on whom delayed reaction was starting to work, shivered as he shook his head. "We should be getting a few reinforcements before much longer, though." Tenderly, he massaged his knuckles. "I wonder why nobody heard all the kerfuffle while it was going on?"

"Why we never heard the car drive away, neither," Jack was quick to point out. "Though that's what it must have done, surely, the way they took off—and it's not as if we can've bin skirmishing for so very long, if the truth be told. Time's a queer, misleading thing, on occasion—and so're the senses, most of all at night. You'd've thought they'd light up their houses, wouldn't you?" with a jerk of his thumb in the direction of the black squares against the steel-grey sky. "Yet I disremember there was that much shouting, after the first, and all over in minutes, if you stop and consider the matter careful-like."

"You can't," said Nigel, grimly, "be too careful, where Murreystone's concerned . . ."

And the other two agreed with him at once.

*   *   *

It was not until day had well and truly dawned that the Bonfire Watch was at last suspended. Even Murreystone would never dare to invade enemy territory when witnesses by the several hundred might observe the invasion: coming from the south, they must pass the post office; from the north, the council houses. The final group of Night Watch Men returned to their homes conscious of a job well done, for the bonfire—and the guy, untroubled on its armchair high above them—remained, as it had done since that one thwarted attack, unassailed.

It was breakfast-time when the Night Watch Men finally went home; it was almost lunch-time when a small female figure, limping on weary feet, leaning for support on a gold-handled umbrella, found its way to an isolated house, and rapped with the brolly on the knockerless door.

Nobody answered. After a pause, during which she looked over her shoulder more than once, the small female rapped again, more loudly.

There came an irritated clattering from above, and a gaunt, red-haired man in his forties peered out of an up-stairs window. "I'm busy," he informed the small one, waving at her to go away. "No tradesmen, no hawkers, no pedlars. Good morning!"

He was about to slam the window shut when a crisp voice enquired from below:

"No princesses?"

John Douglas stayed his hand. He leaned at an acute angle out of the window, and gazed thoughtfully down at the dainty young woman beneath—and blinked as she gazed quite as thoughtfully up at him.

"I think," she said, "you look friendly—I do hope you are. I must have walked miles, and these shoes just weren't designed for hiking—but I simply couldn't risk going to any of the nearer houses, in case they were in league. You wouldn't want to live too far from where you were holding someone hostage, would you?"

"I suppose I wouldn't." Her tone was so reasonable that
Mr. Douglas found himself giving serious consideration to
the possibility that a harmless bookseller such as himself
might at some time hold someone hostage. Then he came
to his senses. *"Princesses?"* He leaned at an even more
acute angle out of the window. Once more he gazed down
at his pint-sized visitor: at the pale, heart-shaped face—the
aristocratic features and the tip-tilted nose—the sapphire
eyes—the bouncing blonde curls . . .

"Hostage?" said John Douglas, with a gulp.

"Captive, if you prefer," said the pint-sized blonde. "Or
prisoner—I don't really mind, now I've stopped being one.
But I do rather feel it would be a good idea to let someone
in authority *know* that I have—stopped, I mean. They're
bound to be interested, I would have said. And yours is the
nicest-looking house for miles—and I'm sure you wouldn't
mind if I used your telephone, would you?"

"Your Royal Highness!" Mr. Douglas slammed the window shut, pelted down the stairs, paused in front of the hall
mirror to smooth his ruddy locks, and, breathing heavily,
rushed to the door to open it, and to usher Georgina inside.

"It was all," explained Georgina, to an enthralled audience
of officials, "thanks to Miss Seeton's umbrella, you
know." She patted the gold handle as she spoke, and
smiled. "When they took her away, poor thing—I don't
know when, but it was after they'd taken us out of the sacks
and given us both some perfectly frightful tea or something,
which they *said* was only herbs, though I have my doubts—
anyway," as at the mention of *herbs* Delphick and Brinton
exchanged glances—"whatever it was, we both fell asleep.
We were pretty tired anyway, with the disappointment and
everything of having tried to get away and—and not man-
aging it."

For a moment, the sapphire eyes lost their sparkle, and
the perfect mouth quivered as Georgina recalled the fright
and disappointment of her recent escape attempt. But royal

nerves are among the strongest, royal emotions under better control than most; the princess was very soon able to go on with her recital.

"We were so hot and dusty in those beastly sacks, being dragged halfway across Kent in the back of that horrible car or van or whatever it was, and we were frightfully thirsty, of course, so we drank the tea because they told us that was all there was . . . And when I woke up, I was . . . alone. Miss Seeton had gone. And so had one of the sacks—they'd put the other one over me as a sort of counterpane, because this new house wasn't anything like as well equipped as the first place they'd—they'd kept me locked up."

Her eyes filled with tears. "I thought that was why they'd moved us, you see—because there weren't the facilities for two people. Just one bed, and one chair—and if they meant to keep us both for any length of time . . . "

She wrinkled her dainty nose. "At least we had decent loos in both places, thank goodness. I mean, I dare say I could have coped, but Miss Seeton—so undignified, at her age. Or it would have been, except that it wasn't, either time—but in the end it didn't matter, because—oh, I do hope you find her soon! I'm so worried—I thought she was positively the dearest old duck, and if it hadn't been for her umbrella I'd never have got away . . . "

"The umbrella, you said, Ma'am?" prompted Delphick, as Her Royal Highness sniffled discreetly, and weakened just enough to reach into her pocket for a handkerchief.

Georgina blinked once or twice, then smiled. "Gosh, yes—such luck for me they left it behind, even if they took her bag. She might," she said, contemplating her aching feet with a whimsical grin, "have had enough in her purse for me to ring for a taxi, or something, once I'd found a phone—but they didn't leave it, so I never had the chance to try." She looked up. Her eyes were twinkling. "Which is probably just as well, because I expect I'd have made a mess of it." Now the grin was the old, high-powered

Georgy Girl beam. "You know how Royalty's, um, not used to handling money . . ."

Her audience laughed along with her. Members of the Royal Family have attendants who habitually carry all cash for day-to-day transactions, while expenses of a more exotic nature are dealt with on account, settled by the Comptroller of the Household at the end of each calendar month.

Georgina soon sobered. "Anyway, once I'd woken up and seen Miss Seeton wasn't there, I started to feel a little—a little twitchy. I wanted to know she was all right—but the horrid man who brought my breakfast wouldn't answer any of my questions. He was in a frightful temper. There was only one man this time—if I'd only known before, I could have worked out some scheme for hooking the beast off his feet and hitting him again, but I didn't . . ." She sighed. "I'd hidden the umbrella under the mattress, you see. Miss Seeton had told me it was her very best, and I knew she was so proud of—oh!"

The blue eyes widened. "Mr. Delphick! You're the one who gave it to her! Miss Seeton told me all about it—how absolutely thrilling to meet you!"

"Er—thank you, Ma'am." Delphick inclined his head. "Most kind of you to say so." He made up his mind. The rest of Georgina's narrative could be—must be—postponed to a later date. Now that she seemed to have talked the worst of the experience out of her system, it was high time to ask her what else Miss Seeton might have told her: what else she might have said that could be a clue, no matter how unlikely, to rescuing her from wherever the kidnappers had chosen to confine her . . .

As he drew in his breath to ask the first question, he realised he'd left it too late.

"I told you this place wasn't as—as civilised as the first one," said Georgina, who was still young enough to relish the notion of being the heroine of a real adventure, even a kidnap. Hadn't she, after all, contrived her own escape, as in the very best fiction? "Not as efficient, for a prison. Bars

across the windows instead of shutters, for one thing, not
that I could loosen them—and they'd put the bars on after
they boarded up the windows, because it was too awkward
for me to wiggle more than the odd nail out of the frame,
no matter how I tried." She looked sadly at the umbrella.
"I do hope Miss Seeton won't mind: I'll have it repaired,
of course. It's the very least I can do, because without it
I'd never have got away, I think."

She sat up, her eyes bright. "The door, you see, didn't
fit as well as the other one—and it didn't have a proper
lock, just bolts, top and bottom. I'd heard him draw them,
so I know there were only two. And at first I thought I'd
see if he came back alone at lunch-time, and catch him
bending from the lower bolt, and hit him—and then I
thought he might have the sense to leave the top one for
last, which would be no help to me at all. Besides, there
might be two of them again by lunch-time. And then"—
her eyes brightened still more—"I realised there was a gap
between the door and the frame, and I poked the umbrella
through to make it wider—and I jiggled the point, and wob-
bled it about—and I don't know what sort of bolts they
were, or why he hadn't twiddled the handle bit up and
round to lock it, but he was in a strange mood, I told you—
and the more I jiggled the brolly, the looser the bolts
seemed to come. And in the end . . . " She smiled a dazzling smile of triumph. "They came. And I went. And,
well, here I am . . .

"Here I am," she repeated, her eyes clouding. "Safe and
sound—but oh, please," she begged, leaning forward with
clasped hands, "*where* is poor Miss Seeton?"

CHAPTER 23

"Well, there goes one worry the fewer—thank the Lord."
Delphick wasn't prepared to stand watching the helicopters
out of sight. The instant the second—the important—one
had risen, rotors clattering, safely into the air, he began to
make his way back indoors.

Superintendent Brinton, with an obscure feeling that you
couldn't just let Royalty vanish into the blue without some
sort of ceremony, stood with his hand upraised in a vague
gesture of farewell, and watched the choppers of the
Queen's Flight (they'd sent three, one for Georgina and two
for her escort) revolve slowly into position—Georgina's in
the middle, the blue-blooded meat in the base metal sandwich—before heading off to London from Ashford Police
Station's hastily-cleared car park. Although it had been explained to them that it was all for Georgy Girl's benefit,
those officers who'd had to move their vehicles out to the
road were not happy about the moving: the war which was
permanently waged between the town's motorists and traffic wardens did not admit of a truce, even in these excep-
tional circumstances. There could well be blood in the

streets before long—good red peasant blood, of course, not blue.

Brinton wondered what sort of welcome young Georgy would get from her loving relatives. Orders had been she was to go straight to Buckingham, not to Kensington, Palace: top-notch doctors and counsellors to check her over, he'd bet. Plenty of fuss and cossetting from Cousin Lilibet (or whatever she called the Queen), and from the Queen Mum, everyone's favourite granny. And—

"Chris! What are you waiting for?" Delphick had halted in mid-stride once he'd realised that his friend wasn't with him. "She's not our responsibility any longer—for which relief, much thanks: I thought the wretched girl would never leave. Now at last we may direct all our energies towards the finding of Miss Seeton—and the sooner, I would remind you, the better."

"Sorry." Brinton, red-faced from a combination of haste and embarrassment, joined his colleague by the door. "It sort of slipped my mind for the moment—not that I take MissEss for granted, you know I don't, but when you think of the number of scrapes she's been in over the years, and how she always seems to survive them—"

"So far," Delphick broke in grimly. "Remember the old saw about a first time for everything? And, talking of old, Miss Seeton is growing no younger, Chris. For heaven's sake let's find out what's been happening while we've had to dance attendance on HRH half the day and pander to the whims of the security boys with their damned debriefing."

He strode off in the direction of the communications room, with Brinton puffing in his wake as he tried to walk and talk at the same time. "Be fair to the girl, Oracle. She gave us enough info to locate the house—the second house, at any rate, and I call that pretty good going, when you think what she's been through." He was trying to cheer his friend as much as himself. "It's not just that she's a complete stranger to the district—but for a kid like her this sort

of thing's hardly the—the run-of-the-mill affair it is for
Miss Seeton, now is it?''

As he caught up with his colleague, he saw the faint
smile of acknowledgement in the cool grey eyes, and nodded. ''You know what she's like, Oracle. Being gassed or
coshed or chucked in the canal's all in a day's work for
MissEss, more or less. Why, she hardly notices it's happened and even if she does she's always sure it must have
been a mistake to begin with—she's never had half the
nightmares she gives the rest of us, I'll wager my pension
she hasn't. If that's what yoga does for you, I'm all in
favour of it. Happy as a sand-boy she'll be when she finally
turns up, you mark my words.''

He was almost starting to convince himself. ''And it
can't be that long—we're sure to find her soon, with the
start young Georgy's given us. She'll be back at the first
house, I imagine—the logical place to take her, keep her
out of the way while they collect the ransom or whatever—
and they'll know by now the girl's escaped. Why, they've
probably let MissEss go already, and it's just a question of
picking her up from wherever she is once she gets to a
phone the way young Georgy did. Nobody's going to pay
a king's ransom for the poor old biddy, and they know it.
I tell you, we're sure to find her soon . . . ''

''If only we knew why they'd snatched her in the first
place, it would help.'' Delphick frowned as he followed
the superintendent—whose headquarters, after all, these
were—into the operations room. ''If only we had more to
go on than Georgina's garbled memories of what Miss Seeton said—if only she'd been able to *draw* something . . .
and then maybe she did, and the princess was too preoccupied to notice—or perhaps it was while she was asleep
. . . if only they'd forgotten to take her bag, as well as her
umbrella . . . ''

He was left to lament alone. Brinton's hurried arrival had
set heads turning. Anyone not speaking on the telephone,
or making notes, or sticking coloured pins into the large-

scale map on the wall, began to gravitate nervously towards the two senior officers as they looked from one face to another, inviting someone to present a more up-to-date report than those they'd been hearing on and off throughout the morning.

But nobody, it seemed, could update any of the reports in more than a negative manner.

"Nothing?" Superintendent Brinton's bark was widely supposed to be far worse than his bite; everyone prayed now that the truth of this supposition would never be put to the test. They couldn't remember when they'd last seen Old Brimstone in such a state. "Nothing at all?"

Heads were shaken in dumb regret; guilty boots shuffled on the floor. "Call yourselves detectives?" bellowed Brinton. "The whole boiling shower of you couldn't detect a— oh, God! What's the use? Never mind bleating you're under strength with two suspicious deaths to investigate. Never mind telling us *again* it's a derelict property that's been on the market so long the blasted estate agent's collected his pension and retired to heaven-knows-where—we know that already! Somebody, somewhere, must know something else! Just keep looking—keep asking questions—ring round every damned estate agent in the country, if you have to—and report to me in my office the instant you hear anything. Anything at all!"

He would have slammed the door on his way out, but Delphick was too close behind him. Brinton groaned, clutched at his hair, and gritted his teeth as he strode off down the corridor in the direction of his office.

"I was so sure they'd have found her by now," he threw over his shoulder to Delphick, hard on his heels. "So—so damned sure, I couldn't believe—" He flung open the door with a crash that had the walls juddering. "You—Foxon! Here, lad—and make it snappy!"

Detective Constable Foxon, his ears ringing, dropped the box of pins he held, and leaped in three urgent strides across the room to his superior. As Sergeant Ranger rose hurriedly from his borrowed desk, Foxon drew himself as close to attention as anyone can who sports the informality of a flowered shirt and a salmon-pink paisley tie. "Sir!"

"Never mind *sir,*" snarled Brinton. "How about *sir, something to report* instead?"

Foxon—who was quite as anxious about Miss Seeton as anyone else, and whose blood pressure was in far better shape than Brinton's—ventured a quick look at Chief Superintendent Delphick. The Oracle's left eye flickered in the merest suspicion of a wink; and Foxon, reassured, allowed himself the luxury of a faint grin before turning quickly back to Brinton.

"Funny you should say that now, sir, because not two minutes ago—of course, it might not be anything to do with all this, but—your, er, standing orders, sir—"

Brinton broke in with a groan. From being red in the face, he turned pale. He clapped a hand to his anguished brow, staggered to a convenient chair, and sat down.

Foxon stared; Bob smothered a grin; Delphick sighed as he observed his sergeant's expression. "Break it to us gently, please, Foxon. What news on the Rialto?"

Foxon looked puzzled. They'd done *Macbeth* at school: he didn't recognise the quotation from *The Merchant of Venice.* "You mean what's the word on The Street, sir? But how did you guess?"

Delphick sighed again. "It hardly strains my oracular powers, Detective Constable Foxon. Your mention of standing orders would have warned someone far less astute than I that there have been happenings in Plummergen of which Constable Potter feels his superior should be apprised . . ."

A forceful and heartfelt blasphemy burst from Brinton's lips, and he shuddered. From his first encounter with Miss Seeton, the superintendent had realised her remarkable, not to say unique, qualities; accordingly, he had issued detailed instructions that PC Potter should advise him—in office hours or out, at home or (heaven forfend) on holiday—of any, repeat any, untoward occurrence in the immediate neighbourhood of Miss Seeton's cottage, or in the general neighbourhood of the village in which that cottage was situated.

Police Constable Potter was a man with much insight into local affairs, with an enthusiasm for his work which meant that, had he so wished, he could long ago have put in for promotion and been moved to a larger beat. Potter, however, was possessed of more than insight and enthusiasm. He had a strong preference for a nice, peaceful life, with which was coupled a certain native cunning. Admittedly, his life had been rather less nicely peaceful since Miss Seeton's arrival in Plummergen seven years earlier: but Potter—whose nerves were stronger than Brinton's—approved of the little art teacher. He considered her an asset to the community, and was gratified whenever her innocent gyrations contrived (as they so often did) to sweep him into their ultimate toils.

This sentiment, he knew, was not shared by his Ashford superior. While Brinton was known to like—even to admire—Miss Seeton, she made him uneasy. She set his blood pressure leaping to heights previously unscaled on medical charts, or so he claimed: and who was Potter, a mere uniformed constable, to argue with a superintendent? He would never dare do anything to invoke the wrath of one set in authority above him; nor did he care to cause anxiety to one whose health was apparently in so precarious a state . . .

Which was Potter's planned defence should Brinton ever discover that an officer under his nominal command had exercised considerable insight and judgement on various occasions in the past, withholding more than one Untoward Occurrence in the neighbourhood of Sweetbriars until it had become absolutely necessary that a report must be made.

As made, just now, it had been.

"A punch-up with Murreystone last night," said Foxon, in succinct response to Brinton's growled instructions to spill the blasted beans without smothering 'em in a load of sauce. "By the bonfire, at the playing-field—seems they had some notion of pinching the guy, then thought better of it when Nigel Colveden and his pals—er, showed 'em it mightn't be such a good idea. Sir.''

Some judicious probing on the part of Delphick—Brinton having been rendered once more speechless by the enormity of his subordinate's intelligence—extracted the full story of the Last-Minute Bonfire-Building Scheme. Further probing—Foxon was never quite sure how the Oracle had managed it, but decided that a Yard training could overcome any number of scruples about betraying one's friends—elicited the retribution proposed to be visited by the Village Watch upon their rivals should Murreystone attempt further skulduggery at tonight's Grand Firework Display and Jacket Potato Roast.

"No doubt," Delphick said, "they were inspired to their attempted guynapping by the abduction of Princess Georgina—though it must be said that Murreystone, even in my limited experience of them, have seldom seemed in need of inspiration to the darker shade of deed. There would appear to be an innate strand of wickedness in Plummergen's near neighbours—but has this current outbreak, do you suppose, anything to do with Miss Seeton?''

Brinton rolled his eyes, but said nothing. Bob ventured the opinion that it might have. Foxon, grinning faintly, said that he had no idea, but that as occurrences went it was certainly untoward (with a flick of the eyes towards his silent superior). And, with MissEss undoubtedly still missing, perhaps it was a coincidence they ought not to ignore. After all, they hadn't had much luck so far going along, well, the normal lines of enquiry; and there were, so Potter had said, quite a few empty properties in the Murreystone area—and if the kidnappers were local, as everyone seemed to be starting to think—and with search parties from Plummergen not exactly official, and wanting as little trouble with the authorities as possible . . .

"So Potter says," supplied Delphick, as Potter's mouthpiece fell silent, blushing. "I'm inclined to agree with you—with him, that is." He glanced at Brinton, brooding on his chair. "One village constable, even in a panda, cannot aspire to a thorough search of a wide-ranging area by himself, no matter how large his band of unofficial volunteers. By the way, are we to assume that such extended and multiple searching explains Potter's . . . slowness to report the bonfire incident?"

"Of course," said Foxon at once, rushing to the defence of his friend. "Er—sir." He saw Delphick's look, and rushed on· "The Colvedens knew last night she was missing, sir, but it was dark, not to mention the bonfire business'd already been set up and they knew they'd be, well, asking for trouble if they left it. So Sir George got them organised for first thing this morning, and off they went as soon as it was light. Potter says the general said they'd set a limit on how long they'd search before giving up, because even if they just checked the places they could get into it would cut it down for the ones that were locked they'd need warrants and stuff for, sir. So, well, that's what they've done, and we've got the list right here. Sir."

Bob passed him a sheet of paper, which he took, then hesitated, and handed to Delphick as Brinton, brushing it aside, lumbered to his feet and stumped across to the large-scale map on the office wall. He stared at it, and grunted.

"Pinned 'em already, have you?"

"Er—some of them, yes, sir, but . . . "

"But our arrival," said Delphick, whose brief reference to the list of locations had told him almost nothing, "prevented your completing the task." The eye with which he gazed upon Detective Constable Foxon was now almost warm in its regard. "Pin on, Foxon—unless, that is, your local knowledge is such that you could guide us to each in turn."

"Between us, sir, I reckon we could," replied Foxon after a moment, as Brinton grunted again, and Bob, adopted local, nodded at his friend's side. "They're none of 'em close to any of the others, unfortunately, so it wouldn't be a quick job to check 'em all out—"

Brinton groaned. Foxon glanced at him, and continued: "But they're in the general area, sir, so it wouldn't be all that difficult to check 'em. If that's what you wanted to do, sir."

Brinton turned from his study of the map to glare at his colleagues. His manor: his responsibility: his word of command, to go or to stay. He let out an exasperated snort at the expectant look on the three faces.

"*Want?* Good grief, there's nothing I fancy more than go wandering around Kent in the dark in winter checking a blasted telephone directory of empty houses on the off chance there's a little old lady tied up in a sack in one of 'em—but it sure as blazes beats sitting on our backsides waiting for news, which is what we'd be doing otherwise, the way things are right now. Dammit, you should be half-way to the car by now, laddie—and you Yard types with him!"

"Right, sir!" Foxon bounded joyously to his desk, took out a set of keys, then leaped to the peg on which hung his leather jacket. "On my way . . ."

Bob Ranger, for all his size, wasn't far behind him; and not far behind Bob came Brinton and Delphick, the former detouring via the operations room to bellow the advice that he was going out on patrol, and was to be informed by radio if there should be the slightest breakthrough in any of the three cases under investigation. Then he thundered in Foxon's wake to the car park, where the engine was already revving for the off. He wrenched open the door, flung himself inside, and buckled the seat-belt as Foxon jammed his foot on the accelerator.

With a roar and a rush, Delphick's car, with Bob at the wheel, caught up with them and sat on their tail. The hunt for Miss Seeton was, with a vengeance, on . . .

For—as Delphick reminded his sergeant, who was too

busy concentrating to reply—find Miss Seeton, and they would more than likely find—with her interpretation of those puzzling sketches—the solution not only to the kidnap of Princess Georgina, but to the murders, as well.

CHAPTER 24

Although many of its citizens, with Miss Seeton's continuing absence, were troubled in spirit, Plummergen contrived to rise above itself for the sake (as some of the more vocal put it) of the kiddies. The Grand Firework Display and Potato Roast had been planned for weeks; the search parties had done all that could reasonably be expected of them, anyone would admit; the police were known to be doing their best—and there was no sense now in spoiling things for everybody else. Besides, wasn't Miss Seeton herself so fond of the youngsters she sometimes taught? She'd hate to have them disappointed. What's more, if they cancelled the festivities as one or two had suggested, wouldn't Murreystone (said those as cunning as they were vocal) choose to see it as Giving In?

It was the final point which clinched the argument. Never mind the truth of the matter: the village knew, only too well, that opportunist Murreystone, gloating, would forever publish it abroad how Plummergen had refused to run the risk of being outdone by a bigger guy, a brighter fire, a more spectacular display from its smaller rival. And no amount of explanation (not that Plummergen would stoop to explain itself to Murreystone, but there were other villages on the marsh who might get the wrong idea) would banish from local legend the Murreystone-inspired accusation of cowardice. Nothing short of a cloudburst, Plummergen realised, could be accepted as an excuse for failing to commemorate the Gunpowder Treason with all due ceremony and celebration; and the committee duly announced that the Plummergen bonfire would be lit, as had originally been planned, at six, sharp.

By five o'clock, the sun had long since set, although in London the sky was never truly dark. There were too many street lamps to cast an upward golden glow against low-lying clouds, too many public buildings with floodlights and with high, uncurtained windows.

From behind the red velvet hangings of her room in Buckingham Palace, Georgina, curled up among cushions on the window-seat, a fleecy blanket draped around her shoulders, gazed without seeing to the shadowed gardens below. There was no question (her cousins had insisted) of her returning to Kensington that night; after all the shocks and disturbance of the past few days, she must have peace, and quiet, and nothing more to worry her. The private wing of Buck House was as peaceful and quiet as anywhere in Town; now that she had done her duty by the security forces, she must retire for a well-earned rest, and have her supper brought to her on a tray just as soon as she felt like it.

Georgina didn't feel like it just yet. She'd managed, with coaxing, to swallow half a cup of tea on landing, but the helicopter flight had been rather bumpier than she would have wished. Her insides still had some way to go to catch up with the rest of her before she could believe herself safe on terra firma again. The aftermath of the trip from Ashford, coupled with the strain of having dutifully repeated, for the benefit of yet another group of detectives, her story for what must have been the umpteenth time, had left her wanting to do no more than sit in silence for a while, thinking.

Princess Georgina might be young and pretty and golden-haired, but she was no dumb blonde. She took her responsibilities as seriously as any member of the Royal Family; and she couldn't help but think of Miss Seeton— whom she'd been so pleased to see in her captivity, who had been so kind and encouraging when she'd most needed it—as the greatest responsibility of her life. She wouldn't, she knew, be able to rest until she'd heard that the old lady had been found . . .

Old lady? Georgina found herself smiling at the very idea. One hardly thought of Miss Seeton as old, for all her grey hair and quiet demeanour. She had been so cheerful, so spry, so—so indomitable in the face of what common sense said had been danger: some old ladies might have threatened the vapours at the prospect of who-knew-how-long in durance vile, but not the Battling Brolly. Not, of course, that the battle had been successful, on this particular occasion, but one had to admit that Miss Seeton's support for the escape attempt had been marvellous, even if at first she'd looked a bit embarrassed about it all. And the brolly! She must be sure to check that the chief superintendent had—as he'd promised—arranged for it to be repaired where her poking and prodding at the bolts of her prison door had damaged it.

Mr. Delphick had given that gold umbrella to Miss Seeton in memory of her earliest adventure—but what other adventures she'd had since then! Not, of course, that she'd seen them as adventures. Georgina smiled again at the memory of how hard it had been to urge her new friend to speak of herself. She guessed that it had only been Miss Seeton's wish to take her mind off their present situation which had persuaded her to say anything at all . . .

And, indeed, even now Georgina's knowledge of Miss Emily Seeton was based less on what Miss Seeton had said than on what the papers had told her of the Battling Brolly, and on what Chief Superintendent Delphick had tried to explain at the earlier debriefing, in Ashford. It had been so confusing, she feared she hadn't really taken it in as well as she ought—but now there was something niggling at the back of her mind. Something about *when Miss Seeton talks about her drawings, you know she's on the right track* . . .

Drawings! Suddenly, Georgina thought of family gossip: of the kidnap of distant cousin Artemis MacSporran, of some crazy plot to overthrow the Crown in Scotland, and of how both had been thwarted through the good offices of—

"The Battling Brolly," breathed Georgina, sitting up, the blanket slipping from her shoulders. "Drawings . . . when she talks about drawings, she's on the right track . . . "

Just what was it that Miss Seeton had said?

"Last on the list," said Brinton, glaring back through the night at the shuttered windows of the empty farmhouse. "And nobody home here, either." Glumly, he watched Foxon score a pencil across the final address on his clipboard sheets, and winced as a distant flurry of crackling bangs signalled the ignition at some festive bonfire of yet another string of jumping-jacks. It was, in his present humour, far too violent a sound for the superintendent's liking.

He scowled at his companions, who were as disappointed as himself by the outcome to their search. "So what do we do now—anyone any ideas?"

In the distance, the silver-sparkling trail of a rocket flashed across the Guy Fawkes sky, and exploded against the clouds in a riot of rainbow stars.

"Ask for an update when you check in," suggested Delphick. "Something may just have come up since we arrived—"

"All of ten minutes ago," snapped Brinton, then swallowed his intended remarks about watched pots never boiling as Foxon reached into the car for the radio handset, and switched it on. The other three crowded close in an uneasy silence, broken only by the rainbow rocket's series of explosions, faint but clear across the quiet, level marshland. After a few frantic moments, Ashford Control crackled into life, and gave reluctant tongue in response to Foxon's quick enquiry . . .

"So *now* what?" Brinton had gone through despair, and beyond. He turned to Delphick, and gestured helplessly. "You're the Oracle, for heaven's sake. Say something!"

Delphick's attention was caught by the flash of another rocket, soaring into the cloudy heavens from the west. There followed a pause, while he pondered; and Bob, shifting from one huge foot to the other, shuffled dry leaves in an agony of frustration. Like Brinton, like Foxon, he longed for action: but there was no sense in going off half-cocked. The Oracle—all of them—had gambled on Foxon's, or rather Potter's, list of likely local houses—and they'd lost. But the Oracle had spent a fair old while talking with Princess Georgina; he'd heard what she'd had to tell him about Miss Seeton, and he'd tried to make her remember everything she could, and more. Now he'd had time for it to pickle in his subconscious, maybe—just maybe—he could tie it all in with those sketches they'd seen back at the cottage, back in Plummergen . . .

"Back to Plummergen," said Delphick, and Bob jumped as the others gasped: had he spoken the thought aloud, or was the old man a mind reader? Or perhaps it was—he grinned, as Foxon and Brinton made *if-you-say-so* noises—the logical thing to do: except that with Miss Seeton, logic was about the last word anyone would use.

"You are entirely correct, Sergeant Ranger." Delphick's dry tones informed his startled sidekick that he *had* spoken that particular thought aloud. "There is," continued the Oracle, above Bob's muttered apology, "no logic whatever to my proposal that we adjourn to Miss Seeton's village—no logic, that is, beyond the perpetually illogical premise that where her ambience is most strong, perhaps there will be found some means to guide us towards the, ah, personification of that ambience. Towards, that is, Miss Seeton herself. Another examination of her sketchbook would not, I believe, in these perplexing circumstances come amiss . . . "

In Plummergen, Sir George—huffing through his neat moustache, conscious (despite his hidden concerns) of the importance of the occasion—struck the ceremonial match, and held it to a strategically-placed wisp of straw. It was thought an omen of good luck for next year's harvest if the fire caught at the first time of striking; and everyone watched intently as the tiny flame licked its way into life, scarlet and crimson and rich, ripening gold . . .

In Buckingham Palace, Georgina slipped from the window-seat, and turned slowly in the direction of her bedside table. On that table were a reading-lamp and a selection of books, a small tin of biscuits, a box of paper handkerchiefs (Royalty is far more practical in its lifestyle than many people realise), and a telephone.

Her hand reached out to the receiver; hovered; and fell back. With a sigh, she shook her head, and quietly scolded herself for her folly—or, perhaps, for her lack of conviction. Had she had a ridiculous, exaggerated idea—or an inspired brainwave? She took a step closer to the telephone—reached out again—paused . . .

From outside, the distant sound of exploding fireworks— the whine of Catherine wheels, the overhead crackle of rockets, the cannon-fire of Roman candles—broke for the first time into Georgina's consciousness.

"Guy Fawkes," she murmured. She smiled. "Guy Forks!"

She made up her mind. Better to appear foolish than, if she was too late proved right, afraid of *seeming* foolish— a coward. Generations of Saxe-Coburg ghosts looked on, and nodded their approval.

"And anyway," said Her Royal Highness Princess Georgina, with her index finger poised and her eyes dancing, "I've always wanted to do this—and it's probably the best excuse I'll ever have in my life!"

Whereupon, with no more hesitation, she began to dial.

Into Plummergen swept the two-car cavalcade, Foxon in front, Bob close behind. From over the marsh they came, racing across the narrow bridge and ready to roar up The Street to the bonfire to find Martha, or Stan, or someone with Miss Seeton's front-door key . . .

But Brinton and Delphick, keen-eyed passengers, spotted the light in the Bloomers' cottage as they passed, and both ordered their drivers to slam on their brakes and stop.

Foxon's reflexes were quick: mercifully, so were Bob's. Four car doors swung open; eight booted feet pounded up the short front path, and only Brinton's barked command for some common sense, dammit, prevented four urgent hands reaching out to seize one brass knocker.

The unorthodox arrival of these clamorous guests brought the Bloomers to the door before anyone had time to knock. It was Stan who opened to them; Martha, the corner of her apron to her reddened eyes, could only stare in dismay at the four official faces on the step, dreading what news they might bring.

"It's not bad news," said Delphick, before either of Miss Seeton's friends could speak. "In fact, it's no news at all, I'm afraid, and I don't propose to insult you with the bromide about no news being good news, because we have absolutely no way of knowing, at present. What we *do* know is that we should very much like to borrow the key of Miss Seeton's cottage—we want to take another look at her sketchbook. I have an idea . . ."

He hadn't; he was hoping, that was all. But the worried Bloomers knew nothing of this, and welcomed his suggestion with relief. Stan, almost before the tall policeman had finished his request, was hurrying down to the kitchen for

Miss Seeton's spare key, safe in its usual place on the board beside the Bloomers' own front, back, shed, and greenhouse keys; he was back as Martha was still only halfway through her sad little speech about not having the heart to go to the fireworks tonight, no matter what folk might say about poor dear Miss Emily not wanting to spoil anyone's Guy Fawkes fun, when they were both so worried about her, and those who said they'd no need to fret on account of her always turning up in the end just didn't understand, did they?

"They don't, indeed." Delphick deemed it wiser (and faster) to agree with Martha rather than waste time trying to explain that neither he nor his colleagues would ever insult the finer feelings of the Bloomers with such a suggestion. "We're as worried as you, Martha, but we are, as I said, still hoping. It's only an idea, I'm afraid, but there just may be something in the sketches that we missed first time around . . ."

And within three minutes they were all in Miss Seeton's sitting-room, poring over the sketches which stubbornly refused to give up their secret. Nobody spoke. Above the tense breathing of the four policemen, the sound of fireworks from outside masked the rustle of pages as Delphick flipped them back and forth, back and forth between the first cartoon—the guy with his battered hat, his cutlery limbs—and the last, the princess in her distant castle with the forces of law and order rushing to the rescue.

"Rapunzel," muttered Delphick, staring yet again at this final drawing as Catherine wheels screamed and whooped somewhere in the distance. "The helicopter flight back to Buck House— well, she was certainly right about that."

"Y-yes . . ." Brinton wouldn't normally have put himself forward as an interpreter when the Oracle was on the case, but when even the Yard's own Seeton expert seemed flummoxed by her drawings, he supposed he ought to be willing to give it a try, if nobody else was prepared to risk it. And he'd crown Foxon if the lad laughed at him afterwards . . . "Overdid it a bit, though, wouldn't you say? I mean—they'll have kept it quiet, won't they, as far as possible? None of this fire-engine-and-squad-car business the way she's shown it, I mean. She'll have thought the sirens were fireworks, most likely," he added, as a rocket howled low overhead and exploded in a high-pitched clatter at the bottom of the garden. "And with all the Guy Fawkes business as well . . . "

It made no sense: he knew it didn't: but somebody had to say something, do something to get the Oracle thinking along the right tracks—and as nobody knew what the right tracks were, it was a case of kicking ideas around until it all came together and he headed off in the right direction.

"Sirens," said Delphick thoughtfully, still staring at Rapunzel. "And Guy Fawkes . . . "

Foxon stirred; but it was Bob who spoke. "Sirens, sir," he said, breaking into the oracular thought process without apology. "Hear them? Heading this way—"

"No," said Foxon, "that's the bells—fire engines, if you ask me. But those others sound like police sirens, all right," and now his superiors could hear them as well. The whooping two-tone constabulary wail, the frantic tintinnabulation of the fire brigade—this last growing ever louder, nearer, speeding past the cottage with a roar . . .

"The playing-field, or I'm a Dutchman," said Delphick. "The Guy Fawkes bonfire—come on!"

CHAPTER 25

Although Miss Seeton's closest friends had been concerned about her disappearance, they were of that class and generation which seldom permits its deepest feelings to show. The Colvedens were not the only people to attend the Grand Bonfire Celebrations determined to put a brave face on things; and more than one person that evening found that thoughts of their missing friend inspired them to follow her excellent example and—the sky being overcast, the outlook uncertain—to carry an umbrella, just in case.

Children in gumboots squealed with excitement as they hurtled through the churned-up mud around the base of the bonfire, around which Nigel and his friends had thrown a stern cordon, remembering Murreystone and the contretemps of the previous night. Only now Plummergen was out in force could the Village Watch relax its vigilance: the bonfire and the guy were safe, their one visible enemy being the low, dense, menacing cloud. Sir George—one eye out for the weather, one for the starter's signal—stood by with the ceremonial matchbox; Admiral Leighton, Dr. Knight, headmaster Martin Jessyp, and other village elders coordinated the distribution of sparklers for the opening extravaganza. Lady Colveden and Miss Treeves (sister to the Reverend Arthur, nominally in charge of cocoa) supervised the jacket-potato detachment and the Hot Spiced Punch. Many were anxious about Miss Seeton; in none was that anxiety evident.

Sir George—huffing through his neat moustache, conscious (despite his hidden concerns) of the importance of the occasion—struck the ceremonial match, and held it to a strategically-placed wisp of straw. The tiny flame licked its way into life, scarlet and crimson and rich, ripening gold; good luck for next year's harvest was assured. Adults stamped their booted feet and clapped; children cheered, and waved sparklers in wild, serpentine coils of burnished light against the dark.

Nigel snatched a brand from the merry burning, and set it to the blue touch-paper of a giant rocket, which coughed, sputtered into life, and roared into the heavens with tumbling silver glitter in its wake, and a series of jewel-hued explosions at the apex of its flight. A deafening cheer went up with the rocket: now, at last, the festivities proper could begin.

Enthroned at the bonfire's summit, the huge guy awaited its doom. Sir George, with a sigh, removed his pork-pie hat and gazed mournfully upwards, bidding a last farewell to his favourite armchair, sacrificed for the good of the village and for the sake of domestic harmony. He cleared his throat emphatically, and blinked.

"Good gad!" He blinked again, and rubbed his eyes, into which tendrils of acrid smoke had been blown by a mischievous breeze. "I could have sworn . . . "

He'd spent many a pleasant hour in that armchair: first in state by the sitting-room fire, then (after too lively an encounter with a wayward spark) in the comfort of his study; then—at her ladyship's decree—in the earthy bohemia of the potting shed. Woodworm, dry rot, and a virulent strain of fungus had finally worked their evil way on both the frame and the horsehair stuffing: even Sir

George could not deny that his chair had long since passed
its prime, but he couldn't help feeling a little sentimental
about that one piece of furniture—although surely that was
no excuse for him to—

"Good gad, I was right!" It hadn't been any whimsical
notion of the chair's making one last, wriggling attempt to
escape its fiery fate: the thing really had moved. Rather,
not the chair, but the guy seated in state upon it . . .

"Stop!" Sir George, hurling his hat aside, bellowed the
command even as he ran across to where Major Matilda
Howett had mustered a small group of wheelchair-bound
patients from the nursing home. "The guy—the guy! Get
it off!"

Wasting no time on explanations, he snatched from her
startled grasp the Howitzer's umbrella, and galloped with
it back to the bonfire, where he began raking furiously at
the bottom branches.

"Help!" he cried, coughing. "Here—help, here!"

The major, like the major-general, had been trained by
the military to respond promptly in an emergency. Her
quick eyes saw what Sir George had seen; her quick wits
urged her to seize a stout walking-stick—his favourite, but
that couldn't be helped—from old Mr. Meredith's knees.
Within seconds, she was at Sir George's side, tugging at
the branches, shouting for more people to join the rescuers.

Lady Colveden, Miss Treeves, and other friends of Miss
Seeton found their brollies wrenched from them by urgent
hands. The smoke and flames were thicker now. Few could
see what Sir George and Matilda Howett had seen; but if
two such common-sense types thought the guy had to be
got off the fire, then got off that guy would be, or they'd
burst in the attempt. Those without umbrellas followed the
Howitzer's example and indulged in a bout of stick-
napping; Lady Colveden and the rest of the catering committee dragged the emergency buckets—woefully
inadequate, never intended for more than a spark-caught
coat, a careless match—to the bonfire and hurled their con-

tents—"Don't!" cried Sir George, but too late—into its very heart.

Smoke surged out in a dense, acrid cloud. A fusillade of coughs, a cataract of tears from smoke-stung eyes. From above—from the guy—a feeble croak, a convulsive wriggle as smoke and heat enveloped its bulky form . . .

But no flames. Not yet. The wild water had suppressed, though not extinguished, the flames: the mischievous breeze was fanning them again into life, but it was at the same time blowing away the smoke. There was, after all, a chance . . . and those who had brought pocket flashlights pointed them towards the centre of operations, and prayed.

The guy croaked again, and jerked back and forth on the chair, which swayed and rocked as, settling a little on the first fire-weakened branches, the top of the bonfire slipped sideways and down—no more than an inch or two, but an inch or two closer to the red-hot peril still beneath.

"Stand back!" The words came in a bellow as loud as any Sir George could command: heredity will out. Nigel Colveden—soaked to the skin, his face cut and bleeding—erupted like a fury from the shadows with, close behind him, Jack Crabbe and Len Hosigg, carrying a ladder. "Mind out!"

"Nigel!" cried his mother, then clamped her lips in Spartan fashion together, and said no more. Sir George was too breathless now for speech, but his heart swelled with pride as he saw his son and heir plunge into the flames and smoke, swarming up the ladder which Jack and Len had thrown against the bonfire's side, stationing themselves—they, too, were soaked and dripping—at its base to catch whatever, whoever might come down, no matter in what condition.

Everyone fell silent. Moved away, if they feared they would be more hindrance than help; moved closer, ready to seize the guy from Nigel's hands and bear it out of range of the still-smouldering fire—if once he brought that guy to safety. But could he do so in time?

Only a muted crackling, the hiss and spit of green wood, was heard as Nigel neared his goal. Some watchers were so tense, they could almost swear they heard bells ringing. As he laid his hand in triumph on the sacking foot, there came a muted outcry, a release of pent-up breath, a groan of general excitement, almost a cheer: and the sound of bells was audible to all.

"It's okay," they heard Nigel say, as he tried to scoop the still-struggling guy into his arms. "Don't worry—try not to fidget . . . "

A swirl of smoke hid him from view, and they heard him cough. Heard, too, above the bells, the sudden swooping two-tone approach of sirens . . .

Torch-beams wavered through the smoke as—cautiously, but as quickly as he dared—Nigel began his descent. Over his shoulder, the sacking guy drooped, without movement: had rescue come too late? Jack and Len, steadying the ladder, reached up; were shouldered out of the way by big Dan Eggleden, head of the human chain organised by the admiral and PC Potter while Dr. Knight and Major Howett, with anxious faces, stood by to administer first aid. Deaf old Mr. Meredith—who'd always been suspected of leading a secret life behind his deafness—released the hot-wire safety switch on his wheelchair, and hurtled across the grass towards the gate, and the road, and the nursing home, where the alarm must be raised, emergency beds prepared.

As he rattled out of the playing-field, he was almost run down by the high-speed scarlet jubilation of a fire engine, its bell clamouring, turning gleefully in through the narrow gateway. As he whizzed up The Street, in his haste ignoring the Highway Code, he narrowly missed being flattened by the panda car approaching from the north. Old Mr. Meredith shouted something rude, and scorched onwards . . .

The crew of the fire engine couldn't believe their luck. A nine-nine-nine call to put out—of all conflagrations—the Plummergen bonfire? It was the best Guy Fawkes message the retained men of Murreystone had had in years.

"Stop!" thundered Sir George, as the oilskinned rivals from over the marsh leaped from their appliance and began to uncoil their hoses. "Stop! No need—panic over. She's safe!" And even in the heat of the moment, he couldn't help the hint of paternal pride as he imparted this information.

"Alarm call to Plummergen playing-field," said the chief officer stoutly. "Bonfire out of control, believed to have caused injury to an elderly party—it's got to be put out, and put it out's what we're a-going to do, so stand aside!"

"She's safe, I tell you!" Sir George almost choked on the words. "Look!"

Had they cared to follow his pointing finger, they would have seen a tumult of sacking and straw on the ground and, in the middle of this tumult, a small woman in tweeds. Her grey hair was rumpled, her eyes seemed out of focus in a pale, drawn face: but she was blinking up at the two persons chafing her limbs, and smiling her feeble thanks to somebody trying to wrap an overcoat about her shoulders.

"Look!" instructed Sir George: but Murreystone did not care to look. This, at last, was their chance, which they had no intention of missing.

"The hose, lads!" commanded the chief officer.

And the lads of Murreystone rushed to obey.

And Plummergen began to murmur . . .

And blue, flashing light filled the sky: light not from an errant firework, but from a police car . . .

Which swept, its siren yodelling, across the grass, and bumped to a halt just as Plummergen's menfolk were flexing their muscles and rolling up their shirtsleeves . . .

Official eyes quickly assessed the situation. And an official voice calmly remarked:

"Hello-ello-ello, what's all this, then? Did we get here too late—or just in time? Pity to spoil our moment of glory, if you ask me. When we've never had a nine-nine-nine call dialled direct from a palace before . . . "

CHAPTER 26

"And neither," countered the Murreystone man at once, "have we." Through the glowing bonfire darkness, punctuated as it was by torchlight beams and the vivid, rhythmic blue of the official beacon, he glared at the glinting buttons and beady eye of the Ashford policeman. "So never you mind *moments of glory,*" he went on, with a sneer. "We've a job to do, with this bonfire here reported out of control all the way from *Buckingham Palace,* no less. So there's nobody going to stop us a-doing our—our loyal duty by extinguishing it, I tell you straight!"

"That bonfire," said the driver of the panda, as Plummergen began to expostulate, "looks as safe as any I've seen, and then some—except," with a cough, as the wind changed, "for the smoke. But even then it's not that near the road it's a hazard to passing traffic, so—"

He broke off—or, rather, was drowned out: partly by the swelling murmurs of discontent from Murreystone (who saw themselves about to be thwarted of revenge by this uniformed jack-in-office), partly by swelling murmurs of annoyance from Plummergen—but mostly by the rumble and roar of two fast-approaching cars across the grass, and the urgent pip-pipping of their horns as they drew near. The Ashford bobby looked round, in some relief: the cavalry was coming! He thought he recognised the sound of the closer of the two cars . . . He was right. Headlights blazing, both vehicles came to a screeching halt, and four doors opened as one. Four large men—no, one was a giant, the others merely tall— leaped out, rushed towards him—and past him, though he tried to catch Superintendent Brinton's eye—rushed on towards the bonfire which was the subject of such heated discussion . . .

And all four, as they ran, clamoured severally: "Police! Stop! Put that fire out! Is Miss Seeton safe?"

"Hey!" cried Sir George, while PC Potter shouted, and the admiral view-hallooed. "Delphick—hold hard, man!"

But it was left to Major Howett to announce, in tones of utter triumph which halted the four in their headlong rush: "Perfectly safe, thank you! What this poor woman needs more than anythin' right now is *peace and quiet*—and she isn't," with a glare, "goin' to get that with you people makin' such a dashed noisy racket all around her."

The Howitzer could be a regular dragon where her patients were concerned. These draconian tendencies were given full rein as she supervised the loading of Miss Seeton— weakly protesting that she hated to be a bother—into the most commodious of the three official cars; after which Major Howett gave firm instructions that the invalid was to be treated with the utmost care during the half-mile trip to the nursing home, and herself followed in the second car, assuring Dr. Knight that she and his wife could cope very well between them, with the night staff and everythin', and that he must stay and keep an eye on the bonfire, just in case, as they'd previously arranged.

The major's forceful eye had not only quelled the rescue rush of Delphick, Brinton, Foxon, and Bob to the bonfire; it had also—at least temporarily—stemmed Plummergen's

fermenting defensive attack upon devious Murreystone, the
fire crew being all too ready to take advantage of a situation
about which everyone kept trying to insist there was no
further cause for alarm. Before the full effects of Major
Matilda's personality had worn off, PC Potter remarked—
at some volume—on the presence of official reinforcements. Sir George and Admiral Leighton loudly restrained
their troops, then muttered sage promises of opportunities
yet to come; Dr. Knight, examining the cuts on a now-
shivering Nigel Colveden's face and the burns on his hands,
expressed himself far too busy to bother with anybody else,
adding that if people proposed committing wholesale
slaughter on one another he was dashed if he was going to
waste good bandages and sticking-plaster on a single man
from either side.

"And this wreck here," he concluded, giving the sodden
Nigel a jovial buffet on the shoulder, "is in danger of death
from double pneumonia, never mind tetanus and blood-
poisoning and multiple bruises." Nigel's teeth chattered,
but he grinned even as he winced. "To jump," continued
Dr. Knight, "head first through a cricket pavilion window,
in my opinion, suggests less an urgent requirement for a
shower than a sudden outbreak of rampant exhibitionism.
Judging by the, ahem, dramatic results of his action, this
patient is suffering from a previously unsuspected circus
performer complex of considerable intensity. My prescription would be a booster jab, a hot bath—which should sat-
isfy any latent craving for cleanliness—and a warm bed, in
that order, to be followed by a stiff tot of whisky and a
sleeping-pill, which together should serve to banish all
thoughts of an acrobatic career. Such treatment to be administered," he added, with a nod for Jack Crabbe and Len
Hosigg, lurking damp (but relatively undamaged) close by,
"to anyone else in the throes of a similar complaint. Immediately."

The doctor's voice was a carrying one, and full of authority. Delphick and Brinton hesitated, exchanged looks,

and then nodded. Brinton thereafter rolled his eyes in the direction of PC Potter and the panda man, who meekly signalled back their obedience to his unspoken command. Sir George and the admiral did not allow their eyes to meet, but they cleared their throats, and otherwise said nothing.

"I believe," said Delphick, "that our wisest course of action is to set a guard around Miss Seeton before another attempt can be made upon her life, and so that a statement may be obtained from her at the earliest possible moment. In the circumstances, those who are already conversant with the complexities of this particular case must be best suited to the task of bodyguard: and, as there are several persons here in obvious need of medical attention, I suggest that we combine two duties in one by giving them all a lift to the nursing home. This will, of course, necessitate the use of more than one official vehicle . . . "

Quite how it happened, Murreystone could never afterwards decide. One minute there were six policemen and three police cars keeping the peace in the bonfire field; then the cars—and the policemen (even Potter, who lived, as everyone knew, so near he had no need to drive)—were gone. The women of Plummergen hustled the children out of the way, and muttered reminders about not spoiling the kiddies' treat; the men of the village closed ranks, and once more rolled up sleeves the untimely arrival of the Law had encouraged them to roll back down.

"Now then," said Sir George, as the leader of the fire crew prepared to renew the offensive, "just what was it you were saying about hoses?"

"I doubt," said Delphick, as they drank coffee and waited for news of Miss Seeton, "whether worse than a good soaking is likely to befall them—and I also doubt they'll seek refuge here with Nigel and company. Once the fire tender has been thoroughly emptied, I imagine they will be allowed to make their escape—whereupon the celebrations may begin in earnest."

"Let's hope we've got something to celebrate, as well."
Glumly, Brinton stirred sugar into his cup. "Potter's a good
man: he'll keep an eye from behind the hedge to see things
don't get out of hand—but what about Miss Seeton, poor
old biddy? In her case, they've already got—out of hand,
I mean, or pretty damned serious, at any rate. She looked
more than peaky, I thought, and there's got to be a first
time she doesn't come bouncing back . . . "

An indignant chorus from Foxon and Bob—privilege of
rank be blowed—drowned out the rest of Brinton's remarks. Delphick smiled.

"There, I think, you have your answer, Chris. Miss Seeton, thank heaven, is a born survivor. The yoga, of course,
will have helped—being drugged and bound without food
for twenty-four hours must come as less of a hardship to
MissEss than it would, say, to young Georgina."

"What a girl!" Brinton forgot lamentation in his amusement. "Something she's always wanted to do, she says –
like pulling the communication cord on a train, except I
don't suppose royal trains have emergencies, really—but to
dial nine nine-nine all the way from Buckingham Palace
like that . . . The kid's made history, I should think."

"A worthy recipient," agreed Delphick, "of the Order
of the Gold Umbrella, should such a decoration exist. Perhaps we might have a word with the relevant authorities."

"Awarded to people who've survived one of MissEss's adventures." Brinton grimaced. "In which case, young Georg-
y'd better be the first person to get it, or I'll—I'll—"

The door opened before he could find words to frame
the threat, and Major Howett marched in, rubbing her
hands.

"Give her a few hours," she said, "and you can pop up
for a quick chat—just one of you, that is. The poor woman
needs a natural sleep now, and to wake up in her own good
time without people explodin' rockets in her ear or half
chokin' her with smoke. Try around mid-mornin' tomorrow—though don't be surprised if she's still a bit woozy.

After a sensible breakfast, mind you, if she can keep it down, she could well surprise us all.''

''In the past, she frequently has,'' Delphick agreed, as his companions expressed their relief at the major's advice. ''If we must wait,'' he went on, ''then naturally we will. But if you could tell us whether Miss Seeton has said anything about how she came to be in her recent predicament . . .''

Matilda Howett shot him a shrewd look. ''She hasn't said much at all.'' She paused. ''Not much that made sense, that is . . .'' She seemed to be considering his request for information very carefully; and nobody made any attempt to hurry her to a decision. The sound of late-night fireworks filtered through the curtained windows of the comfortable little room; a sudden loud bang overhead made everyone jump. The major frowned at the noise, then coughed. After a further contemplative pause, she continued:

''But then, she was very fidgety, don't you know. Twitchin' a good deal—and we were tryin' to calm her down, so we could well have missed it even if she did. Say anythin', that is.''

''Twitchy,'' repeated Delphick. ''Her fingers?'' He knew a hint when he heard one.

''Dancin','' replied the major at once. ''Almost as if the poor soul was playin' the piano in her sleep. And mutterin' about . . .'' For the first time in their acquaintance with Matilda Howett, the four policemen saw her blush. ''About,'' repeated the Howitzer firmly, though her maiden cheeks were pink, ''about drugs, and—and about havin' to—to go to the powder-room . . .''

''Aaah,'' said Delphick, as light, at last, dawned: and he heaved a great sigh of triumph.

''These are from Bob, these from Chris Brinton, these from my humble self. And Foxon''—Delphick hid a smile—''has been revealed as possessing a far more practical streak than I'd ever given the boy credit for—he sent you this.''

Gravely, he handed Miss Seeton in turn three bunches of flowers, and a bronze chrysanthemum in a decorated pot. "I observe," he went on, as Miss Seeton blushed above her woolly bed-jacket, "that you have some truly splendid floral specimens here—let me guess," as Miss Seeton blushed still more. "By Royal Command, perhaps?"

Miss Seeton murmured in some embarrassment of the great kindness of Her Royal Highness, then perked up to say how very, very glad she was that the poor young thing had been restored in safety to her family.

"And all thanks to you—to your umbrella, anyway," amended Delphick, as Miss Seeton voiced a muted, but startled, protest. "Has Georgina explained that it was , . . a little damaged during her escape attempt, and that it will be returned to you as soon as it has been repaired?"

"So very kind," said Miss Seeton, still muted and pink. "Indeed, most gracious, when really, there was no need—to go to so much trouble, I mean. I can only be thankful that, even if I could be of no particular help or comfort to Her Royal Highness during her—during our, that is, I suppose I should say, although I can hardly feel that it can have been in the least deliberate, in my case . . . during the incarceration, if that is not too melodramatic a term . . . that it should have been of use. My umbrella, I mean. Thankful. Except, of course," blushing with sudden, dreadful realisation, "that I would naturally have arranged for it to be repaired just as soon as I could—and it would have been no trouble at all, Mr. Delphick, I assure you."

"I believe you," Delphick said quickly: he couldn't bear any longer to see her blush and fluster her way through this tortuous apologia. "And you must believe me, Miss Seeton, when I say that I feel every bit as—as honoured as yourself to think that in some small way the umbrella I gave you has served a purpose of which neither of us, in the beginning, could ever have dreamed."

"Indeed not." At the chief superintendent's matter-of-fact tone, Miss Seeton was almost her old self again, with

a smile in her voice and the beginnings of a twinkle in her
eye. Only the pallor of her face, and a slight hollowing of
her normally smooth cheeks, showed that she had so recently passed through the grim experience of being drugged
close to death, then set still closer to death—by combustion—than even the drugs could contrive.

"An honour," said Miss Seeton, in the assured tones she
would use when teaching, "for us both, Mr. Delphick—
but oh, dear," and assurance turned to anxiety. "I fear I
had forgotten, in the pleasure of being allowed a visitor—
though the dear major—and the Knights, of course—have
been more than kind, and I was most certainly not suggesting that she—I mean they—had forbidden . . . "

At this point, Miss Seeton's innate honesty brought her
to a blushing halt. Ever since the marriage of Anne Knight
to Detective Sergeant Bob Ranger had installed Major Matilda Howett in Plummergen's private nursing home, the
Knights—whose names were on the mortgage as owners
of the property, whose signatures were on the cheques
which paid wages and rates and running expenses—had
bowed to a far superior force, and acknowledged themselves the merest ciphers. The whole village knew that Major Howett was—to mix naval with military metaphor—the
captain of the ship, if not the admiral of the fleet. Her word
was law, her command absolute. Under the old regime,
Miss Seeton would have been permitted without argument
to discharge herself and go home straight after breakfast,
as she had on more than one occasion in the past. The bed
(she had insisted) should be left for others in greater need,
the nurses freed to continue with more pressing work . . .

"I had forgotten," said Miss Seeton, recovering herself
with a gulp, "that you might reasonably expect to be at
work today, rather than waste your time—not, of course,
that it is not always a pleasure to see you, Chief Superintendent, but when there are so many demands on . . . "

"Not as many as there were," he told her cheerfully.
"Nor on Superintendent Brinton's, either. Things have

been happening while you were, shall we say, sleeping it off under Major Howett's, ah, protection. The kidnappers have been found—thanks to you, Miss Seeton, as I said earlier. And it may not come as any great surprise to you that it was, indeed, they who were responsible for the death of the caterer Donald Bragbury—and, I'm sorry to say, for the subsequent death of one of their own employees . . . ''

CHAPTER 27

"The KarriKlozzet company," said Delphick, above Miss Seeton's shocked exclamations of dismay, "has been in financial difficulties for some time. Caroline Kelshall did wonders, mind you, with the firm she inherited from her husband Caradoc—put it on the map, built it up to the third largest portable powder-room supplier in the country—but Caroline isn't growing any younger, and she hasn't been in the best of health." He smiled. "Not everyone, Miss Seeton, is blessed with the stamina and physical fortitude which your yoga has imparted to you—nor, I might add, does everyone possess your strength of character and your high moral scruples." He sighed. "Few, alas, do. I only wish they did—except, of course, that if they did, I'd be out of a job." There was a wry twist to his lips as he spoke. "Human nature, however, being what it is, I rather think I'll be in gainful employment for the rest of my working life . . ."

Miss Seeton, likewise sighing, said with regret that she feared the chief superintendent was right. She clicked her tongue, and shook her head. For anyone to—to contrive the death of another was bad enough. Wicked, indeed: but the added wickedness of the—the betrayal of trust in causing the death of one's own employee . . .

"Luke Hadham," Delphick said. "He'd started with Kelshalls when they were just an ordinary builders' merchants, and he went along with old Caradoc when he branched out into KarriKlozzet. He knew pretty well as much about running it as Caradoc himself. He watched the children grow up, watched Caroline take over when Caradoc died, offered advice from time to time, especially when things started to go wrong—advice which sometimes she took, and sometimes she didn't. The layoffs, for instance: he was very much against that idea. He would have preferred reducing overall hours, so that everyone would at least keep some regular income, to reducing staff numbers—but Caroline wouldn't listen. She considered herself the ultimate boss, you see, even though Caradoc left more shares in the company to his children than to his wife: but the children have always been completely under their mother's thumb. So what Caroline Kelshall said, went—with everyone except Luke.

"Poor chap." Delphick shook his head. "He'd begun to think of himself as an éminence grise, which in some ways he was—but he was also, once the Kelshalls decided to turn to crime as a way out of their difficulties, a danger to them. He knew them all so well, you see. Not just the everyday work routines, but their personal foibles, their nervous habits—and some of them grew very nervous, in the course of their illicit activities. He knew enough, in short, to know when they were up to something, or at least to have strong suspicions that something wasn't right. He noticed when they kept sneaking away for their secret meetings to plot the abduction of young Georgina; he went on noticing whenever one or other of them took time off to give their prisoner her food; and maybe he said something, or perhaps tried a little blackmail—they're not saying—but it's clear the Kelshalls decided that he had to go."

In other circumstances, he would have smiled. "Killing

two birds with one stone, it might be said. By the so-called bomb attack on their premises they not only removed the threat of Luke Hadham, they also removed—reduced to smithereens, in fact—all evidence of their original scheme for Georgina's kidnap. A scheme which . . . ''

Miss Seeton began blushing once more. Delphick hurried on: " . . . which your encounter with the radiation meter only served to bring forward, Miss Seeton. Believe me, they would have gone ahead anyway: their plans were all laid, and it was just that they were sufficiently quick-witted to take advantage of the—the inevitable confusion which resulted from the setting off of the alarm.''

"Oh, dear," breathed Miss Seeton, falling back on her pillows in guilty dismay. "Oh, dear . . . ''

"Their original scheme," he went on quickly, "would have been far less dignified for the princess than the actual quick sack over the head and subsequent hustling to a nearby car. Peter Therfield, the husband of Caroline's daughter Cleopatra—Caroline might be the lady boss herself, but she didn't hold with other females going into the business world, or taking too much responsibility upon themselves; that's why she recruited her son-in-law to take Cleopatra's place—anyway, Therfield, acting as a substitute for his wife, either bribed, or blackmailed, Donald Bragbury into spiking young Georgina's drink at the opening reception.'' He grinned. "Blackmailed, probably—Bragbury's wife, or rather widow, is hardly . . . ''

Delphick, himself happily married, shuddered in sympathy for the marital burden borne by the late Mr. Bragbury. "Let us say, Miss Seeton, that Mrs. Bragbury does not give the impression of having been the most affectionate of helpmeets. For Donald to take a mistress would have been hardly surprising: almost predictable, indeed.'' Once more, Miss Seeton sighed. Delphick nodded.

"Caroline Kelshall is a shrewd woman. She must have looked for a weak point in the caterer's armour, guessed at the likelihood of another woman in his life, and instructed

Therfield to arrange to have the wretched man slip a diuretic in Georgina's lemonade.'' Miss Seeton clicked her tongue, and murmured with great disapproval of royal dignity. Resting on the bedclothes, her clasped hands gave a sudden twitch.

Delphick nodded again. "That, of course, was the basis of their plan. Where else should a poor sufferer from waterworks trouble go to relieve her sufferings than to the lavatory? And when Royalty visits, it is not necessarily subjected to the indignities of the common cloakroom, particularly in a place which hasn't long been open, where all the niggling little problems of the plumbing haven't been entirely ironed out. The country-wide supplying of de luxe portable toilets for royal occasions is a serious business, or so I have been given to understand.''

Miss Seeton's fingers had begun to dance, despite their owner's clasping them tight, during the latter part of the Oracle's explanation. Kindly, he ignored the way she tried—and failed—to still them. "The particular closet the Kelshalls had supplied that day was altered to have an extra door, camouflaged very cleverly in the wall behind the wash-basin, and connected by a most ingenious system of levers to the ballcock in the cistern. As soon as the princess pulled the chain, the noise of rushing water would cover the sound of the levers unlocking the hidden door. When she turned on the tap to wash her hands, the door would open—and bingo.''

"Ingenious," agreed Miss Seeton, as Delphick came to a temporary halt, "but—but discourteous, in the extreme, and hardly a—a responsible attitude . . . ''

Her disapproval had, for the moment, quietened her restless fingers: a quietening which Delphick remarked with interest, though he still said nothing.

"To be fair to the Kelshalls," he continued, "they did their best throughout the remainder of their, ah, involvement with the princess to ensure that her washing and sanitary arrangements were of the highest standard that could, in the circumstances, be achieved. Kidnappers, believe me, are not often so considerate. Perhaps if we had paid more attention to this unusual fact once Georgina had been safely recovered, we would have found you rather more quickly than we did.'' His smile was apologetic. ''I must tell you, Miss Seeton, that we—that the police—are only too sorry you had to be subjected to such . . . unpleasantness. We're deeply thankful that the outcome of your adventure wasn't a good deal more serious than it proved, in the end, to be.''

''Oh, dear.'' Miss Seeton turned pink with mingled guilt and dismay. ''Poor Nigel—he has already been in to see me this morning, and his face—such a dreadful shock. And his hands, with their bandages . . . I remember so little, I fear, of what occurred at the time, although dear Major Howett has since explained . . . Nigel himself told me almost nothing, beyond the fact that''—the embarrassed note gave way to a hint of amusement—''the major had refused to allow him to go home before breakfast . . . ''

''Nigel,'' said Delphick, ''is a born knight-errant. When there is a lady in distress, would you suppose his courage to fail him? As of course last night it did not. But,'' he added, as Miss Seeton blushed again, ''does it surprise you that his courage *did* fail him when faced with Major Howett's . . . professional resolution? In order to resist the major in, let us say, full cry, one would need to be more than courageous. One would have to be rash beyond belief, as well as totally lacking in common sense.''

''Nigel,'' said Miss Seeton warmly, ''is a very intelligent young man, besides being''—a little sniff escaped her, and she blinked rapidly several times—''a true gentleman.''

''Indeed he is.'' Delphick grinned. ''And bright enough to know when he's beaten by superior odds: so I'm not surprised he stayed here overnight. He wouldn't have dared do anything else.'' He chuckled. ''Not unless he was quite out of his mind, that is; and Nigel is far from crazy.''

Miss Seeton's fingers suddenly twitched again. Delphick couldn't help glancing at them; then he dragged his gaze away, and prepared to go on with his exposition.

There was no need to upset Miss Seeton by telling her that it had been the media notoriety she so greatly disliked which had made the Kelshalls suspect her of knowing more than she in fact did. They might, without that notoriety, have been able to ignore the several uncanny coincidences which had occurred: Miss Seeton's having been in charge of the child who presented the bouquet to their victim; her insistence on searching, as they'd seen it, the booby-trapped lavatory; even her waving of her umbrella in what anyone less guilty must have recognised as an innocent signal for assistance—that same umbrella which had provided so convenient a distraction after the alarm went off that they had been able to swoop upon the princess so much sooner than they'd expected . . .

They *might* have ignored all this: but, in fact, they hadn't. The newspapers' insistence on coupling the name of the Battling Brolly with Scotland Yard, the local knowledge that the soubriquet concealed Miss Emily Dorothea Seeton of Plummergen, had pricked the uneasy consciences of the Kelshalls, leading them to case the village joint under the pretext of admiring the many penny-for-the-guy displays along The Street. One of these guys had worn a hat which could only have belonged to Miss Seeton: try as they might, they couldn't escape her.

Had they balked at killing her outright? Had they left it to chance—to the strength of the barbiturates in the doctored tea? The same devious mind (thought Delphick grimly) as had planned the diuretic spiking had planned *that,* he'd wager. Miss Seeton was a small woman; the post office guy had been an unusually fine specimen, sufficiently large to accommodate easily two bound, living limbs within one sacking leg, one pinioned torso within its enormous body. It had been a close-run thing. Though the clues towards her ultimate rescue had been plain in her sketchbook, the police—he himself, renowned throughout the force as the Seeton expert—had failed to interpret them in time. It had been the quick wits of Nigel Colveden which had saved her . . .

Plus her own undoubted stamina, of course. The yoga: how many people of her age could have gone as long as she had without food or drink, yet still have the strength to move and cry out when the effects of the drug had finally worn off?

"Worn off," muttered Delphick, and caught Miss Seeton's curious eye. *Had* it been intended that it should wear off in time—should give her a sporting chance? They'd have the truth out of the Kelshalls, sooner or later. He wouldn't tell Miss Seeton, of course; there was evidence enough to convict them without that last knowledge—but for his own satisfaction he needed to know whether it had been a deliberate gamble on the kidnappers' part, or an honest-to-badness in-the-heat-of-the-moment mistake . . .

"A mistake," Miss Seeton broke into his thoughts with a nod and a smile, startling him: he hadn't realised he'd been thinking aloud. He wondered how much he'd said: she didn't seem too worried—but then, she never did.

"A mistake," said Miss Seeton, smiling. "Naturally: why should anyone, especially someone I have never met, wish to harm me? And, as you implied, it is most fortunate that my knowledge of yoga enabled me to overcome the discomfort and inconvenience rather more easily than, for example, might have been the case with Her Royal Highness. Except, of course, that she is so much younger—but one must be thankful that she was spared the experience. After all," she explained, with a smile, "I was, remember, among friends—a most fortunate circumstance. So very alarming for the poor child to have woken up surrounded by complete strangers, no matter how well-disposed towards her—as, of course, they would be. Nevertheless . . . "

Only Miss Seeton could regard her abduction and drugging and narrow escape from death as a positive advantage. One day, Delphick mused, there would be some occurrence which even she couldn't fail to regard as dangerous, unpleasant, and deliberately aimed against herself: one day. But not, he hoped, just yet . . .

"And more than fortunate," he told her, "that you'd set us on the right track with your drawings—the powder-puff, in particular, encouraging us to look at those who had provided the portable powder-room." Once more Miss Seeton's fingers danced on the bedclothes. The chief superintendent kept a fascinated eye upon them as he continued:

"I really must apologise again, Miss Seeton, for having failed to understand soon enough what you were telling us—me, that is. The catering arrangements, the Karri-Klozzet connection—they were all there, but we were, I fear, much too slow in a proper interpretation of them, with the result that we had to rely on everyday police work when these were far from everyday crimes. The gamble paid off, but it was a crazy risk to have taken . . ."

That twitch again. He couldn't bear it. "Miss Seeton, is there something you feel you should be telling me—us? The police, I mean—ah, there is. I thought so," as there came another convulsive leap. "I see that you have been the recipient of several get-well cards: would it disturb you to rough out a few ideas on the back of that monster there, for instance?"

Miss Seeton, across whose face a look of relief for her friend's understanding had flashed at his words, now looked regretful. She murmured of dear Mr. Potter, or rather Amelia and her mother, who had so kindly brought . . .

"The wrapping from my bunch of flowers, then." Without waiting for her to demur, Delphick seized his bouquet and deftly unrolled the patterned paper, disclosing blank whiteness on the other side. "My ballpoint pen," he said, "and a firm surface, that's what you need—as these flowers," with a quick gesture pulling the over-the-bed table towards her, and collecting the floral assortment with one hand as with the other he dug his pen from his pocket, "as

these flowers need water. I'll just have a word with Major
Howett . . . ''

"I apologise for troubling you, Mrs. Potter." Delphick
stood on the doorstep of the police house with a roll of
paper in his hand. "But if I might have a quick word with
your husband, I'd be most grateful."

"Why, he's not here." Mabel Potter seemed astonished
that anyone should think her spouse neglectful of his duty.
"Bin gone these twenty minutes or more, he has, doing his
rounds. Course, there's the radio"—she saw the involun-
tary shake of his head, and went on quickly—"but if it
might be something I could help with . . . ''

Delphick hesitated. While he had been talking to Miss
Seeton, Bob had kicked his heels downstairs, too much in
awe of the major to grumble at being denied the bedside
of his adopted Aunt Em. It was Miss Seeton herself who
had broken the impasse. She'd been dressed and waiting
by the time Delphick had returned to see what manner of
sketch it had been to set her fingers dancing; and Major
Howett, with stern warnings about overdoin' it, had con-
sented to her patient's discharge on condition that she went
home by car rather than on foot, as she'd wanted. A delighted Bob had done the honours in the Yard's unmarked
car, leaving Delphick to puzzle alone over the wrapping-
paper sketch his ballpoint pen had produced . . .

"It's this drawing of Miss Seeton's," said Delphick, as
Mabel Potter closed the door and led him into the office,
realising that he came on police business. "Even with hind-
sight, I can't for once quite make out what she's trying to
express, and I wondered . . . ''

Together, he and Mabel Potter gazed at the image of a
hospital bed, neatly made. The corners of its sheets were
mitred, its counterpane was crisp and smooth—apart from
that part beneath the long-armed table, on which stood a
large and ornate vase of flowers, and a bowl of what had
at first appeared to be mixed fruit, but which closer in-

spection showed was an assortment of nuts. Directly under the table, the folds of the counterpane were scooped back by a man's hand: a man who, in police uniform except for the helmet, crouched under the bed and peered out, his face wild and working—peered out from beneath, not a helmet, but an enormous, upturned china chamber-pot . . .

And the man had the face of Police Constable Potter.

Delphick looked at Mabel. Mabel looked at the drawing. For some while, she did not speak.

Neither did Delphick. Then, as Mrs. Potter seemed to be struggling with herself, he sighed. "It's my fault, I dare say." He took the sketch and rolled it up again. "Preferring all the loose ends to be tied up, I mean—one can't, every time, have everything. I believe that, while I was talking to her, I said something about someone-or-other being, well, crazy . . . It was she who spoke of your family's kindness in sending her a card—and the vase of flowers is obvious, of course, though I confess I didn't notice any nuts, or even fruit, while I was there. We must, I think, assume it is the shock of her recent experience which has—has somewhat distorted her usual good sense. I do hope you aren't too offended . . ."

But Mabel wasn't in the least offended. Her struggle had been not to erupt into giggles rather than not to explode in anger; and now the struggle was lost. She laughed out loud. "Bless you—sir," she added, "Potter's used to it—and so'm I, being married this long. What else could we expect? *And* young Amelia, now she's started school." She saw Delphick stare, and giggled still more.

"He," said Mabel, indicating ballpoint Potter under the bed, "looks barmy, don't he? Potty, you might say—and that's what she's drawn, see? Grew up with 'em making jokes like that at school, he did. Water off a duck's back." She twinkled at the chief superintendent. "Why," she quizzed him, "does a madman hide under the bed?"

Delphick struck himself lightly on the forehead as she waited, grinning, for his reply. "Of course! Because he thinks he's a little . . . oh, dear, to be caught out by that old chestnut. I haven't heard it in years—but what, in a case like this, could be a more apposite conclusion?'' He joined Mabel in her laughter. ''Why, she's even drawn the blessed chestnuts for us, to tell us it's a joke . . . ''

Delphick and Bob—leaving Brinton to charge the Kelshalls and begin the laborious task of getting the paperwork in order—returned to London, confident that they had tied up every loose end.

But they weren't, for once, altogether right.

It was some days later that—unknown to anyone directly concerned with the case—the true meaning of Miss Seeton's final sketch was made plain: although those who made it so, being no great friends to Miss Seeton, would have been most annoyed had they realised the truth.

''Too clever of Eric, I think.'' Mrs. Blaine beamed, all sulks and tantrums forgotten. ''No, Eric, don't blush—you shouldn't hide your light under a bushel. I'm willing to admit,'' said Mrs. Blaine bravely, looking about the post office to make sure her magnanimity didn't go unnoticed, ''that I was wrong. Though you must admit that to use my best sieves and buckets to wash the clay—''

''Body,'' corrected Miss Nuttel, in knowledgeable tones.

Mrs. Blaine tittered. ''I'm sorry, Eric. Body. That's the technical name for it,'' she explained, whether or not anyone wished to know. ''To rinse all the stones out of *the body:* clay from deep in our garden, of course, because Eric keeps the topsoil in such splendid condition—''

''Heart,'' came the next correction from Miss Nuttel. Mrs. Blaine scowled, then quickly recovered herself.

''Keeps the soil so splendidly,'' she amended, ''that she had to dig positively *yards* down before she reached the subsoil. And then all the straining, and rinsing—''

''Slurry,'' said Miss Nuttel.

''And drying in great plaster-of-Paris beds,'' said Mrs. Blaine, ignoring her. ''And then having to cut it with wire

over and over and over again to squeeze all the air out—''
"Wedging.''

Bunny shot Eric a very nasty look. "And then to have our own—that is, a home-made potter's wheel, *and* a kiln—and Eric taught herself all about electricity from the book, which I think too clever for words . . . ''

Somebody sniggered, remembering how all the lights had gone out in Lilikot, and the Nutty outcry there had been.

"Anyway,'' said Mrs. Blaine, proudly, "to think we might never need to buy a plate or a pot or a vase ever again!''

And, on this note of triumph, the Nuts departed.

There was a pause. The sniggerer sniggered again, more loudly. "Make your own plates—they're mad,'' she concluded. "Nutty as fruitcakes, they really are!''

But another conclusion—had the speaker but known it— was even more apposite: providing, as it did, the punchline to Delphick's—to Miss Seeton's—last little joke.

"Potty,'' she said: and nobody disagreed.

ABOUT THE AUTHOR

Hamilton Crane is the pseudonym of Sarah J(ill) Mason, who was born in England (Bishop's Stortford), went to university in Scotland (St. Andrews), and lived for a year in New Zealand (Rotorua) before returning to settle only twelve miles from where she started. She now lives about twenty miles outside London with a tame welding engineer husband and two (reasonably) tame Schipperke dogs. Under her real name, she writes the mystery series which stars Detective Superintendent Trewley and Detective Sergeant Stone of the Allingham police force.